The Lab, the Witch, and the Simulation

John Gabriel

ISBN: 979-8-9997432-1-3

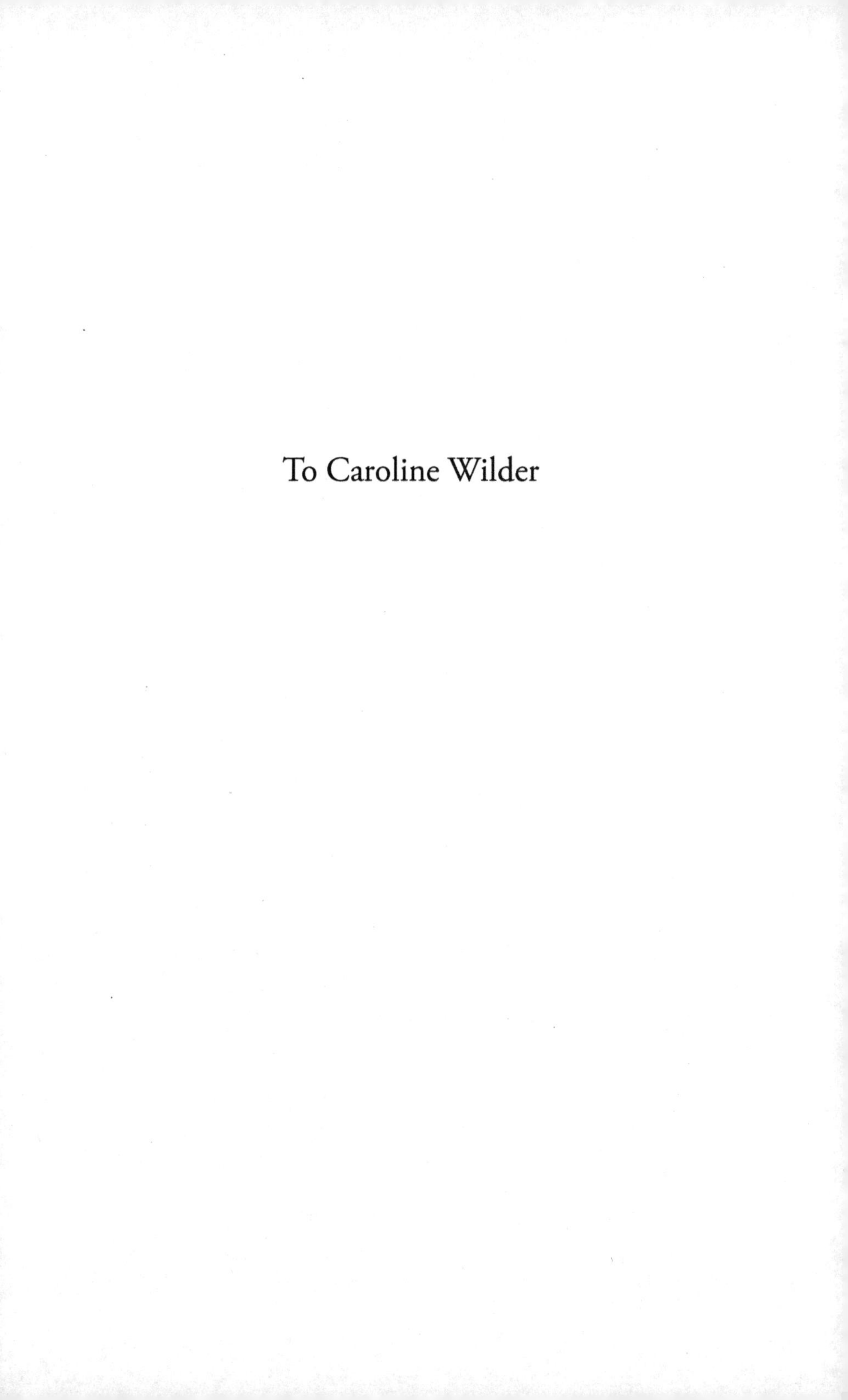

To Caroline Wilder

Prologue

Molly Williams stepped through the threshold and emerged as her original self. She swept her hand behind her to see if she still had wings. She knew how illogical that was, after watching four girls with wings lose theirs. But, just this once, Molly wanted her logical side to be wrong.

She wanted to feel the wings, soft as glove leather, that had hung cape-like from her shoulders and back. Molly wanted to unfurl them fully and view their opalescence one last time. But she couldn't. They were gone. *My beautiful wings,* Molly thought. With a sigh, she stepped into the darkness to join her friends.

One of them lit Molly's way with a flashlight, saying, "I already regret leaving. I never dreamed I would ever fly like that!"

"I did," said a second girl, "literally. This world is my favorite recurring dream come true."

The two remaining girls said, almost in unison, "We have to come back here someday!"

What? Molly started to say, *And risk our lives all over again?* But she changed her mind. *They know as well as I do we're never coming back. Let them enjoy a little moment of joy. Don't we deserve it after last week?*

Wait, had it only been a week?

1
NovaCamp

IT HAD BEEN six days. It was last Sunday afternoon when Molly arrived in San Francisco. By 4:30, she was searching for the baggage claim area at SFO, trying not to look like a fifteen-year-old kid on her first solo trip away from home. She shouldn't have worried; all she had to do was follow the signs along a straight path. Then, with her suitcase recovered, Molly just needed to find her ride.

Just past the baggage area, a sign proclaimed, "Welcome, Campers, to NovaCamp #1." Printed in full color on thick card stock, it featured an aerial shot of the LTG campus beneath the NovaCamp logo. The logo, an eight-pointed star, was apparently meant to represent a supernova.

But NovaCamp wasn't about Astronomy; it was about digital technology. Molly was going to spend seven weeks at the largest tech firm in the world, developing software alongside LTG programmers. And it was all free, thanks to Molly's score on a test open to every tenth-grade girl in Alabama.

Next to the poster and its easel stood a young woman, dressed in an orange NovaCamp T-shirt and holding an iPad. Her sandy blond hair hung in long pigtails beneath a headband with two flashing antennae.

"Hi. I'm Diana Newcomb. Are you here for NovaCamp?" She beamed at Molly with a smile so genuine it totally compensated for the silly headband.

"Yes, Ma'am, I'm Molly Williams, from Birmingham."

"Hello, Molly. Welcome to California! I'm sorry I didn't recognize you. New glasses?"

Molly had forgotten that her NovaCamp picture was taken before she'd gotten glasses. "Yes, Ma'am, I just started wearing these."

"They're very attractive."

"Thanks. My mom was pushing for contacts. She said I'd look too nerdy in glasses, but I decided to lean into it."

"You made the right decision. I love those oversized frames, and that tortoiseshell looks great on you." The hues of green and red in the frames did bring out Molly's hazel eyes and auburn hair.

"You make nerdy look cool," said someone behind Molly. The voice was flute-like and melodic, a child's voice. Molly turned around and was surprised to be looking into the eyes of a girl her height. Those pale blue eyes seemed enormous, and not just because of her delicate build.

"This is your roommate," Diana said. "Claire Turner, from Boulder, Colorado."

"Hi, Claire. Nice to meet you." *So nice,* Molly thought. *I only came because LTG let me change roommates.*

"Nice to meet you," Claire said. "They put us together because we're the closest in age. I'm still fourteen, and Diana said you're fifteen. Did you skip grades, too?"

"No, I just started early," Molly said. "My birthday is September 1, so I turned five on the first day of eligibility for kindergarten."

Claire nodded. "So we're a year and a half apart, but still the youngest girls here. Usually, juniors are already sixteen when school starts."

"Oh, I'm well aware. I feel like I'm the only person I know who isn't driving."

Claire's big eyes grew a little wider. "Doesn't that suck? For me, it will be a graduation gift!"

Diana laughed with the girls at this. "I hate to interrupt, Molly, but there was at least one other camper on your flight. Did you see any potential campers leave your plane?"

"No, Ma'am, I'm sorry."

"Was Jo Beth Taylor on your flight?"

"I'm positive she wasn't." Molly heard the edge in her voice, but if Diana noticed, she didn't let on. Molly tried again. "I don't know why she canceled, but I'm positive she did. Her seat was right next to mine."

"Good," Diana said. "They told me she canceled, but I wanted to be sure. I wouldn't want the poor kid wandering around SFO by herself."

"You don't need to worry about Jo Beth," Molly said. "She watches out for herself."

Diana nodded. "Gotcha." She was still beaming, with only a millimeter rise of one eyebrow. "In that case, we're waiting for just two more campers, and then we'll head off to Wonderland."

At that moment, a tall girl ran up to them, her short afro bobbing up and down with each effortless stride. Even at rest, her stance, relaxed but perfectly balanced, suggested power held in reserve. "I'm so sorry," she said and flashed a big smile at Diana. "I promised my Gran I'd call the second we landed. We talked so long I thought I might have missed you guys."

"We wouldn't leave without you!" Diana said. "Besides, we're waiting on at least one more camper. Aren't you Aaliyah Peterson, from Macon, Georgia?"

"Yes, Ma'am."

"Hi, Aaliyah! I'm Diana Newcomb. Welcome to NovaCamp. This is Claire Turner from Boulder, Colorado, and Molly Williams from Birmingham, Alabama."

Aaliyah turned to them. "Hey guys, so glad to meet you! Molly, were you on Flight DL726?"

"I was."

"I thought I saw you getting on the plane. We were on the same flight! When I fly back to Macon, maybe we can get seats together," Aaliyah said in a single, breathless stream.

"Let's do that." It felt strange to think of Macon as close to home, but the world seemed smaller now than it did this morning.

Diana pointed up to the flight information board. "Your roommate just landed, Aaliyah. But it always takes them a long time to unload the luggage, so I expect we'll be waiting a while."

"No way I trust baggage handlers with my stuff!" Everyone turned to see the speaker. She wore torn jeans and a black leather jacket and had purple hair with a burgundy stripe. She stood there, one hand on her hip and the other holding her "stuff" — a large khaki backpack.

"You must be…" Diana said.

"Katrina Rizzi, from Chicago."

"I'm Diana Newcomb; I'll be your counselor this summer. This is your roommate, Aaliyah Peterson."

Katrina gave a slight head shrug. "Wassup?"

Aaliyah smiled broadly. "Hi, Katrina. And this is Claire Turner and Molly Williams."

At that moment, Diana's cell phone rang. "Oh! Excuse me, girls; I need to get this." She stepped away before answering.

Katrina turned to the other girls. "So, where you guys from?"

After Molly and Claire answered, Aaliyah did. "I tell everyone I'm from Macon, Georgia, but I'm really from an unincorporated area outside of it. Way out in the sticks. I hope you're not disappointed getting stuck with a country girl for a roomie."

"Hell no! I can tell you're cool. Honestly, I'm relieved. I was sure they'd stick me with the other girl from Illinois. What a freakin' poser!"

Diana rejoined them. "Girls, we're good to head out. Jo Beth Taylor arrived on campus about two hours ago, so all one hundred campers are accounted for. I guess you and I can stop worrying about her now, Molly."

Molly wished that were true.

"Diana," Katrina asked, "are we there yet? My butt is killing me!" Katrina had claimed the back seat of the van for herself and her large backpack. Everyone else had stowed their gear in the cargo space. Molly and Claire sat in the middle seat, and Aaliyah was up front, next to Diana.

"We're close. Maybe four miles from the LTG exit, and traffic is light. So don't worry, we'll be there soon."

"I'm enjoying the ride," Aaliyah said. "I've never been in an electric van before."

Claire asked, "Diana, do you know how big our teams will be?"

"That depends on the particular project, but they want to keep them small, probably four or five girls on average."

Claire frowned. "Darn! I wanted a big team so I could make lots of friends."

"I'll be your friend," Molly said.

"Me too," Aaliyah and Katrina said at the same time.

Claire's eyes lit up and then quickly dimmed. "Are you guys being sarcastic?"

"No!" Molly said. "Why would you say that?"

"Because that's the way girls usually say they'll be my friend."

"That sucks," Katrina said. "Let me guess, are those girls popular?"

"They sure are. That's why I asked them." Claire said. "Did I do something wrong? You sound angry."

"Yeah, I'm angry, but not at you, at those stuck-up bitches!"

Claire's mouth flew open as if she'd never heard the b-word before. Then she tried to compensate by hardening her voice. "Yeah, they are! And they don't even know how to code!"

"Exactly!" Aaliyah said. "It's important to have something in common with your friends. At my school, I couldn't find anyone interested in computers, but I also love sports, so I've made some friends through that."

When Claire made a face, Molly spoke up. "It doesn't have to be sports, just something you enjoy talking about. For me, that's art."

"Whoa," Katrina said. "If Claire wants to be popular, art and computers are the last things she should talk about!"

Molly laughed. "Good point, but when it comes to friends, I'll always choose quality over quantity. I don't have to be 'popular' to be happy."

"Preach it, girl," Katrina said. "Your average high school kid just isn't on our wavelength. But all the NovaCampers will be. We can all enjoy not being outcasts this summer!"

"And Claire," Aaliyah said. "I bet you've got some gamers back at your school — you could hang with them."

"Oh, I'm not allowed to play video games!" Claire said. "My mom says they're a waste of time."

"A crazy profitable waste of time!" Katrina said. "The gaming industry has nearly half a trillion dollars in sales. That's why I want to work on one of LTG's game dev projects."

"Me, too," said Aaliyah. "I'd like to try my hand at coding a game. I have some ideas, but the 3D modeling part scares me."

"Oh, I can help you with that," Molly said. "I love modeling! I'll show you my favorite tricks and model libraries."

"Show me, too!" Claire said. "I want to be a game developer."

Then Diana pointed to the exit sign they were approaching. "Look, girls. We're here!" She took the exit ramp and crossed back over the highway. Up ahead, unmistakable for anything else, was the LTG campus. Each building was a different bright primary color. They looked like Lego blocks left behind by giant children.

Molly had read every article she could find about the campus and had scrolled through hundreds of pictures, but that didn't prepare her for the real thing. She hadn't grasped the sheer scale of the place. Not just more buildings, but more sidewalks, gardens, fountains, and trees than she had ever imagined. But more importantly, this was not a picture. This was her home for the next seven weeks. *And also Jo Beth's!*

Molly shook her head. Here was this amazing campus, this rare opportunity, laid out before her like a buffet, and all she could think about was something that happened three months ago. It was an image Molly couldn't unsee: her father's guitar, a gift from his father, lying in pieces at Jo Beth's feet. That mistake, that one lapse in judgment, was Molly's personal ghost, ever-present, even today.

"Here are the dorms," Diana announced. Two three-story buildings stood side by side, identical except that one was orange and the other, lime green. Diana parked and led the girls into the green dorm. In the lobby, she handed out their room keys. "Aaliyah and Katrina, you're in room 208. Claire and Molly are in room 215. I'm the Second Floor counselor, and I'm in room 201. We're on a tight schedule because Orientation starts in thirty minutes. The other girls know where the Exhibition Hall is since they had a campus tour earlier. So I'll walk the four of you over there. Just drop off your bags and be back here in fifteen minutes."

Claire and Molly located their room upstairs. They rushed in, only to find a small dorm room painted light gray with boring furniture. Claire, at least, found something to get excited about. She spotted a note on one of the desks with the Wi-Fi password and instructions for side-loading a special app just for NovaCampers.

"Oh, my Gosh, Molly! The Camper's App has a calendar full of camp activities and a social app for friending campers and counselors." Still staring at her phone, Claire turned in a circle. "There's a map of the campus that tracks our position and even knows which direction we're facing. By the way, can I have that bed, please?" referring to the one Molly had just put her bags on.

It made no difference to Molly. They were identical beds, each in a corner on either side of the sole window. "Sure, Claire, that's fine!" Molly moved her bags and started downloading the Camper's App.

Claire headed for the door. "I'll see you in the lobby. Don't forget to lock up when you leave."

Molly loaded the app and was about to leave when she heard a knock on the door. She opened it, and there stood Jo Beth Taylor.

2
LTG

Jo Beth had her hands up in peace. "I know I'm the last person you want to see."

Absolutely the last, Molly thought. This was the first time they had been face-to-face since Jo Beth destroyed that guitar. At school, Molly had seen her from a distance, but she had managed to maintain a safe distance until today.

"Just give me two minutes, and I won't bother you again all summer."

I wish!

"I want to explain what happened," Jo Beth said.

"There's nothing to explain. You lied to me. Again," Molly said. Her voice was calm; she wasn't upset at all. *That's good,* she thought. *If I can stay chill with Jo Beth in my face, I might actually have a great summer!*

"But it wasn't a lie — I really wasn't going to NovaCamp! So I canceled the plane trip and went to Miss Jarrett to make it official. I thought it would be simple, but she went right into counselor mode and kept at it until I changed my mind. She made me realize I was throwing away the chance of a lifetime."

Molly rolled her eyes. "Seriously? It was the school counselor's fault! It's funny how nothing is ever *your* fault. And keeping it a secret from me; was that Miss Jarrett's idea, too?" The sarcastic remark echoed down the hall. *God, I hope none of the other girls hear this.*

Jo Beth lowered her eyes. "No, that was my bright idea. I should have told you, but I kept putting it off. Part of me was afraid you'd bail if you knew I was coming."

"I've known for weeks, and I didn't 'bail.' I admit I thought about it, but, like you said, 'Chance of a Lifetime!' Besides, LTG's a big place; we can probably go all summer without seeing each other. I'm certainly going to try." Molly checked the time on her phone and showed it to Jo Beth. "You don't want to be late for Orientation."

Jo Beth didn't budge. "They put me upstairs, so I can't promise you won't see me, but I do promise I'll leave you alone."

"That's good enough," Molly said, but she had thoughts. *You can see me all you want, but this is the last time we talk. When you break your promise and speak to me, I won't respond. I have nothing more to say to you.* Molly looked over at the elevator, a not-too-subtle hint.

Jo Beth continued. "And don't worry that we'll be on the same project. Miss Jarrett checked with LTG, and they said there was only a 5% chance we'd end up together. If that happens, they said I could switch to a different project, and I promise I will."

"Uh-huh." *Does she really think I'm stupid enough to believe that, after what happened the last time I trusted her? But it's good to know we can switch projects.* Molly checked her phone a second time, and Jo Beth finally took the hint, exiting down the stairs. That left Molly alone with her thoughts. She had kept her cool, and that was a win, but this was only the first round.

After Orientation, Molly joined her friends for dinner in the Cafeteria.

"I can't believe that speech didn't piss you guys off!" Katrina said.

"It didn't make me feel very welcome!" Molly said. "It wasn't so much what Mr. Campbell said as the way he said it."

"I know!" Claire said. "But nothing Mr. Crankypants said will keep me from having fun this summer. Take this 'cafeteria', for instance. It's more like a food court, the best food court ever! They even have a McDonald's!"

Katrina shrugged. "I do like Ronald's coffee, but," she held up her pizza slice, "this 'Hacker's Heaven' deep-dish is lit! And these guys are open 24/7! One more reason I don't want to be sent home, but I hate all these bullshit rules. Like the 'tell no one' rule! Whoever heard of a summer camp where you can't tell your friends what you're working on?"

"But this isn't an ordinary summer camp," Aaliyah said. "We're working on *real* LTG products — products other companies would love to find out about."

"And other countries, too," Claire added.

"So you're OK with Campbell spying on us?" Katrina asked. "He said they're monitoring our communications!"

"I'm sure he didn't mean that," Molly said.

Katrina cocked an eyebrow. "Oh, he meant it, alright. I'll prove it to you! Remember how he said 'no Snapchat'? Watch what happens when I try to use it." She pulled out her phone and opened Snapchat. "I'll hit 'Camera,' and… See," she said, holding the phone up. "The 'Camper's App' hacked our phones!" A large red and yellow box hovered over Snapchat. It said,

<Function Disabled>

"Whoa! I bet it's reading our texts and emails, too!" Aaliyah said.

"And tracking our phone calls," Claire said. "It would be easy for a company like LTG. They could do it like the CIA: an AI scans every conversation for certain keywords. If the AI gets a hit, it passes it on to a human to evaluate."

"Which means what, exactly?" Molly asked.

"It means you can talk dirty to your boyfriend as long as you don't leak any LTG information." Everyone laughed. Claire blushed at her own joke.

"Claire, I've known Molly less than a day," Katrina said, "and I already know she doesn't talk dirty to anyone! Besides, Southern Girls don't kiss and tell, do they, Aaliyah?"

Aaliyah laughed. "I'll tell you anything you want to know about my boyfriends as long as you don't tell them about each other."

"Yes, please," Claire said. "I want to hear it all!"

"I'll tell you about my adventures, too, Claire," Katrina said. "I bet they top Aaliyah's!"

Aaliyah winked at Katrina. "Claire, you may end up learning more than you bargained for."

Claire's pale cheeks glowed pink, even as she giggled with delight.

Thankfully, that seemed like the end of the conversation. Molly had expected to be teased about being from Alabama — that was all in fun. But this sharing personal stuff? She didn't want to go there.

Molly looked up when the table went silent. All three girls were looking at her. Molly sighed. "Oh, you want me to share, too?"

"No, not if you don't want to." Katrina waved her wedge of pizza back and forth, sending a greasy olive slice into the air.

"Thanks," Molly said. "I guess I don't want to 'kiss and tell.' You'd probably find it boring, anyway." Not probably, definitely. Her only "boyfriend," Daniel, had asked her to choose between him and wearing glasses. Easy decision.

Katrina shrugged it off. "That's cool. Forget about it."

"Of course!" Aaliyah added, and Claire smiled and nodded. Then Claire noticed the runaway olive slice had landed on her tray. Every muscle in her face contracted. Her eyes bugged out, and her mouth stretched impossibly wide, making her look like a blue-eyed frog. Everyone laughed, even Claire.

The next morning, Molly and her friends headed back to the Exhibition Hall. Like everyone else, they were wearing their bright orange NovaCamp T-shirts. The counselors had similar T-shirts, but with the word “STAFF” added in giant letters.

When the doors opened, a sea of orange poured into the spacious hall. All but the first ten rows were roped off, so Molly and her friends claimed the first group of four seats they could find. They had visited for some time when Molly realized they'd been sitting there for fifteen minutes.

Finally, the lights came down, and Michael Bradford walked on stage. Molly had seen his picture on TV and the Internet, but from a few yards away, he made a different impression. He was about Molly's size and couldn't have weighed much more. He looked like a teenage boy with a fake goatee.

Wearing designer jeans and a bright orange and green Hawaiian shirt, he jaunted across the stage with the cocky confidence of a high school quarterback. He went to the front of the stage and sat down with his legs dangling over the edge.

“Hello, ladies!” he said, his amplified voice echoing in the large room. “I'm Mike. Not ‘Mr. Bradford.’ Mike! I'm so excited to be kicking off the first annual NovaCamp, a very special opportunity for some very special young women — you! When I look out at your faces, I see the future of our industry. Heck, the future of humanity! I know you can achieve great things, and we want to help. After all, you are the Future!” He pulled his shirt open to reveal the slogan on his T-shirt, “The Future is Female.”

“I'm sure you're all eager to find out what your project is, so here's what we're going to do. When we finish here, I want you to find a nice, private place outside to look at your phone. Then we'll send you a personal text message with the location and room number you should report to. Remember that you can use your app to guide you anywhere you want to go on campus, like this.”

The screens behind him switched to a live screenshot of the app, showing the steps to locate a building and then a room.

"OK. I think that does it. Thank you for coming to NovaCamp, and have a great summer!" The campers all rose to their feet, clapping and cheering. Bradford stood back up, waved to the crowd, and walked off, already buttoning his shirt. The applause tapered off, and the campers headed for the exits. Once outside, they scattered out across the lawn like children on an Easter egg hunt.

Everyone's phone chimed at the same time. Molly's text said, "Exeter East, Room 313," with a button that opened the app for her.

That's how it began.

Exeter East was a white tower that Molly had imagined as a gigantic Lego block that landed on its short end. Now that she stood outside the entrance looking straight up, the illusion vanished. Its height surprised her, and she wondered how many floors it had.

Not that it mattered; Molly would be spending her summer on the third floor. She couldn't wait to check it out. After all, LTG was famous for creative, fun workspaces.

The elevator's control panel revealed there were seventeen floors. She chose the third floor and arrived in seconds. The doors opened in the center of a long hallway lined with glass-fronted conference rooms. The left half had ten rooms, five on either side. The right half was identical, except for the smiling woman three doors down.

"Welcome to room 313, Molly! I'm Brittany Keller, and you're the last member of our team." Black shoulder-length hair with blunt bangs framed Brittany's face. She was probably in her twenties. Her black-rimmed glasses and white lab coat had made her seem older, but her youthful voice gave her away.

"Come in and introduce yourself."

When Molly reached the glass wall, she made the mistake of looking inside. Of the five girls seated around the table, only one looked up: Jo Beth Taylor. Molly stumbled just enough that all the other girls looked up, and Molly knew all but one. There sat Katrina, Aaliyah, and Claire.

Katrina rolled her eyes as if to say, "Nice entrance," but Jo Beth's reaction was all that mattered. She looked as surprised and miserable as Molly. *Don't panic,* Molly told herself, and somehow managed a smile as she walked through the door.

Brittany invited her to have a seat, and then everyone introduced themselves. The girls Molly knew went first, followed by the one Molly hadn't met yet. A petite brunette with a pixie haircut, Emma Nelson was from Trenton, New Jersey.

Then it was Molly's turn. "Hi, Emma. I'm Molly Williams, and I'm from Birmingham, like Jo Beth. In fact, I go to the same school as Jo Beth."

"Wait," Katrina said. "Both of you go to the same school? How could that happen?"

"Maybe it's because we both nailed that bizarro entrance exam," Jo Beth said.

"Did you like my questions?" Brittany asked with a playful grin.

"You wrote the entrance exam?" Katrina asked. "I thought you were a medical technician!"

Brittany looked down at her coat and laughed. "The lab coat! I think that will make more sense when we get upstairs. And I didn't write the whole test, just the 'bizarro' questions. They helped us determine aptitude for our project. No one else scored close to the six of you. That's how we ended up with two girls from the same school. Incidentally, I sure hope you two get along, because teamwork is crucial on this project."

"We definitely do," Jo Beth said before Molly could answer. "We're writing a video game together, and we're always sharing tips and hacks. That's why we hoped we'd be on different projects. Can I transfer to another team?"

"Oh," Brittany said. "Well, you can transfer, but I don't think you'll want to, once you see what we're doing. This is a major breakthrough, paradigm-shifting technology!"

Emma spoke first. "What exactly is this amazing technology?"

"I'm dying to tell you, but the boss made it clear he gets to do that. He'd fire me for even hinting at it."

Katrina scoffed. "I think you might be overselling it!"

Brittany shook her head. "I'm really not, but I can't blame you for being skeptical." She pursed her lips and looked at the manila envelope in front of her. "Why don't we go upstairs and check it out? If any of you still think I've oversold it, I'll help you transfer to a different project. Fair enough?" She upended the envelope, pouring six security badges on the table. Each displayed a color picture of the camper, her name, and a barcode.

Yes! Molly thought. *I'm not going to be on the same project as Jo Beth! If she doesn't leave, I will. There's no way I'm spending this entire summer on a project with her!*

"Do all campers get badges?" Aaliyah asked. Molly picked hers up and wondered when they had photographed her. She had on her NovaCamp shirt, so it must have been today.

"They do," Brittany said. "Most buildings on campus have some security. Our lab has the most. Let's go see it." She led them back to the elevator. When everyone was inside, she selected the button marked "Roof." Molly started to ask if she'd hit the wrong button when the elevator spoke:

"Restricted access, scanning occupants. All occupants have proper clearance."

"Was that RFID or facial scan?" Emma asked.

"It's both," Brittany said. "There are three types of security built into that badge. With biometrics, that's four-factor authentication to reach our floor. Without our badges, we'd get no further than the twelfth floor."

"But why," Katrina asked, "are you taking us to the freaking roof?"

Brittany grinned as the doors opened. "I'm not. Welcome to the eighteenth floor, the one that doesn't exist."

3
The Lab

THE EIGHTEENTH FLOOR was the exact opposite of the third floor. *This* was a data center. Instead of carpet and conference rooms, it had raised floor tiles and glass walls. Behind that glass, hundreds of server racks blinked in the dim light.

"Wow!" Molly said. "How many buildings do these servers support?"

Brittany laughed. "Not even all of this building. This is 100% dedicated to your project." She turned to Jo Beth. "The boss is going to give you a tour and then disappear. If you still want to transfer after that, please don't say anything until he's gone. I'd much rather ask for forgiveness than permission."

They continued to the end of the hall, to a door marked "Restricted Access." Brittany pointed to the security camera above it. "Welcome to the most secure area in all of LTG. That door only unlocks if the camera recognizes you."

Once inside, the girls encountered a bank of eight computer racks, no doubt networked to the server farm outside. These racks were too stuffed with servers to allow any glimpse of what lay behind them. Whatever it was, it required an astronomical amount of bandwidth. Two large fiber cable bundles rose from each rack to the ceiling, where they converged somewhere out of view. What was all that bandwidth for?

It would be a while before Molly found out. Brittany came to a halt and turned to face them. She stood between the end of the server racks and a round lunch table, blocking the path around the racks. "I know you're all dying to see what's behind those servers," Brittany said, "but there's someone I want you to meet first."

"Here I am," said the lanky blond man appearing from behind the racks. A broad smile lit up his face, but that light never reached his eyes.

"Everyone, this is Harold Reston, the head of our project."

"Welcome to the Sandbox project!" Harold gestured to the area behind the servers. "It's no exaggeration to say this is the most important project at LTG, possibly the entire tech industry."

"And you named it The Sandbox?" Katrina asked.

"Mr. Bradford named it 'The Sandbox' because it's limited only by your imagination. You even program it with your imagination. Have any of you heard of a BCI?"

"A Brain-Computer Interface," Molly said. "Everyone's working on one, but it's still a decade or more in the future."

"That is the general consensus, Molly, but the consensus is wrong. We've not only developed a fully functional BCI; we've tied it to an immersive virtual reality. You haven't heard about our breakthrough because the entire project is top secret. So secret, it doesn't exist. Outside of this room, only two people have any knowledge of the project."

"That's why we're standing out here!" Jo Beth said. "You don't want us to see the tech until we sign a non-disclosure!"

"You and your guardians have already signed an NDA. LTG *will* come after your parents if you reveal any trade secrets, so I need your personal guarantee you won't tell *anyone* what we're doing."

"Even our parents?" Claire asked.

"Especially your parents." He paused. "If you can't keep this a secret, I need to know right now. Do any of you think that will be a problem? Please be honest with yourselves."

The girls looked around at each other, expectant and excited. Aaliyah broke the silence. "We've got this."

"Good. Let me introduce you to the rest of the team." Harold turned to his right. "Come on, guys, just a quick introduction, then you can get back to work."

A young man about Molly's height strode into the room. He had bronze skin, a solid build, and sun-bleached hair that reached his shoulders. "Greetings!" He gave them a laid-back wave.

"This is Uriel Page, ladies. He and Brittany keep the simulation running. They develop and maintain bleeding-edge software on the most powerful computer cluster LTG has ever built. When you're plugged into the system, they will monitor both the system and your vital signs at all times."

"Did you say 'plugged in'?" Claire's voice rose high enough for a cartoon mouse.

"Oh, that's just our little joke, Claire," said the woman now standing beside the server racks. "It's a 'Matrix' reference." She stiffened a little when everyone focused on her, but she didn't lose her warm smile. "Our tech is totally non-invasive. We don't even use sticky electrodes. You just put on a cap."

"This is Genevieve Wallace," Harold said, "master programmer and your guide in the Sandbox. Come join us, Genevieve."

Genevieve came a step closer. She was pale and thin, with light, almost white hair that hung straight down the back of her lab coat past her waist. Rapunzel. She took the time to look each camper in the eye before saying, "Welcome to the Sandbox, ladies. You are going to love this!"

As the silence that followed grew longer, Harold's brow grew more furrowed. "Hmm, weren't you, hmm, going to highlight the system's design and capabilities?"

"I was, but I can't wait to see the look on their faces when they see what we've built."

Harold's nostrils flared so briefly that Molly almost missed it. After a lengthy pause, he shrugged his shoulders. "Then it's time for us to see the lab! Will you do the honors, Genevieve?"

"Of course!" Genevieve pivoted around to face the lab, her hair tracing a bright arc through the air before falling back into place.

As a line formed behind Genevieve, Molly found herself stuck at the very end. When Katrina said, "Holy Crap!" all Molly saw were some workstations to her right and a small office in the corner. It wasn't until she rounded the servers that Molly understood Katrina's reaction. They had seen only half of this system. Another eight computer racks lined the far wall. Their cables joined the others to create a spiderweb of fiber optics across the ceiling.

Everything below the web could have come from an alien spaceship. Seven ultra-modern silver recliners faced each other in a circle. On the seat of each lay a plastic helmet and its coil of cable. The cables ran up to a fiber patch panel, suspended spider-like from the center of its web. So all this processing power and bandwidth supported these seven caps! Molly had to see the tech in that helmet.

"Please don't touch that, Molly," Harold said just before she did. Molly jerked back her hand as if she'd burned it. He covered the distance in two long strides and picked up the helmet. "Always handle it like this, where we've reinforced the edge. Otherwise, you might damage the sensors." He pointed to the clear, stubby bristles that lined the inside.

Harold held up the helmet so everyone could see. "This is our BCI cap. It interfaces with the sensory and motor cortices of your brain. This technology generates a Virtual Reality directly in your mind, without goggles, motion detectors, or gloves."

"Neural Reality," Molly said.

Harold froze with his mouth open, cutting his eyes at Molly and then Genevieve.

Genevieve grinned back. "You read the same profiles I did. These young women are going to keep us on our toes." She turned to Molly. "Harold was hoping to surprise you with that term."

"Oh, I didn't come up with it myself. I think I heard it on YouTube."

Claire and Aaliyah giggled, and Jo Beth said, "Way to twist the knife," in a stage whisper, making Molly blush.

Harold cleared his throat. "Anyway, you'll all experience Neural Reality for yourselves this afternoon. But first, we have to calibrate the caps to you. Genevieve's team will walk you through that, and I'll check in on you after lunch." He turned to leave.

"Excuse me!" Claire called out. "Mr. Reston, sir, excuse me? I wanted to ask what sort of clinical trials this technology has passed."

Harold turned around, attempting a pleasant face. "Miss Turner, I assure you, the safety of this technology is the last thing you should worry about." He gave a paternal nod and left.

Brittany turned to Jo Beth. "Well, what have you decided? Are you staying with us?"

Jo Beth started to answer, but stopped to peer sideways at Molly.

It took Molly a second to realize Jo Beth wanted her permission. *Damn it!* Molly thought. *Why do I have to decide?* She looked down at the cap in her hands. *I really want to be on this project, just not with Jo Beth. And if I tell her no, then I'm the bad guy.* Molly reluctantly nodded her assent.

She started to put the cap back when Aaliyah said, "Can I see that? I'm not sure it will fit over my natural hair."

Genevieve walked up and said, "It should fit fine, but let's try it now. There are straps on the front and back to keep it in position. If you girls watch us, this will help you adjust your own caps."

After helping Aaliyah, Genevieve pointed to the chair. "Did you girls notice the number '2' here and on the cap? Once we assign you a number, we'll calibrate that specific cap to your brain. But to calibrate the cap, we need you over here." She walked past the chairs to the second row of servers. "We've set up six cameras to capture your movements while we record your neural activity."

"These numbers are really classy," Jo Beth pointed to the six sticky notes on the floor.

"At least you get to be Number One." Uriel handed her the cap marked "1." He positioned Aaliyah in front of the '2' sticky note and then handed out the other caps. Soon Molly was wearing cap #4 and trailing a long white cable that draped behind her and looped up to the ceiling.

When everyone was in position, Genevieve stood in front of them. "What you're about to do might seem silly at first, but if you don't take this procedure seriously, your Sandbox experience will be horrible. Please try to copy me the best you can, without adding extraneous movements."

She led them through a series of moves: balancing on one foot, knee bends, and cross-toe touches. Then Uriel and Brittany came over to help. Each of them played tennis ball catch with two campers. Molly and Claire were assigned to Uriel.

Claire couldn't conceal her excitement over this. She blushed and giggled, and talked nonstop. Uriel had to remind her that talking would spoil the calibration. Claire sulked in silence for the rest of the exercise.

The final activity calibrated their hearing. With their eyes closed, the girls raised their left or right hand to show which side they heard music from. After a few minutes, Genevieve announced that they were finished. "Put your caps up and help yourselves to the pizza Brittany ordered. After lunch, we'll go into the Sandbox."

Molly smiled. *I wondered why I kept thinking about pizza!* Brittany had stacked five pizza boxes on the break table. Thanks to the lab's aggressive air handling, Molly didn't smell them, but she knew even a few molecules could plant a subliminal idea. When Brittany opened the boxes, there was no mistaking the delicious aroma.

Brittany also set out napkins, cups, and two-liter bottles of Coke and Sprite. "There are bottled waters in the fridge, if anyone wants one." She pointed to the refrigerator in the corner.

Molly got a big slice like the other girls, but she didn't want to start eating before Brittany. "Aren't Uriel and Genevieve coming?" she asked.

"I'm afraid we've got too much data to process. We're going to eat at our desks." Brittany had already grabbed a pizza box and a liter of soda when Claire stopped her with a question.

"Brittany, did you see the clinical data that proves the caps are safe?"

Katrina rolled her eyes. "You're not letting that go, are you, girl?"

"Hey, I want to know, too," Molly said. "We don't want unsafe technology in our brains!"

"And neither do I," Brittany said. "I haven't seen the clinical trial results, but Harold told me we passed with flying colors. And I've monitored Genevieve's brainwaves and vital signs before, during, and after every simulation for a year. That's shown me how safe it is. And I'll be monitoring all of you the same way. So relax and have fun in there. I've got you."

"Thank you!" Molly and Claire said.

Now Molly tried the pizza. It tasted even better than it smelled. She quickly put away three slices and almost grabbed one more before she realized she was already full.

From here, Molly had a good view of one of Brittany's monitors, but she didn't recognize any of the software running on it. Of course, she wouldn't. This hardware was light-years beyond anything she had seen, so why would they use run-of-the-mill software? *Remember, Dorothy, you're not in Kansas anymore!*

"Earth to Molly." Aaliyah waved her hand at her. "I was saying that you and I came in on the same plane, but we didn't know it."

"That's right."

"I was wondering," she drew closer to Molly and whispered, "why didn't you and Jo Beth fly together?"

Molly looked across the table to see if Jo Beth had heard, but she couldn't have. She and Katrina were debating the merits of Python over other languages. "That was the original plan," Molly said and paused, unnerved by how familiar all this felt.

Two months ago, she and Jo Beth would always sit together at lunch to discuss NovaCamp. They had been friends since second grade and often sat together, but never with such urgency. First, they made sure they had plane seats together and would be roommates.

Then they made big plans for the camp itself. Much of it was guesswork, since this was NovaCamp's first year, but that didn't dampen their enthusiasm. Whatever the summer held, they knew it would be fantastic.

But that was before the guitar.

"Then everything changed," Molly heard herself say out loud. When questions formed behind Aaliyah's eyes, Molly improvised an explanation. "Her dad's company does a lot of business in the Bay Area, so he flew her here on the company jet."

"Ooh, fancy! But I bet you're excited she's on the team."

Molly hoped her face wouldn't betray her. "Oh, she has mad programming skills. I know she can help the team a lot." Molly didn't doubt that, but she had serious doubts about their ability to get along.

After lunch, Uriel gathered the girls around Genevieve's recliner. "While Brittany and Genevieve confirm the calibration data, I'm going to demonstrate adjusting the recliner. Then I want all of you to try it."

Following Uriel's lead, Molly positioned her cap, sat down, and eased her chair into the prone position. She remembered adjusting her seat back in the plane yesterday, just before the 757 launched her into the clouds. Now she was taking off again, on a different kind of ride. She studied the web of cables above her and smiled.

No one spoke. Only Uriel, and only briefly, as he moved from chair to chair, checking on each camper. "That's good." "Perfect." "Right." "Very good."

"What's wrong, Claire? Are you uncomfortable?"

"I'm nervous! What if you throw the switch when I'm not ready?"

"Don't worry. I'll count down from five and throw the switch on zero, so you won't be surprised."

Genevieve spoke from her chair. "Don't forget I'm going with you, Claire. Not just this time, but every time you enter the Sandbox. I promise it's safe, and you'll have fun."

"Thank you," Claire said.

"Everyone ready?" Uriel asked. "Here we go: Five, Four, Three, Two, One…"

4
Neural Reality

The ceiling disappeared. Molly wasn't lying in the lab; she was sitting upright in a large white room. She heard gasps and murmurs as her teammates joined her in this strange world. Despite her curiosity, Molly turned slowly; Uriel had warned them about rapid head movements.

They were sitting in massive navy-colored club chairs arranged in a semicircle. There were no pictures and no other furniture, only a white carpet and walls. A floor-length beige curtain concealed most of the wall to her left. Everyone looked exactly like they had in the lab, except they'd lost their caps and cables. It all seemed so real, too real.

Molly knew intellectually that the people seated around her were simulacra, sophisticated computer models. But all her senses insisted they were real. Every detail of their appearance was true-to-life: Aaliyah's lithe physique and mocha skin, Emma's intense green eyes and jet-black hair, even Katrina's purple and burgundy hair. But these were just physical characteristics. Somehow, the simulation had also captured those ineffable qualities that made each girl uniquely human. Uncanny.

Katrina's face wasn't visible yet because she was looking at the curtain on the wall. "Pay no attention to the man behind the curtain!" she said, but when Katrina turned toward Molly, her skin turned pale, and her eyes wobbled. "Whoa!"

"Are you okay?" Molly asked.

"Not sure. I turned too quickly, and I feel like I'm gonna puke."

"Look at your hand," Genevieve said. "Breathe deeply and try to relax."

Everyone was quiet for a few seconds. Then Genevieve said, "Your vital signs and neural activity look good, Katrina. Are you better now?"

"Yeah, I'm okay; it passed quickly. What happened to me? And how do you know what my vital signs look like?"

"Brittany added a heads-up display to my avatar so I could monitor your health in real time. I can drill down into the display whenever I need to check how you're doing."

Genevieve stood up and walked to the center of the half-circle. She looked realistic but somehow different. The lab coat was missing, but there was some other change that Molly couldn't quite put her finger on. Then she saw it, a subtle difference in Genevieve's posture, as if whatever weighed her down in the lab was absent here.

Genevieve continued. "What happened, Katrina, is that you moved your head quickly before the system had finished fine-tuning your cortical map. We do everything we can in the lab, but the final phase has to occur here. You and your avatar will need a little time to get used to each other."

"No shit! I'm guessing that's why you stuck us in these grandma chairs, right?"

Genevieve laughed. "Exactly! When you take your first steps in here, you'll appreciate how sturdy Grandma builds them! Let's start with a little coordination test. Jo Beth, just give me this sign," she touched index finger to thumb tip, making the OK sign, "then we'll go around the room."

Jo Beth signaled okay, and Aaliyah signaled okay. Claire gave an OK sign, and Molly did the same. Now it was Katrina's turn, but she held up a finger. "What is this ugly-ass thing on my left hand?"

At first, Molly thought Katrina had given Genevieve the bird, but that was her fourth finger, the ring finger. And there was a ring on it: a purple, plastic-looking band with a red button where the stone should have been. It *was* ugly, just like the one Molly now noticed on her left hand.

Genevieve raised her left hand and showed them her ring. "These rings are important, and I'll tell you why right after Emma gives me the OK signal." Emma did, and Genevieve continued. "This is what we call the 'exit ring.' When you're ready to leave the Sandbox, all you do is push that button, and you'll instantly go back to the lab."

"Is that the only way to leave?" Molly asked.

"It's the only safe way. You might think we could drop your neural connection, but that would surprise the brain. The ring removes any surprise and gives your brain control. Because the last thing you want to do is surprise the brain. We learned that the hard way."

"What happened?" Aaliyah asked.

"Something that will never happen again. That was in the earliest days when we were still learning. We got our signals crossed, and they pulled someone out with no warning. But that can't happen now. You and only you control your exit."

"But what if I lose the ring, or it breaks?" Molly asked.

"The ring is a permanent part of your avatar. If your avatar is functioning, the ring is functioning. And your avatar will never malfunction."

"Can we stand up now?" Jo Beth asked.

"Not just yet. You have to know the rules! One, move slowly. Two, hold onto the chair for support. And Three, stay there until I've checked on you in person. Okay? Let's try it!"

Molly told her right hand to grasp the arm of the chair. It obeyed perfectly; she even felt the sticky-smooth texture of faux-leather upholstery. But it all seemed artificial, like she was doing things by remote control. This was going to take some getting used to!

Molly scooted to the edge of the chair and planted both feet on the floor. She tried to stand up normally, still holding on with her right hand. That didn't feel right, either. It took a visual inspection and shifting her weight from foot to foot to convince Molly she wouldn't keel over.

Emma never got that far. She lost her balance and fell back into her chair, arms windmilling in vain. "OK," she said to no one in particular. "Next time, I'll try that slower."

Genevieve came over to help her. "Take your time and be patient with yourself." She turned to address the group. "I picked these sturdy chairs because they'll support you while you work on your balance. You shouldn't let go of the chair until you're positive you don't need it."

Molly stood for a while, waiting to get comfortable with this foreign object posing as her body. She tried lifting and replacing her feet in place. Most of the familiar sensations were there, but something felt off. It got worse when she tried to take a step.

Molly lifted her left foot to extend it forward, but the brief imbalance was overwhelming. She drew the foot back. Standing straight, balancing on one foot, shifting weight: once-routine tasks now seemed monumental. And the more Molly analyzed her movements, the more awkward they became. *I'll never get this*, she thought, shaking her head.

Genevieve saw that. "By now, your cortical maps should be complete. But these avatar bodies are not the ones you grew up with, and will take some getting used to. Trust me, this will soon feel perfectly normal. Just be patient."

It took a while, but once Molly completed her first successful step, the second and third were easier. A series of baby steps followed, each steadier than the last. At some point, Molly realized she wasn't going to fall and tried walking with her hand near but not holding the chair. She followed that by walking next to the wall and then across the most open part of the room. Molly couldn't help but notice that Jo Beth was now walking freely, too.

"Please tell me there's more to do in here than walk around these chairs," Katrina said.

"Time for the big reveal." Genevieve walked past them to the curtain. "I'll do this slowly to give you time to adjust." She pulled the curtain back about two feet, and it did take some adjusting. An entire world was hiding behind that curtain.

A sliding glass door led to a concrete patio and a lush green yard sloping out of sight. Above, enormous cumulus clouds filled a brilliant blue sky. In the distance, vast grasslands stretched to a distant mountain range.

When the curtain was fully open, Molly came close for a better look. They seemed to be on the side of a small hill. At the base of the hill, a gentle hollow cradled a meadow, carpeted with clover. Slender wildflowers waved in the wind while yellow butterflies fluttered over them.

Aaliyah went right to the glass door. "Is that real or just an image?"

"Those distant fields and the sky are a backdrop. Everything on the hill and meadow has three dimensions and feels solid. See for yourself." She slid the door open for Aaliyah, who rushed past the patio and onto the lawn. At first, she seemed sure to fall, but like a newborn foal, she progressed from wobbly to graceful in a few dozen steps.

"Hey, wait up!" Katrina went outside, and Emma and Jo Beth followed her onto the grass. Molly walked out, but stopped on the patio to see what was going on with Claire.

"Are you OK?" Genevieve asked her.

"I'm fine," Claire said. "This is amazing, but it's almost too much of a good thing."

"That's exactly how I felt the first time. We can stay in the clubhouse if you're more comfortable here."

"Thanks, but I think I've got my bearings now," Claire said and stepped outside. Without hesitation, she walked onto the lawn and knelt to feel the blades of grass.

Genevieve joined Molly on the patio. "I'll give all of you some time to get familiar with this new reality."

Molly was wondering what to do when she noticed Aaliyah waving at them from the meadow.

"Is she waving at us?" Claire asked Molly.

"Oh, I guess she is!"

"She wants us to join her. Come on."

Molly tagged along and discovered that walking down the hill was harder than she expected. When they reached the meadow, Aaliyah grinned at them. "When Genevieve was talking just now, how loud did she sound to you guys?"

"About normal," Claire said. "She was probably talking a little louder since she was outside."

"You guys saw where I was standing. I could barely hear her."

"Well, that makes sense," Molly said. "You were far away."

A huge smile lit up Aaliyah's face. "To quote Morpheus, 'You think that's air you're breathing now?' We're in a simulation, you guys! There's no air; there are no sound waves. All of that is simulated!"

"Oh," Molly said, "I hadn't thought of that!"

"They've programmed virtual sound waves that account for how 'loudly' we speak and how far apart we are," Aaliyah said. "Impressive!"

Molly felt her cheek. "I think there's virtual wind, too!"

"What?" Aaliyah rose on her toes, stretching into the wind. "I feel it. That's amazing!"

She was still in that position when Genevieve called out from the patio. "Come back inside now, please. I've got something to show you."

With a sigh, Aaliyah eased back on her heels, still grinning. "Darn, everyone is heading back," and she took off with quick, long strides.

Claire leaned near Molly and whispered, "Did you notice just now that Aaliyah got so excited she sounded short of breath?"

"She did, didn't she? Do you think that's muscle memory?"

"Like her motor cortex is constricting her vocal cords out of habit? That could be, but it's so realistic — it sounds like she's barely got any air in her lungs! I'm dying to know what's going on. I need to find a way to ask Genevieve without embarrassing Aaliyah."

She and Molly headed up the hill to join the other girls on the patio. Genevieve waited for everyone to arrive before making her announcement. "I think you've all mastered how to navigate the Sandbox. But that's just the beginning — the next step is to understand how we created all of this. Let's take a look under the hood."

5
The Clubhouse

GENEVIEVE LED THEM back inside the clubhouse. It had undergone a dramatic transformation. The clean white walls were now turquoise, and the white carpet had become a gold shag. The club chairs had disappeared, replaced by an orange mid-century sectional. Across from that stood three pinball machines.

The words "Sandbox Derby" in gaudy script flashed across the top of all three boxes. They were identical except for the names over the scores. Aaliyah and Emma were on the left machine, Claire and Molly in the middle, and Jo Beth and Katrina on the right.

Genevieve turned to address everyone. "Your Sandbox projects will succeed or fail based on their realism. The Sandbox has a next-generation physical engine, but that's only half the battle. What makes a pinball machine convincing is the details: the mass of the ball, the elasticity of the bumpers, and so on."

Emma drummed the right flipper button on her table in a machine-gun-like burst. "Are you using photosensors and solenoids?"

"No, but I could have; the physics engine supports basic circuits. But in this case, I programmed them to mimic the real thing."

Emma nodded her approval, while Katrina spread her arms out in mock frustration. "Are we going to play these, or just talk them to death?"

Genevieve laughed. "Go for it!" The simulated air erupted in clicks, clacks, and clangs.

After three balls each, neither Molly nor Claire had broken 50,000. "Let's call it a draw," Molly said. "I'm ready to do some programming."

"Good, have a seat." Genevieve indicated the sectional where Emma and Aaliyah were already sitting. "We'll start the lesson as soon as Jo Beth and Katrina finish."

"Did you program all this while we were out?" Molly asked.

"No, I just restored the room to its usual configuration. The layout earlier was a temporary one to help you with your first steps."

"So these objects already existed somewhere?" Molly asked.

"Of course. Everything in the Sandbox, including your avatar body, is a file stored in computer memory."

Claire pointed to the pinball machines. "Will we be able to create objects like that?"

"You can build anything you want," Genevieve said. "A pinball machine is just a collection of simpler components."

"Frankly," Emma said, "I was hoping to build something you can't find in any shopping mall."

"And you will, as soon as you learn how. It's my job to teach you the fundamentals of Sandbox world-building. Once you're comfortable with the rules and the tools, you'll be able to create whatever you want." She paused while Katrina and Jo Beth sat down. "For instance, here's a design for a world I've thought about building."

Genevieve nodded at the pinball machines, and all three faded away. In their place appeared a glowing green dot, no larger than a BB, pulsing in the air. The dot grew into a shimmering, translucent green sphere before unfolding like a flower. Fully open, the petals merged and began to morph into into an elaborate landscape.

The sprawling scene first revealed the meadow outside, then the hill, and the clubhouse. A winding river appeared behind the hill and entered a deep valley beyond that. A great mountain range grew, and on the side of the tallest mountain, a medieval castle took shape. On and on, the scene grew, an imaginary world rich in detail and ripe with possibilities.

This world hung in the air for several seconds before slowly disappearing. First, the color faded from every surface. Next, the surfaces themselves dissolved, leaving only a green wireframe. That last remnant flickered like a neon sign, then it, too, vanished.

The campers remained silent, their eyes fixed on the absent image. Finally, Emma said, "That's more like it!"

"You can teach us how to do that?" Aaliyah asked.

"Absolutely. Today, we'll focus on creating an object; tomorrow, we'll cover all the ways you can combine and alter objects. Then you'll have all the tools you need to create entire worlds."

Genevieve pulled a pinball out of her pants pocket and held it up for all to see. She tossed the ball upward a short distance, caught it, then tossed and caught it a second time. The third time, she tossed the pinball forward. The ball traced a perfect parabola in the air before landing in the thick carpet with a solid thud. "Now, try to create a 3D image of the ball like this." Like magic, a new ball appeared, floating in front of Genevieve. "Don't be shy," she said. "See if you can create a visual image of a pinball in front of you."

Molly looked around, expecting silver spheres to pop up in front of everyone. All she saw was a lot of concentration and frustration. *It must not be that easy,* she thought. *I'd better get started.* Bing! As soon as Molly thought about the ball, one appeared.

"Don't try so hard," Genevieve said. In response, both Emma and Aaliyah created pinballs.

"Remember that you're actually back in the lab, and this is all make-believe," Genevieve said. Soon, Claire had a ball, then Jo Beth, and finally, Katrina.

"That's great," Genevieve said. "Let's take a second to appreciate what you've accomplished. OK, now I'd like you to pick up the ball with your fingers."

Molly reached for hers, only to have it pop like a soap bubble. She noticed Claire's ball didn't pop, but it didn't cooperate, either. Instead, it disappeared and reappeared as Claire moved her hand through it.

"Not funny!" Jo Beth said. "They're just projections — you knew we couldn't pick them up."

"My hand went right through mine, and Molly's..." Claire saw Molly's face and didn't finish the sentence.

"And mine popped like a bubble." Molly's voice fell in a sigh.

"Don't worry," Genevieve said, "that's a good sign. Your brain has accepted this world as real, so it rejected that ball for acting unreal. Trust me; you're going to master this quickly."

"But why bother? What can we do with a ghost ball?" Jo Beth asked.

"I'll show you." Genevieve looked at her left hand and turned it palm up. Instantly, a shining screen appeared in her hand. It looked like the screen of a computer tablet, but only the screen; no case, no buttons. She held the display up for everyone to see.

"That's a badass tablet," Katrina said. "I want one."

Genevieve smiled. "You have one. Just like the exit ring, a coding screen is part of your avatar. Instead of wearing it, you access it with a hand gesture. It disappears if you close your hand above it." Genevieve swept her free hand over the screen and brought her fingers together in a loose fist. The screen disappeared.

"And it appears with this gesture." She flipped her hand palm up, and the screen reappeared. "See if you can make yours appear."

Katrina mimicked the palm-up gesture, and a coding screen appeared in her hand.

"That's great, Katrina. Now make it disappear." When Katrina hesitated, Genevieve said, "Don't worry, it will always exist in the

Sandbox because it's part of you. These gestures just determine if it's active or not."

Katrina made the screen disappear and immediately retrieved it again.

"Good job," Genevieve said. "Now, everyone try it."

Molly performed the retrieve gesture, and a glowing screen blinked into existence. She tried the hide gesture, and it was as if it had never existed.

After everyone had hidden and retrieved the coding screen several times, Genevieve continued. "OK. Put away the screen for now and try to imagine that ball again."

Molly jumped at this second chance. Seconds later, she was smiling back at herself from the ball's shiny surface.

"Now," Genevieve said, "while you hold the ball with your mind, use the hand gesture to get your screen back."

Molly retrieved her screen without looking at it, afraid to take her eyes off the ball.

"I promise the ball won't disappear if you look at the screen," Genevieve said. "Your mind is more than capable of doing two things at once. Good. You'll notice there are only two buttons to choose from: Create and Retrieve. Choose Create."

Molly tapped the button, and the entire screen blacked out. A white square appeared in the center, slid out of the screen, and formed a wireframe cube in front of her. Despite Genevieve's promise, Molly checked to verify her ball was intact. The cube followed her gaze and slipped around the pinball to enclose it.

Genevieve's instructions matched what was happening. "Use your imagination to position the Container cube around your object. This binds it to whatever properties you select."

Then Molly noticed the new page on her screen. The upper left corner had a blank box labeled "Name," and under it, a thumbnail of the pinball. Below were sliders for various properties, such as hardness, mass, and elasticity. Molly noticed that just thinking about a property caused the slider to adjust to the left or right. She looked at the Name box, and it changed to "Pinball."

Molly guessed she could save her new object by thinking of pushing the Save button, and she was right. Immediately, the ball crashed to the floor with a plop.

"And that is how a ghost ball becomes a real ball," Genevieve said. "Once you save the new object, it replaces your mental image. Your floating image becomes a solid, heavy object." One by one, the other silver balls joined Molly's on the floor.

"That was great, girls; why don't we call it a day?" Genevieve said. "By the way, how long would you guess we've been in the Sandbox?"

"Forever," Katrina said. "At least five hours."

"Gee, I think it was more like three," Claire said.

"There's no correct answer," Genevieve said. "I'm just curious what you perceived the time to be."

"I'd say right in the middle," Jo Beth said, "about four hours." Molly and Aaliyah shook their heads in agreement.

"So, somewhere around four hours?" Genevieve looked down at her screen. "It was actually only an hour and twenty-two minutes."

"What?" said almost everyone. Katrina said, "Bullshit!"

"No, it's true. We'll get back to the lab at about five o'clock. Since everything in the Sandbox happens in the synapses of your brain, it happens quickly. That's what we call the Time Dilation effect. On average, the real time is about one-third of the perceived time. Just something to be aware of. Now, let's talk about leaving the Sandbox.

"Remember how disorienting it was when you arrived here? Going back the first time can be just as confusing. So we're going to do this one at a time, and Uriel and Brittany will make sure everyone lands safely back in the lab. Let's start with you, Aaliyah. Visualize yourself reclining back in the lab and send yourself back."

Aaliyah smiled, touched the exit ring, and faded out of existence. Molly had expected Aaliyah to disappear, but didn't realize it would be so hard to watch. She had assumed it would be like ending a Zoom call, but that wasn't what she experienced. She had seen her friend, standing right next to her, cease to exist.

It got better. Emma went next, and then Jo Beth, and then it was Molly's turn. She reached for the ring, hesitated, but then touched it. Molly stared at her hands, expecting them to fade away. Instead, the room and everyone else turned transparent.

Then she was looking at Uriel's face. "Big breath." He demonstrated, giving her a detailed look inside his nostrils. Normally, this would have grossed Molly out. Today, it barely registered with all the other sensory information bombarding her. Molly inhaled and felt her rib cage expand, felt the firmness of the recliner against her back. She smelled the slight hint of ozone in the lab air. When was the last time she'd noticed this sort of thing? Genevieve had said they could feel disoriented — talk about an understatement! Molly had just exited an artificial world and entered the real one. Why did it feel like the exact opposite?

"Wiggle your fingers. Stretch a little, and then we'll get this cap off of you." Uriel guided her hands to the cap, and she lifted it off herself. "I'm going to slowly raise you up to a sitting position," he said, "then I need you to sit here a few moments while I help the others."

"Wasn't that the coolest thing ever?" Aaliyah was already out of her chair and standing between Molly and Katrina. "Just think of all the FLOPs it takes to render that world in real time."

Molly heard the words and thought she understood them, but she wasn't quite sure what to do with them. Aaliyah's words, like everything in this moment, seemed strange, out of place. Molly smiled at Aaliyah, hoping to pass for normal while she waited to feel that way.

Katrina also seemed unfazed. "It renders everything with very high resolution, in stereoptic vision, and the depth of field is always perfect."

"Can you believe it?" Aaliyah asked, breathless with excitement. "We're going to build our own world!"

"Or worlds," Emma said. "It might be exciting to see what we can come up with individually."

"No, I want to work with all of you," Claire said.

"I'm sure we'll do both kinds of work," Molly said.

Claire sighed. "That would be okay, I guess."

"Sure it will," Aaliyah said. "Don't worry, Claire, it will all be fun."

A few minutes later, the girls headed over to the cafeteria, talking about the Sandbox the whole way. As they entered the building, Molly realized she no longer felt disoriented.

The girls ordered their food in a hurry, eager to resume their discussion. They sat together in the far corner of the cafeteria where no one would hear them. At first, there was a lot of speculation: how the cap worked, the simulation's hardware requirements, and its possible applications in the real world.

"I'm still pinching myself," Aaliyah said. "I never dreamed I'd get to work on a project this secret and this important."

"It sucks that I won't get to mention it on my college applications," Jo Beth said.

"It sure does," Katrina said. "But you couldn't ask for a better experience than this."

"I don't know," Claire said. "I think it would be better if there were boys."

"Strong disagree!" said Jo Beth, while the other girls nodded in agreement. "Our school is big on group projects, and I always try to avoid the boys. They just don't get teamwork."

"Jo Beth's right," Katrina said. "I'm guessing you don't have any brothers, Claire. I have one, plus three sisters, and they're all younger than me. We all get along fine, except for Martin. Youngest kid, but just because he has a dick, he thinks he gets to run everything."

"How old is Martin?" Molly asked. "My little brother is ten."

"Oh, so's mine! What an irritating age."

"I think I would have liked a brother or sister," Claire said. "It can be lonely growing up as an only child."

"I agree," said Aaliyah. "I supposedly have a half-brother somewhere, but I doubt I'll ever meet him. I haven't talked to my mom since I was six. My Gran raised me."

"Personally, I like being an only child," Emma said. "I wouldn't want an older sibling who tried to parent me, or a younger one I had to parent."

"Try parenting four of them," Katrina said. "My parents are always at work, so I've been babysitting since I was ten years old."

"No wonder you cuss so much," Aaliyah said.

Katrina laughed. "Damn straight!"

They all talked and made plans for over three hours. They would have talked even longer, but Molly was exhausted and told them so.

She got ready for bed as soon as they reached the room, and Claire followed suit. Molly was about to doze off when Claire said, "Do you mind if I ask you a question?"

"I don't mind. Should I turn my light on?"

"No, thanks. I'm about to fall asleep. But I have to ask: are you and Jo Beth really great friends? I noticed you didn't talk to each other all night."

"Oh, is that right?" It wasn't exactly a lie, but Molly felt her ears turning red.

"Come on, spill! What's going on with you two?" Claire turned on her light and sat on the edge of her bed, eyes wide and eager.

6
The Castle

MOLLY SIGHED AND rolled over to face her roommate. With her eager expression and Hello Kitty pajamas, Claire could have been a six-year-old on Santa's lap. *The last thing I want to do is hurt her,* Molly thought, *and I'm not going to lie to her, but...*

But she knew she couldn't share her deepest secrets with Claire. That was just too risky.

"You asked if Jo Beth and I are good friends. No, we're not. I know Jo Beth told Brittany how well we work together, and that's true. Jo Beth is a born coder, but that doesn't make us best friends. More like "work friends."

Claire twisted her face into a big question mark. "So, you're not angry with her?"

"No," Molly said with excess conviction. *Why'd she have to ask me that? Of course, I'm angry with Jo Beth. She acts like we did nothing wrong. Like she made everything okay with her big checkbook. If only life were that simple!*

Claire's eyes narrowed. "I can tell you're holding something back, but I'm not going to take it personally. I'm pretty sure you have trust issues. I mean, you wouldn't even tell us about your boyfriends."

"That's because I've never had one." Molly felt her ears warming again, this time with the lights on. She wondered: did she have trust issues? Wasn't this more like setting boundaries? "Some people are just more private than others," she said, "but I didn't mean to hurt your feelings. I do trust you! I trust everyone here. Well, except for Mr. Reston."

"Harold! Oh yeah, he's hiding something."

"I get that same feeling," Molly said, "and I worry it might be tied to our safety. But he's just Management, and I know the Techies have our back. They'll keep us safe in there!" *At least,* she thought, *I hope so.*

"You mean Genevieve, Brittany, and Uriel? That's true, isn't it? And I trust them completely! I guess that's why I feel so safe in there." Claire crawled back into bed and turned off her light. "Goodnight, Molly."

Molly sighed quietly in the dark and wondered if she could have been more honest with Claire. She was still wrestling with that when she drifted off to sleep.

Molly woke with a start. Was that a scream? She was about to write it off as her imagination when she heard it again. Claire was screaming, "Help! HELP!"

Molly switched on her light. "Claire?"

Claire was trapped in a nightmare, whimpering in terror, flailing at the air. Molly knelt next to her and managed to touch Claire's shoulder without being hit by one of her wild punches. "Claire, wake up!" Molly blocked a backhand to her temple, held on to the fist with her right hand, and rubbed Claire's shoulder with her left. "Wake up, Claire. You're having a nightmare."

Claire's eyelids flew open, revealing wild eyes, dilated almost to blackness, fixed on some invisible terror. Molly released her fist, and Claire turned in her direction, still panting. "Molly?" she said, her voice a brittle shadow of itself. "Thank God!"

"You're fine now. It was just a bad dream."

"Where are we? We're not in the lab?"

"No, that was hours ago. You're safe in bed. Were you dreaming about the lab?"

Claire shuddered. "I was in the Sandbox. You and Brittany were trying to wake me and help me exit, but I couldn't leave. I was trapped in the simulation, some new, horrible version of it. It was a huge, infinite nothing, and I was falling through it, just falling and falling. It was awful."

"That sounds terrible," Molly said. "But it wasn't real. It was just a nightmare. You're safe here."

"Safe here," Claire said. Her brow relaxed, her eyes focused, and she raised herself to a sitting position. After examining the ceiling, the closets, and the door to the hallway, she turned back to Molly. "That was a dream, wasn't it?"

"Just a dream, Claire. Are you okay?"

"I'm OK." She paused for an extravagant yawn. "And I'm sleepy!" Claire lay down and pulled up her covers. "Thank you, Molly!"

A minute later, Claire was asleep. Molly got into bed and switched off her light, hoping she could sleep. She couldn't. Hours later, that vivid image of endless falling still haunted her. Staring up into the darkness, she wondered why.

Molly was late for breakfast and had a choice of where to sit. Emma and Jo Beth were eating at one table; Claire, Aaliyah, and Katrina were at another. Katrina waved her over, so Molly joined them. When Emma looked up, Molly smiled, but Emma didn't smile back.

"Why are they sitting by themselves?" Molly asked.

"They're roommates now!" Claire said.

"You missed all the excitement last night," Aaliyah said. "They moved Emma's old roommate upstairs, and put Jo Beth in 204 with Emma. Poor Diana had been waiting hours for us to get back from dinner."

"But she was chill about it," Katrina said, "unlike that counselor from upstairs."

"I'm glad NovaCamp did that," Claire said. "I felt sorry for Jo Beth and Emma, having to keep our project secret from their roommates. That's a lot to ask."

"It is, and that was a risk Harold wasn't willing to take," Katrina said. "He's not looking out for them; he's looking out for his job."

By nine o'clock, the girls were all back in the lab, preparing to enter the Sandbox. Molly had just gotten comfortable in her recliner when Uriel began his countdown. "Three, Two, One."

And then she was in the clubhouse, standing with the others around the same 3D map they'd seen the day before.

"Ready for another lesson?" Genevieve asked. "Yesterday, you learned how to create a simple object from scratch. Today, we'll build more complex objects. Once you're comfortable doing that, you'll be ready to build your own projects. A model like this is a group of miniature objects. But two parts of this model have much more detail than the others because I created them full-size. Can you spot them?"

Molly was raising her hand when Claire called out, "I can! The castle — it's super detailed!"

"Right, and the other one?" Claire's face went blank, so Genevieve turned to Molly. "Didn't you raise your hand, Molly? Have you got it?"

"I think it's our clubhouse and the area around it. The proportions seem to be exactly the same as those out there." Molly turned to the glass door behind her. In the sun-kissed meadow, the butterflies flitted from one swaying wildflower to the next. It seemed so real.

"That's right, Molly." Genevieve swept her hand over her screen, and most of the model disappeared. That left a circle of land containing the hill, the clubhouse, and the meadow. She pointed at the circle. "The castle is stored in memory, so this is the entire simulation right now."

"But that can't be," Claire said. "There are miles of grass stretching to the horizon."

"That's just an image projected on the dome that surrounds the simulation. Like this." As Genevieve spoke, a wireframe dome spread over the scale model. "It looks realistic, even up close, but it has no substance or depth."

"That's like a CGI background in a movie or TV show!" Aaliyah said.

"Exactly! Now, back to this castle." Genevieve made another gesture over her screen, and the dome-covered model disappeared. A large model of the castle took its place. "On the outside, our castle is complete, but inside, it's just empty rooms." She turned the model semi-transparent and revealed the floors. "It's based on Harlech Castle in Wales, one of the best preserved Thirteenth Century castles. I thought it might be fun to fill all these rooms with authentic medieval furniture and objects."

Emma said, "I hate to complain, but interior design? Really?"

"I get that," Genevieve said, "but this isn't about design. It's about mastering the Sandbox, and if you work with me, we can accomplish that in one day."

"What are these two giant rooms?" Jo Beth asked.

"On the first floor, there's the Banquet Hall," Genevieve said, "and on the second floor, the Throne Room."

"We could have two teams," Jo Beth said. "One could work on the Throne room and the other on the Banquet Hall."

"If that will make it more interesting, sure. But this is not a competition. Don't expect me to declare a winner."

"Then I want to work with Molly." Jo Beth turned to look at her. "If you could stop hating me for a minute, you'd see that we still make a good team."

Molly stared at Jo Beth. *What the hell?* she thought."I don't hate you, but I think I'll pass." This earned Molly a sharp look from Emma.

"Come on!" Jo Beth said. "Don't you think it's time to bury the hatchet?"

Molly scanned the confused looks around her and then shrugged. "Fine, it's not that big a deal."

"I'll be the third wheel," Emma said.

"And the three Leftovers will take on the Drama Queens." Katrina gave Aaliyah and Claire a group hug. Claire's eyes grew to an alarming size, and Molly chuckled despite herself.

"Before you split up," Genevieve said, "I want you to follow me outside for a final lesson." She walked past the girls to the patio.

Molly followed, only to find herself face-to-face with the impossible. The sunny landscape she had just seen was gone: the meadow, flowers, and butterflies. All gone, replaced by this monstrous fortress, casting its cold, black shadow on everything else. It stopped Molly in her tracks. She stood staring at it, unable to comprehend.

Someone was waving their hand in front of Molly's eyes, and a soothing voice called her name. Even before Molly recognized Genevieve, her presence had a calming effect. "It startled everyone, but it really clobbered you. Why is that?"

"I had looked out there just a few seconds earlier, when it was all meadow. I'm sorry."

"No, I'm sorry! I should have warned you before I added the castle. I'm so used to the way things work in here that I forget how unnatural it is. It's my job to protect all of you in the Sandbox, and I let you down. I promise that will never happen again."

"Do you need a break, Molly?" Claire pointed to the sectional.

"No, thanks; I'm fine now. It was like reality just broke. But I'm good now. Really, let's go see the castle."

Outside, Molly searched in vain for any sign of the meadow. Even the lowest part of the hill had been devoured by the ugly embankment surrounding the castle. As they walked up that incline, the castle no longer upset Molly, but she still didn't like it. It was too warlike, too much like a medieval fortress. "I wish Uriel had found us more of a fairy-tale castle."

"Yeah," Jo Beth said, "this is seriously lacking in curb appeal. But I suppose we could paint it bright colors, give it a facelift."

"Paint it?" Genevieve's voice rose in pitch. "Uriel spent so much time tracking down good photos of the actual castle; I wouldn't want him to find out we painted it."

"Could we clean it?" Aaliyah asked. "I bet it looks pretty good under all that grime."

Genevieve nodded. "Eight centuries of grime! Uriel won't mind that, and it should improve the 'curb appeal' a lot. Any ideas on how we can clean these blocks?"

"All these different stones are the same color," Molly said. "I'm guessing there's a parent class they inherited that color from."

"Go on."

"If so, we can 'clean' the stones by making that parent color brighter. Can we use the terminal screen to look for that parent class?"

"That's what the 'Retrieve' button is for." Genevieve pointed to her screen. "You take a picture of what you want to retrieve. The database does an image search and pulls up the object. Search on one of the stones, and if there is a parent class, it will show in the properties, see?"

"Not really," Claire answered. "It's so tiny."

"Sorry!" Genevieve grabbed the top of her screen with her right hand and raised it in the air. Then she pulled the bottom left corner down and over, making the screen a high-tech chalkboard. She pointed and continued, "Clicking on Castle_rock brings up the class, and clicking on the property Color pulls up this editor."

"Oh, I see now!" Claire clapped her hands in delight. "That looks like Photoshop."

A few seconds later, the entire castle sported fresh-quarried stone. "What do you think, Molly?" Jo Beth asked.

"It's a big improvement, but could we also fly banners from the towers?"

"Of course we can!" Genevieve led them up the stairs of the nearest tower. While the rest of the team tried to agree on a design, Claire produced a banner by herself. On a triangle of royal purple, a white unicorn reared up on its hind legs.

Aaliyah created flagpoles ten meters long, and they soon had five banners waving in the wind.

Katrina nodded her approval. "Good job, Boulder. I'm glad you're with the Leftovers and not the Drama Queens."

"Those names aren't funny," Molly said.

"Yeah, they are," said Katrina.

"It was funny," Jo Beth said, "emphasis on *was,* and I *can* be a drama queen, but it's time to move on. We're going to be Team 2, and you guys can be Team 1." Katrina scrunched her mouth to one side before giving a reluctant nod.

"Now that that's settled," Genevieve said, "I'm assigning the Throne Room to Team 1 and the Banquet Hall to Team 2. I promise to spend equal time with each team, but I'll start in the Throne Room. Let's get started."

Genevieve led the way down the stairs and into the Throne Room. Molly followed them, but Emma and Jo Beth continued down the stairs. Emma turned around with a big smile on her face. "Come on, Molly! Your team is down here!"

The instant they reached the Banquet Hall, Emma's smile disappeared. "What the Hell, Jo Beth? You promised to chill out until I could talk to Molly. Instead, the first opportunity you get, you start something in front of Genevieve!"

Jo Beth shrugged. "I don't see what the big deal is."

"The Big Deal?" Emma yelled, then composed herself and continued in measured tones. "I didn't sign up to ambush Molly like this. I said I'd talk to her one-on-one, in private. Now you've dragged the whole team into this. That's unfair to Molly *and* me."

Jo Beth started to speak, but Emma raised her index finger in warning. "Brittany told us how important teamwork was to them, and you just told Genevieve you two don't get along!"

Jo Beth grimaced. "OK, that was dumb. It's just…" She turned to Molly. "I mean, we were best friends for, like, ten years, and you refuse to forgive me. Hell, you won't even talk to me! Molly, I'm so sorry! How many times do I have to say it?"

"Why can't you forgive her, Molly?" Emma asked. "After all, it was an accident."

Molly glared at Jo Beth. "You told her it was an accident?" Molly heard the fury in her voice, felt the blood rushing to her face. She knew she had lost her temper and should try to control it. But first, she had to say this, "Emma, she grabbed it by the neck and smashed it on a chair!"

7
The Banquet Hall

Emma seemed to freeze. "No. That can't be right!" She fixed Jo Beth with narrow eyes. "You said it was an accident."

Jo Beth cleared her throat. "Yeah, I shouldn't have said, 'accidental.' I meant unintentional — I just lost control." Emma crossed her arms and glared at her.

"Well, it's true!" Jo Beth said. "How could I know that my asshole dad would pick that moment to call and cancel our trip to Europe? After he swore he'd never do that? 'This time is different,' he said. 'Nothing is more important than taking this trip with you.' But of course, he backed out again. Everything after that is a blur, like I was watching it happen but couldn't stop it."

The look Emma gave her was ice-cold. "So getting bad news and throwing a temper tantrum is what you call an accident?"

"OK, already. Not an accident, but it *was* random as hell! I'd been asking for a solid year to play that guitar, and then, three chords in, my father calls. So, yes, I lost my shit and smashed it on the chair."

Emma nodded. "That, I believe. Now tell me the truth about giving Molly's dad a guitar. There's no way you gave him a '39 Martin D28. I researched those, and they're crazy expensive."

Jo Beth responded by glaring back at Emma. The standoff lasted almost a minute before Molly said softly, "She can afford it, Emma.

Her dad is the richest man in Alabama. And my dad said it was super-valuable."

"Thank you," Jo Beth said and turned to Emma. "Yes, I can afford expensive toys, but the money's not the point. The point is that Mr. Wilson loved his guitar, and I felt I should replace it with a guitar that I loved."

"And Dad appreciated it," Molly said, "but it can't *replace* his guitar. That was a gift from his father."

Jo Beth nodded. "Fair. But your dad still forgave me. Why can't you?"

"Because we don't deserve forgiveness!" The angry words echoed in the giant hall. Emma made a "keep it down" gesture, and Molly did. "I should never have taken Dad's guitar off the wall, and you shouldn't have acted like a five-year-old. What kind of friend does that?"

Jo Beth stood there, stunned.

Emma broke the silence. "You guys have *got* to work this out! But not now! Now, you need to make sure our project isn't canceled."

"How are we supposed to do that?" Jo Beth asked.

"Simple. Pretend you like working together. Lose the drama and sarcasm. Be polite to each other."

After a pause, Molly nodded. "I can do that."

Emma turned to Jo Beth. "Can you?"

Jo Beth looked like she was swallowing something noxious. Then, with an eye roll, she said. "Fine!"

"Good," Emma said. "Let's get to work on this room!"

"It definitely needs work!" Jo Beth said.

Molly hadn't thought about the room before now. Jo Beth wasn't wrong. Six halogen work lamps on tripods lit the walls and floor, all of it dull gray sandstone. Overhead, soot-blackened oak beams cast fathomless shadows across the ceiling.

Jo Beth crossed the room to inspect the back wall. "What if we put a giant mural on this wall?"

After she and Emma caught up with Jo Beth, Molly took a hard look at the sprawling blank space. A picture started to form in her mind. "Oh, I'll do it! I bet I can put the colors directly on the surface without brushes or tubes of paint."

Emma inspected the wall and then Molly. "Are you sure you want to take on a project this size? Have you ever done something like that?"

"Molly's super-talented. You should see the scenery and character art she did for our game proposal. You and I can work on everything else." Jo Beth turned and headed toward the opposite wall. Emma was still looking at Molly.

"Did that compliment sound sincere to you?" Molly asked under her breath.

"I'm sorry, but it did." Then Emma left to catch up with Jo Beth.

The thing is, it sounded sincere to Molly, too. It was like Jo Beth was two people. This one, who used to be her friend, and the crazy person who accused Molly of hating her in front of the whole team. *Pick a lane!*

Molly got to work. When she closed her eyes, the entire scene was clear in her mind. But as soon as she opened her eyes, she saw a blank wall and only a portion of that. How could she lay out the mural when she could only see half of her canvas at a time? After looking back and forth like a referee at a ping-pong match, Molly let out a sigh. She wanted a scale model, but first she'd need some way to measure the wall. It occurred to her that Aaliyah's flagpoles were ten meters long.

Molly retrieved her screen and created a five-meter version of the flagpole. She increased the length until it reached the ceiling at six meters. She repeated the technique and found the width was eighteen meters. Molly drew a rectangle two meters high by six meters wide in the center of the wall.

At once, the rectangle's dull gray disappeared in a flood of blues, browns, and greens: all the colors of nature. Without conscious effort, her initial idea for the layout took shape exactly as she had imagined. Molly laughed out loud. *I definitely don't need brushes or tubes of paint*! At this scale, she could tweak the layout and identify which parts needed more work.

The first thing she wanted to change was the perspective. Quick as thought, colors bled and swirled and coalesced into a new composition. The result was better, but the paint wouldn't stop moving. As soon as a change occurred to Molly, it appeared on the wall, spawning a new idea, which became another change. It was an endless cycle.

Molly turned away from the chaotic wall to clear her mind; she had to find a way to control her thoughts! She knew how to steady a paintbrush tip; now, she needed to steady her mind.

To start, Molly washed all the color out of her thoughts. That limited the wild kaleidoscope to grayscale, but it still twisted and squirmed like a living thing. It took practice to calm her thoughts and focus on a single area of the sketch. At first, she had to use her hands to mask the scene down to a workable size, but soon that was unnecessary. Once she finished the grayscale, she would add color.

The inspiration for the mural was Genevieve's 3D map, but the details were all Molly's. The point of view was roughly where she was standing now, but reimagined as a grassy hillock. Molly had moved the castle to a majestic mountain that dominated the right third of the painting.

Along the left side stretched a dense forest of ancient oaks. Genevieve's forest had been evergreens, but Molly had something different in mind. To convey mystery, solemnity, and timelessness, only an old-growth oak forest would do. Clad in the dark greens of early summer, towering over their surroundings, hiding a secret world beneath their thick canopy, it had to be oaks.

Besides, she was eager to push the limits of this "virtual" style of painting. She didn't have to prepare her paints, clean her brushes, or even paint the same thing twice. Instead of painting hundreds of separate trees, she could mentally Xerox a single one. As needed, she could adjust their size or make other alterations.

A peaceful meadow stretched from the forest to the mountain. Molly painted the same wildflowers, grasses, and butterflies as those outside. A wide river snaked through the meadow and continued to the horizon. The foreground featured the top of the hill, with the six Sandbox campers facing the viewer. Each wore chain mail, wielded a sword, and held a large shield emblazoned with the unicorn coat of arms.

Molly stood back and inspected her work. Satisfied with this scaled-down version, she retrieved her screen and captured the painting. She named it smallMural. Then she copied it, named the new object Mural, and changed the dimensions. Just like that, her painting covered the entire wall! It seemed like cheating. What would Da Vinci or Michelangelo have thought? They both loved technology, so there was that. But they also painted with painstaking realism, which her blown-up image sorely lacked.

"Wow! Have you finished already?" It took Molly a moment to register the comment and another to process who had interrupted her. It was Emma, standing in the doorway as if she'd just entered.

"Oh, I'm just getting started. If you come closer, you'll see how much detail it needs. Did you go out?"

"I went upstairs to settle a little disagreement. Jo Beth thinks castles were lit by torches, but I said candles. We agreed to let Genevieve decide since she knows all this castle stuff."

"And what did she say?"

"Yes." Jo Beth joined them. "What did our Fearless Leader say?"

"She said torches were mainly used outside, contrary to what you see in the movies."

"In that case, pretend you don't see this." Jo Beth waved at her screen, and a flaming torch appeared in her hand. Molly leapt back. She told herself it was instinct, but Emma was just as close to the flames and hadn't jumped. Emma didn't look at her, but Jo Beth did, with wide, hurt eyes.

Jo Beth opened her mouth to speak, but didn't. Then her features softened, and she nodded. "I'm sorry, Molly. I guess it's more realistic than I realized." She turned her attention to the torch and studied it in silence. "Those flames were harder than I expected." She turned back to Molly. "I'm open to suggestions."

Molly was reluctant to take the bait. After a long beat, she answered. "Well, the colors and brightness look perfect, but the contours might be too hard and the motion a little too tame."

"Interesting," Emma said. "I thought the same thing. Natural combustion of an impure medium is going to be chaotic, anything but tame."

"Can you help me with that, Emma?" Jo Beth nodded at the mural before heading to the back wall. "Didn't I say it would be amazing?"

Molly knew she should say something nice, but the words didn't come. She just stood there watching her teammates walk away. Molly returned to the mural, wondering how she would add the missing detail. To her surprise, it just happened.

Anywhere Molly looked, smudges of color snapped into sharp detail. It was like a magical focus knob, but one she couldn't control. Molly's gaze kept darting around the scene, scattering tiny drops of clarity in a blurry ocean. She would need a methodical approach if she ever hoped to finish.

After several attempts, Molly found an effective solution: the "wallpaper" technique. She started at the top left corner of the wall and worked straight down, not letting her eyes stray to either side. By keeping her eyes straight ahead, she kept the strip's width from varying too much. When she reached the bottom, she took two steps to the right and repeated the process.

This worked so well that Molly finished the left half of the mural without a break. But she needed one now. She took her glasses off and rubbed her eyes. Then it hit her: these weren't her real eyes; they couldn't get tired! This was like Aaliyah getting short of breath — the simulation was fooling them. Or was it just force of habit? She still didn't know, but it didn't matter: her brain was tired, so she was taking a break.

With her glasses back on, Molly explored her teammates' handiwork. They had built a table, the longest Molly had ever seen: two yards wide and seven yards long. Even more impressive was how authentic it looked. It even felt ancient, like real hand-hewn oak, rubbed dark and smooth by decades of hard use. *How had they done that?*

The twenty oak chairs were equally sturdy and worn. They looked genuinely medieval, as did the ten unlit candles in shallow wooden candlesticks. Emma, with her back to her, was busy studying the candle on the far left. Jo Beth was also looking at candles. She had five of them, each as thick as a soup can, atop an iron floor candelabra three feet taller than she was. "That's a lot of candles," Molly said.

"We need a lot," Jo Beth said. "There's not a single window in here. In the real world, this room would need dozens of candles, at least eight of these monsters. We're planning to replace Genevieve's ugly work lights with natural candlelight. But I thought you might want us to wait until you finish your mural. Here's what it will look like." She glanced at her hand terminal, and seven more candelabra appeared across the room.

"That won't bother me. I'd rather paint in the light we're going to have. You can swap them out now if you want."

"I want," Emma said from behind her, "but they still need work. This has been hard, but I'm almost there." Her eyes darted across her screen, and the candle nearest her sprouted a flame. "No, wait." She studied it and made an adjustment. "And that's too fast." She made another change. "There! How's that?"

"That's perfect!" Molly said and meant it. The flame flickered exactly like a real candle flame.

"Here's the best part." Emma turned to the first table and tapped her screen. All the table candles grew flames.

"Wow!" Molly said. "Each flame has a different pattern."

"That's because the patterns are random. Now I feel bad for complaining about Genevieve's castle idea. I hadn't realized how much chemistry and physics I would use. This is actually fun!"

"Oh, I have to show you the torch flame!" Jo Beth said. "You won't believe it!" She led Molly over to the stairs. There, on the side of the doorway, an iron bracket supported a flaming torch.

The change wasn't noticeable from a distance, but up close, the difference was startling. The flame had gone from okay to amazing, from a representation to the thing itself. Molly couldn't take her eyes off it. She thought back to Emma's advice about the first torch: it needed "to be chaotic." *That was it!* Emma had harnessed the chaos, or maybe Jo Beth had; that seemed a better fit. Either way, they had injected life into this fire by ceding some control. That seemed important.

"What a fantastic mural!" Genevieve said from the doorway.

"Oh!" Molly hadn't heard her come down. "I'm not finished!" She whipped around and started back to her painting. After two steps, she stopped herself and turned back to Genevieve. "I haven't finished the right half, but it shouldn't take too long. If that's okay."

Genevieve smiled and made a "help yourself" gesture. "Of course, and there's no rush. I didn't expect you guys to be finished; I came down now because Emma asked me to. Take your time." Genevieve turned her attention to Emma and Jo Beth. "What did you need help with?" she asked.

That was the last thing Molly heard. As she approached the mural, all her senses and thoughts locked like a radar on the task ahead. She studied the remaining nine meters of work. Molly wished she hadn't promised Genevieve it wouldn't take long.

Molly needn't have worried; she soon got her rhythm back, and the strips of detail came faster and faster. By the end, she was moving sideways at almost a walking pace. Once she reached the end, Molly examined her painting from right to left, searching for spots she'd missed. She couldn't find any, so she backed up several feet and repeated the process, going left to right. She still didn't spot any problems. Molly smiled as she saved her work to the Mural object. Now she could join the others.

The three of them were in the far corner, where Genevieve was admiring one of the candelabras. Molly was impressed, too. She felt like she was standing in a real medieval banquet hall. The oak table, surrounded by chairs, had gained a twin beside it. Set end to end, they spanned the length of the room, leaving about two yards of clearance from either wall. There were forty place settings, each consisting of a wooden plate, a tankard, and a single utensil, a knife. The flickering candles, twenty on the tables and another forty on the candelabras, filled the room with ancient radiance.

Genevieve noticed Molly and asked, "Are you ready to show us your mural?"

"I think so. I'm pretty proud of it." Molly turned around and…

It was gone. She was looking at a blank wall.

8
Backup Files

PEOPLE WERE TALKING, but Molly didn't hear them. With her heart pounding in her ears, she pulled up her screen and searched for the Mural object. It had to be there! That was only logical; it was why she had saved it, so there would be a copy in memory to persist beyond this session. But her gut told her it was gone.

And Molly's gut was right; it wasn't there. She searched for smallMural and couldn't find it, either. She felt as if the room were spinning, dissolving into white. For a split second, she thought she saw the lab's wire-covered ceiling in front of her. Then it was the Banquet Hall again. She was still in the castle. The wall was still bare.

"You all saw it, right?" she asked. "It was real! I saved it to the computer, and now it's gone!"

"Now, don't panic," Genevieve said. "Are you sure you're spelling the object name correctly? Maybe you made a typo when you saved it. I've done that."

"Well, I didn't!" Molly heard how angry she sounded and tried to steady her voice. After two deep breaths, she continued. "But even if I had, it's the only object I've made today, so it should be easy to find."

"Then we need to see Brittany. She makes frequent backups and can pull up everything you created today. So, one way or another, we'll get your mural back." She turned to Emma and Jo Beth. "I need to exit with Molly, but it will only take a minute."

By the time Molly had her cap off, Genevieve, the real Genevieve, was standing beside her chair. "Are you doing better now?"

"I think I am." Molly was surprised to realize it was true. Maybe she had left some of her hurt and anger in that virtual world.

"What's wrong?" Brittany came over from her workstation.

"Can you pause what you're working on and retrieve an object for Molly? It represents her entire morning's work. Also, please change our settings so that all objects are write-protected."

"Of course."

"Molly, I have to go, but whatever this is, Brittany can fix it." Genevieve returned to her chair. With practiced ease, she swung herself into position while she whisked her long, silvery hair off her back and across her shoulder. As she pulled the cap over her head, she said, "Thank you, Brittany." A second later, her whole body went limp, as if someone had stolen her soul.

"I've never seen anyone enter the Sandbox," Molly said. "Is she OK?"

"She's fine, sweetie. What about you? Do you know what happened to your object?"

"I wish I knew! I assumed it was a system glitch, but if objects aren't write-protected, maybe someone deleted it! Why would you set up permissions like that?"

Brittany's cheeks flushed pink. "You're right, Molly. Every DBA knows that only the creator should have write permission! I even asked about that, my first week here. The application is supposed to keep this from happening, so I let it slide, but I should have fought for it. I'm doing it now, but I know that's too little, too late. I'm so sorry."

"I don't blame you, Brittany. But if someone did delete the objects, wouldn't it show in the transaction logs?"

"It should. What are the names of the missing objects?"

"Mural and smallMural."

Brittany brought up a list on her monitor. "Well, this is good news — they're both in our last backup! I'll kick off the recovery process first and search the transaction logs while it runs."

Brittany's search took less than a minute. "OK, here's where you created smallMural and then copied it to Mural. Here's where you saved it… Huh! There's no mention of those objects after that. So why aren't they still there?" Brittany turned around, and her face was paler than usual. Her eyebrows had arched over her glasses and disappeared under her bangs. "This is either a major system failure or malware, and neither one is possible!"

"Could a hacker bypass the firewall to install a rootkit?" Molly asked.

"Absolutely not. The Sandbox has security that's orders of magnitude beyond a standard firewall. Which means if it *was* a hacker, it was an inside job."

"One of the campers?" Molly asked.

"That's impossible for hundreds of reasons. But it's just as impossible that this system is suddenly glitching after a year of flawless operation. I'm stumped!" Her monitor dinged as a message appeared on the screen. "But on a positive note, your objects are back, see?"

Molly studied the display. "I was afraid of this. They're the same size, so this is the first version of Mural, before I added all the detail." Brittany looked so disappointed that Molly added, "But that won't be hard to fix. Thank you, Brittany! I guess I'll go back in and finish it up."

Molly found herself standing in the Banquet Hall again, but this time, she had the room to herself. *Thank goodness!* Until she replaced her original, she would feel as incomplete as the mural. The image before her was named Mural, but it was the very first version of it, a copy of smallMural. She would have to add all that detail back a second time.

The blurry faces of the six knights kept staring at her, so she started there. It was just a matter of recalling the heroic expressions she'd used before, so most of that went smoothly.

Until the last face, which was Jo Beth's. Molly tried to picture the original version, but it just wouldn't come to her. When she attempted to paint Jo Beth anyway, the result was barely human – a face of genuine evil. *Real life*, Molly thought, *try again and paint what she actually looks like*. The result mirrored Jo Beth's face this morning when she talked about her father. That furious face was realistic, but as useless as the first. So Molly painted a third version, trying to visualize the Jo Beth who had once been her friend. Instead, Molly painted the face of a hurting, wounded child. Would this person have stooped to destroying her mural moments after complimenting it?

That was three exhausting attempts and nothing Molly could use. At this rate, she would never finish. Molly repainted the angry face, softened the jaw and lips, and moved on to the rest of the mural. She repeated the "wallpaper" approach and found it went even faster than before. When Molly finished, she saved her work as Mural and, as an extra precaution, saved it twice more with misleading filenames.

She turned around to head upstairs and saw Jo Beth coming over from the staircase. Molly held up her hands. "Can we please not do this now?"

"Do what?" Jo Beth asked, walking up to her.

"Seriously? You weren't about to tell me you didn't do this?"

"But I didn't! You have to believe me!" Jo Beth's face was so close that all Molly saw were those frantic brown eyes.

Molly backed away, one hand up to maintain some distance. She studied Jo Beth's face; all that emotion had to be real, didn't it? But then Molly remembered Brittany's embarrassment a few minutes ago. That was real human skin blushing, a natural, autonomic response. Jo Beth had a computer-generated expression on her computer-generated face.

"We do need to talk about this, but not now, not in this place. Let's discuss it this afternoon, in the real world."

Jo Beth nodded. "That's all I wanted!" She looked down, lost in thought. When she looked up, her face was almost calm. Jo Beth pointed to the mural. "I'd say anything to get on your good side right now, but I swear," she placed her left hand over her heart. "It's perfect. I love it."

That was the third time she had complimented Molly today, and each time, she had sounded sincere. Was Jo Beth that good an actor? "You know," Molly said, "I love it, too, but you're right. I'll never know what people really think of it. They'll have to say something nice because I got so upset. I'd like their honest opinions."

"Then be grateful Katrina is on our team. If she doesn't like it, she'll straight up tell you!"

"That's right, isn't it?" Molly said. "Oh, I hope she really hates it!" They both laughed then, laughed as if nothing had changed between them. The familiar sound echoed off the stone walls and struck Molly's ears like an out-of-tune chord. She stopped laughing.

After a long silence, she said, "Well. I'm ready to see the Throne Room. I bet it's impressive!"

Jo Beth raised one eyebrow. "Oh, it's *something*, alright!"

"What does that mean?"

With a wry smile, Jo Beth gestured toward the stairwell. "I don't want to spoil it for you."

Genevieve was waiting for them when they entered the Throne Room. "Don't tell me you're finished already!" When Molly nodded, Genevieve said, "That's terrific! We all want to see it, but we knew you'd want to see this room first." She stepped to the side and gave Molly her first look at the space.

Molly's mouth fell open before she could stop it. All she could think to say was, "This is amazing!" And it was. After hearing Genevieve stress thirteenth-century accuracy, Team 1 had channeled twentieth-century Disneyland. That would have been hard to do downstairs, but here, it actually worked.

The ceiling was twice as tall as the Banquet Hall's. Sixteen stained glass windows filled the entire room with natural light. Each opening was roughly two yards long by eighteen inches wide. Their subjects came straight from a fairy tale: queens, kings, wizards, knights, and dragons. The walls were a rich cream color that basked in the warm sunlight. The ceiling had eight sections, alternating between pale pink and robin's egg blue. Mighty oak beams separated the sections.

The far wall featured three king-sized banners hung point down. They had the same unicorn design as the flagpole banners, but rotated to accommodate the vertical position. In front of the banners sat six identical thrones in a semicircle. Oversized and over-the-top, they featured purple velvet and gilded wood. The other campers took seats, and Genevieve pointed to the remaining throne. "For you, Molly."

"This is wild!" Molly sat down. "But I have to ask: what happened to the thirteenth century?"

"Good question!" Genevieve beamed like a proud parent. "Claire, why don't you tell Molly what happened?"

"Don't you just love it?" Claire pulled her shoulders up and squeezed her elbows into her ribs, giving herself a little squeeze. "It makes me feel like a real princess!"

"I do love it!" Molly said. "So, is this my assigned seat, er, throne?"

"No assigned seats," Aaliyah said. "We're all equally important, and one throne is just as good as the others."

"Which is the way we approached the entire project," Katrina said. "We created all the objects together, as a team."

"Which didn't stop Katrina from telling us what she thought," Aaliyah said. "Remember how you said these thrones looked 'ridiculous'?"

"That's true, but I have to admit, I like them now. I think being a queen suits me."

"Oh, it does, Your Majesty," Molly said.

"Thank you, Your Majesty. Art thou ready to go downstairs? I'm dying to check out the Banquet Hall."

"Of course," Molly said, and soon she was leading them down the stairwell. As soon as she exited the staircase, she verified that the mural was exactly as she had left it. She felt her back and shoulders relaxing, releasing the tension she hadn't realized was there.

Everyone seemed to love the mural, and if they were only being nice, they were very convincing. Even Katrina gushed. "I can't imagine being able to paint like that! It's amazing."

After the third glowing review, Molly spoke up. "As much as I appreciate the compliments, you need to check out the rest of the hall."

"I don't know if anyone noticed, but Emma and I have skills, too!" Jo Beth winked at Emma.

"We noticed," Aaliyah said, "all of this is incredible. It's like going back in time!"

"I love these flames," Claire said. "We talked about having a giant fireplace, but thought it would be too hard to get the fire right."

"I'd be happy to help you build a fireplace," Jo Beth said, "provided we're keeping the castle."

"If we're keeping it," Molly said, "could we move it somewhere else? Here, it ruins our little meadow."

"I hear you!" Genevieve said. "For now, the castle has served its purpose, so I'll save all this in memory and put the meadow back the way it was."

"Couldn't you move the castle to the other side of the meadow?" Aaliyah asked.

"It wouldn't fit. If we moved the castle more than a few meters, it would poke through the dome. Brittany and I could expand the simulation, but let's wait until I know what kind of projects you'd like to do. We'll talk about that after lunch, so be thinking about what appeals to you."

"Is the dome something we could examine up close?" Molly asked.

"Of course," Genevieve said. "It's right behind the castle."

"I want to see!" Claire said.

"I think we all do," Katrina said.

"That's a great idea. You should get familiar with the dome before we expand this world. Let's take a field trip." Genevieve headed to the archway that led outdoors. But instead of passing through, she slammed into an invisible boundary. Then Katrina collided with it, too. The other campers froze in their tracks.

"We're trapped!" Claire screamed.

9
Downtime

"YOU'RE NOT TRAPPED," Genevieve's tone contained a rare hint of irritation.

Katrina rubbed her forehead and spouted a few choice obscenities. Then she began groping for the barrier. "Is the entire exit blocked?"

By this time, everyone was feeling the air with their hands. "You know we look like a cut-rate mime troupe," Jo Beth said. "I think it's safe to say we're not leaving through here. Could this be the dome, Genevieve?"

"No, the dome isn't a physical barrier. It's only an image designed to give the illusion of unending space. You could walk right through the dome, but there would be nothing behind it. I don't know what this is, but at least it's not our only exit. Let's take the stairs."

This time, Genevieve stopped short of the stairwell and tested the air with her hands. Her palms banged against another invisible barricade. She turned around slowly, and whatever she was feeling, it didn't show on her face. "Let's stay calm. This is odd, but it shouldn't be hard to fix." She pulled up her screen, navigating through page after page of streaming code.

Molly was trying to stay calm, but it wasn't working. A dark castle had appeared out of nowhere, her mural had vanished off the wall, and now they were all trapped! Molly told herself that it wasn't real, that her body was safe in the lab, but fear still throttled her throat like a fist. "Can we just go back to the lab, please?"

Genevieve looked at her. "Of course, Molly. You've had quite the day, haven't you? Girls, let's go back. And today, we can all go at once."

Molly touched her exit ring. The castle walls shimmered and disappeared, replaced by the comforting geekiness of the lab. She filled her lungs with a glorious breath of real air. Then she realized Harold was staring down at her with concern. "Are you OK?" He offered her his hand.

"I think so." Molly grabbed his hand and pulled herself up. *This doesn't mean I trust you*, she thought. "How did you know something was wrong?"

"Your vital signs spiked. An alarm text goes out to all of us whenever the levels get too high. All of you had high levels, but yours were the highest."

"You weren't here earlier."

"You're right, and I should have been. That's why I stuck around once I got back. Brittany filled me in on what happened to you, but this time, it affected everyone." He turned to face Genevieve, now standing next to him. "What happened in there?"

"I haven't had time to determine..."

"I didn't ask why it happened. I asked *what* happened." She hesitated, so he turned to the nearest camper. "What happened in there, Emma?"

Emma looked up at Genevieve, who nodded her approval. "We couldn't leave the castle. The doorways looked normal, but some invisible barrier blocked us."

"And you felt trapped. That explains the rapid pulse! Everyone OK now?" Harold checked each girl's expression in turn.

"Everyone's fine, Harold." Genevieve's voice, usually soft and melodic, had acquired a distinct edge.

"Genevieve, your vitals spiked too, even with all your experience. Imagine what it did to these girls on just their second visit! And this is less than two hours after that incident with the mural! What is going on?"

Genevieve gave a slight shrug. "I have a hundred theories, but I won't really know until I go over the data."

"Well, I want to know as soon as you get that hundred down to a workable number. In the meantime, Brittany, Uriel, and I will sift through the logs ourselves. We should have it solved by suppertime." He looked over at Uriel and Brittany and saw their skeptical faces. "It is a lot of data. How about 1:00 tomorrow?"

"1:00 tomorrow," Genevieve said. "Even if I have to stay up all night."

Harold turned to the campers. "I'd like you to take the rest of the day off and try not to worry about the Sandbox. Be here tomorrow at 1:00, and we'll update you on what we found. I don't want anyone going back in there until I'm satisfied it's safe."

As they left Exeter East, Aaliyah asked, "Can we eat outside today? The weather is so gorgeous here. In Macon, right now, it's 90 degrees Fahrenheit and 90% humidity!"

"Outside sounds wonderful! I'm feeling claustrophobic." Molly had meant that to be funny, but that's not how it came out. She turned to check Jo Beth's reaction, but she looked genuinely concerned. Katrina and Emma nodded in agreement.

"I'm fine with eating outside," Emma said, "but it's too crowded near the cafeteria. We should discuss what happened in the Sandbox, so let's find somewhere private."

"Oh, I've got it!" Claire sprang into the air, waving her hands. "Have you seen the koi pond? There are picnic tables there that hardly anyone uses."

***

The entire north end of the LTG campus was a natural area. Most of the walking trails and picnic areas surrounded a large pond. One of the trails led to a Japanese garden with its own small pond, stocked with Japanese ornamental carp, or koi. This is where the girls bought their lunches.

They arrived to find four tables, two on either side of the pond. Only the nearest table was occupied. An LTG employee sat there, wearing earbuds and programming on his laptop. Claire led them across the wooden footbridge that spanned the pond. Halfway across, she paused to point out the koi circling beneath them. Molly lingered there as the rest of the group continued across the bridge.

So these were koi! She hadn't known their name, but Molly recognized them from Japanese art. As beautiful as those paintings were, they could never match the creatures themselves. Nature's colors were richer and more complex. Not paint applied to paper, but pigments locked deep inside living cells, encoded in their DNA. Not an image in a frame, but living things gliding through water, through shadow and light.

Their scales held the light like pearls and might display any color. Molly spotted cobalt blue, silver, black, gold, white, orange, and crimson. Some of the fish bore multicolored patterns while others flaunted a single bold hue.

The koi oscillated their bodies in gentle sine waves, moving in effortless harmony with their environment. They all swam at the same languid pace, whether they were slender youth or portly elders over a yard long. And as they navigated their silent world, a tranquil soundtrack played above. Water lapped against the piers while songbirds signaled each other across the pond.

Molly stood alone on the shaded bridge, absorbing all of this. For the first time since she stepped off the airplane, Molly's mind was still. She disappeared into the moment itself.

How long that moment lasted, Molly didn't know, but by the time it passed, her friends were eating lunch. *I would love to paint this pond,* Molly thought. She took a mental photograph and crossed the bridge. "Neat find, Claire. I love it here."

"You did good, Boulder." Katrina raised her Dr. Pepper in a toast but then turned serious. "Guys, those glitches have me worried. I bet Harold will keep us out of the Sandbox all week — just when Genevieve was going to let us start our own projects!"

"I'm more afraid he'll put us in before it's fixed!" Claire said. "Do any of you trust that guy? He's totally sus!"

Emma shook her head. "I was withholding judgment, but now it's obvious the man is out of his depth. He's not qualified to tell us the Sandbox is safe. I want to hear it from Genevieve. The second she says it is, I plan to start prototyping my flying car."

Jo Beth stared at her. "You designed a flying car?"

"I call it the AeroCar — it was my intern project at Princeton. I built a working scale model, but I want to build a full-size prototype I can fly. We projected the cost at a quarter-million dollars, but in the Sandbox, all I need is time."

"I want to fly in it!" Molly said.

"Seriously?" Claire said. "You can't want to go back in the Sandbox."

"Of course I do. I know I freaked out when the castle had us trapped, but I was still upset from losing all that work. Once they find the bugs, and Genevieve says it's safe, I'll be the first one to put on my cap."

"And I'll join you," Aaliyah said, "but I still haven't decided on my project. How do you choose among infinite possibilities?"

"Choose whatever's the most fun," Jo Beth said. "Something you can't do IRL!"

"Really?" Claire said. "All of you want to go back after what just happened?"

"I agree it was freaky," said Katrina. "But tech this advanced is bound to have a few hiccups. So what if we had to use our exit rings to leave the castle?"

"What if next time the rings don't work?" Claire asked.

"Hmm." Katrina furrowed her brow. "Can I get back to you on that?"

"We could avoid that risk," Aaliyah said, "if we knew what procedure the ring triggers. Then we could execute the code from our hand terminals."

Katrina smiled and pointed at Aaliyah. "There you go — problem solved."

"We should develop a risk management plan," Emma said. "They don't seem to have one."

Aaliyah smiled. "I love that idea. Of course, we don't know every risk, but we've seen plenty so far, and we can help Genevieve address them!"

"Sounds good," Molly said. Jo Beth nodded her approval, and Katrina said, "Let's do that!" Claire remained silent, arms crossed and mouth tight.

"What's wrong, Claire?" Molly asked.

"I think risk management is *their* job, but if you guys want to go back in, let's help them make it safe."

An hour later, the girls had finished their risk plan. Claire had written it down on her phone and read it back to the group. "If that sounds good to you guys, I'll text it to all of you."

"No need," Emma said. "I wrote them down, too, and I think it would be best if just one of us presented the plan. I'll do it, since I have the most experience in negotiations."

"Says who?" Katrina asked.

"I do. Has anyone else here talked their principal into letting her spend four days a week at the local university?"

"Has anyone else here helped an FBI agent bust a hacker ring?" Katrina countered. "Listen, Professor, we've all done amazing shit. We wouldn't be here if we weren't exceptional. But at NovaCamp, we have to get used to being among equals. This team doesn't need a leader — we've got six of them!"

"Personally, I'd rather not show up to the lab unorganized. The best way to demonstrate that we speak with a single voice is to have a designated spokesman. It's more professional."

"We're sixteen-year-olds at summer camp," Jo Beth said. "We're not supposed to be professional!"

Emma looked around the table, then sighed. "Fine. I yield. By the way, being loud and stubborn isn't leadership."

Katrina rolled her eyes. "Good talk! Anyone up for a swim?" She stood. "I'm going to grab my suit and check out that Olympic-sized pool in the fitness center."

Everyone stood up except Jo Beth. "You guys go ahead. I want to ask Molly something."

The other girls headed across the bridge, and Molly sat back down. "What's up?"

Jo Beth waited until the others were out of view. "You said we'd talk about the mural this afternoon. You don't think I did that, do you?"

"Oh, right! No, I believe you. I'm sure it was a glitch, which is even worse. I hope Genevieve has some solutions for us tomorrow."

"Oh, me, too!" Then Jo Beth chuckled. "It's pretty ironic — you're the only person who's said she believes me. The other girls don't like how I've been acting."

Molly hesitated but said it anyway. "Why *are* you acting that way? Back in the dorm, you said you'd leave me alone this summer! What happened to that?"

"The Sandbox happened." Jo Beth said. "When I asked to be on the same team as you, I never dreamed it would be this hard! It's a constant reminder that I will never be forgiven. And I understand why; I do. This morning, you said I don't deserve forgiveness, and you're right. I don't deserve it, but I..." Tears sabotaged her, and she looked away. When Jo Beth spoke, her voice had withered to a frayed thread. "But I still want it."

Who was this person? She bore no resemblance to the overconfident Jo Beth that Molly knew. This was someone in pain, a pain Molly understood. That look in Jo Beth's eyes was how Molly felt every minute of every day.

Jo Beth was waiting for a response. Molly told her the truth, "I don't know what to say."

"You could say you forgive me, even if I don't deserve it."

And that would take her pain away? Just three words? How can I forgive her before I've forgiven myself? Molly wasn't sure that made sense, but did it even matter? She knew it would make Jo Beth feel better, and there was no reason for both of them to be miserable.

Molly took a big breath and then exhaled. "Neither of us can change what happened. It's in the past, and hanging on to it just hurts us both. So... I forgive you."

Jo Beth drew back, a puzzled look on her face. "For real? You're serious?"

Molly nodded. *Hey, I'm surprised, too.*

Jo Beth stared at her. Then her eyes lit up, and she broke out in a giant grin. "You mean it?"

"Of course."

"Yes!" Jo Beth pumped her fist and continued grinning at Molly. Too animated to stay seated, she jumped to her feet and walked away from the table. She stopped after a few steps and stood with her back to Molly, rocking and fidgeting. Soon she returned and, looking embarrassed, sat back down. "Ready to go? There's something on my laptop I'm dying to show you."

Molly had stood but promptly sat down again. "Oh, what's that?" she asked, trying to sound nonchalant.

"Our video game: I've mapped out a whole new level for us to build and even coded two of the challenges. I wanted to get your input before I go any further."

"Right now? Won't it wait until we're back home?"

"It won't take long. Just let me show you what I've done! We can meet later to plan our next steps."

"Jo Beth, I want to give NovaCamp my full attention while I'm here."

Jo Beth started to frown, but caught herself. "Please? I'm asking you as a friend."

"And I'm asking you as a friend: give me some time. Space and time."

Jo Beth froze, staring blankly. Then a crimson glow flared from her cheeks to her ears. "I should have known you didn't mean it. You'll never let me forget what happened!" She was on her feet and headed for the bridge before Molly could react.

Jo Beth thundered across the bridge and down the footpath. Within seconds, she had passed out of view and beyond hearing. Overhead, the birds continued singing in the trees. Below, water still lapped the bridge piers; koi still glided beneath the surface. Molly still sat at the picnic table, in the shade of a Japanese maple, taking it all in.

If Jo Beth had stayed to listen, Molly would have explained that she wasn't excited about the game right now. It seemed silly to spend time on that instead of learning everything she could at NovaCamp. She didn't get to explain this before Jo Beth stormed off. That conversation would have to wait until Jo Beth cooled down.

For now, Molly breathed in the sweet, loamy air and rose to join her friends at the swimming pool.

10
The Aerocar

THE NEXT MORNING, Molly and Claire were running late and had to eat breakfast by themselves. When Molly mentioned how much she enjoyed the koi pond, Claire's eyes lit up. "You know what we should do? The NovaCamp app has a list of cool things to see and do at LTG. Let's check out some of them!" So they spent the entire morning exploring the campus and didn't see the team again until lunch.

The six of them sat together, had a normal conversation, and then walked over to Exeter East. Molly couldn't get a read on Jo Beth. She didn't apologize, but she didn't act upset, either.

When they got off the elevator, Harold was waiting for them. He led them into a conference room where Genevieve was already sitting. "Girls," he said, "I have good news! The team has discovered what happened with those doorways yesterday. Would you be so kind, Genevieve?"

"After Molly's mural disappeared, I thought it would help to lock down all the existing objects. I forgot that the doorways have a procedure to keep the butterflies out. Tightening security probably caused the doors to lock us out, too."

"See?" Harold said. "I told you it wasn't necessary to reenter the simulation to find the glitch. All it required was a code review." He didn't notice Genevieve shooting daggers at him. "I know we disagreed, but it was the right call to stay out of the simulation until we fixed the problem. Sometimes the boss gets it right." He looked at the campers for confirmation, and Molly tried to keep a poker face.

Harold sat back in his chair. "So, with that problem solved, I see no reason not to proceed. Any questions?"

"No questions," Aaliyah said. "But we have some safety ideas we'd like to run by you."

"Fire away."

"Are coding screens only for building content, or could we use them for messaging, too? We'd like some way to contact each other and you folks in the lab."

Harold looked at Genevieve. "Is that doable?"

"That object already exists. I'll show you how to use it as soon as we're back in the Sandbox."

Harold turned back to Aaliyah. "What else did you think of?"

"We want to be absolutely sure we're never trapped in the Sandbox. Of course, we know we weren't trapped yesterday, but that's how it felt. We asked ourselves, what if the next glitch is worse? What if the exit rings fail, too? Can you give us the code behind the rings so we can execute it ourselves?"

Genevieve smiled and picked up her phone. "That one is more work, but I'm sure Brittany can isolate that code for you. I'll get her started now, so you'll have it today." She finished the text while she was speaking.

"Those are excellent ideas," Harold said. "What else have you got?"

"I wanted to ask," Molly said, "what would happen if you had to pull us out of the Sandbox from this end? Genevieve told us it's not good to surprise the brain. Could it cause brain damage?"

Harold's mask slipped for a millisecond, then returned, smirking. "Molly Williams, did you just ask if you were in danger of brain damage from NovaCamp?" He snorted. "Of course not!"

“Do you have procedures in place for retrieving someone who can’t come back on their own?” Claire asked.

Harold cleared his throat and turned to Genevieve, who gave him a look so hard that he turned back to Claire. “Well, of course, we do. But it never hurts to reevaluate that sort of thing. Will you look into that for us, please, Genevieve?” She nodded without looking at him.

“Anything else?” Harold asked Claire.

“Nope. I think we’re ready to go.”

“Why don’t we launch in fifteen minutes?” Genevieve said. “That will give us time to put most of your ideas in place.”

Molly arrived back in the Sandbox, sitting exactly where she sat for the pinball lesson. They all were, with Genevieve standing in front of them.

“The six of you really impressed me today. Instead of being intimidated by those glitches, you worked out a mitigation plan. That was brilliant, which didn’t surprise me, because I know how bright the six of you are. But it was also brave, and I respect that. So, today I’m going to drop the teacher act and address you as colleagues.”

“This sounds serious,” Aaliyah said.

“That’s because it is.” Genevieve paused to retrieve an office chair and sat down to address the girls at eye level. “As bad as these glitches are, I’m relieved it wasn’t something worse. Harold sprung this NovaCamp scheme on us just six weeks ago. When I told him it would take four times that long to debug all these worlds, he just said, ‘Do what you can.’”

“What worlds?” Claire asked.

“The 95% of the Sandbox you haven’t seen yet. I was ready to show it to you when that glitch trapped us in the castle. The team and I had worked frantically to track down every bug so the site would be safe for you. But somehow we must have missed something. That’s the only explanation for the glitches.”

"I knew there were still problems!" Katrina said. "That butterfly program doesn't explain how Molly's mural disappeared."

"No, it doesn't even explain the barriers in the Banquet Hall. Changing permissions wouldn't alter that routine one bit. But I let Harold think that so we could come back. The only way I can fix this problem is in the simulation."

"Please let us help," Molly said.

"Thank you, Molly. If we had more time, I'd walk all of you through the code, and we'd repair it together. But alone, I can fix it in a fraction of that time. I'm sorry, but the best solution is for the six of you to stay here and work on your object building."

"How long will you be gone?" Claire asked.

"I have a strong hunch where to look," Genevieve said, "so I'm going to say two hours top, in perceived time."

"But I'm not sure we're safe here," Claire said.

"You should be safe now, thanks to Brittany's hard work. She's installed the TxtMessage app on your screens, so if anything comes up before I return, you can message me."

"What about the exit ring code?" Aaliyah asked.

Brittany's already found it and packaged it up. I'll send it to all of you now."

Genevieve gestured over her screen, and a red exclamation mark appeared in front of Molly. "Each of you should see an exclamation mark," Genevieve said. "It's your 'text received' alert." After a few seconds, the image faded away.

Molly opened her screen, and the texting app was already active. There was the text from Genevieve, with the ring code attached. It took her less than a minute to get familiar with the texting app and save the code.

"I'm so glad you've got those two objects already," Genevieve said. "Now that you can contact me, I feel better about leaving."

"How exactly are you going to do that?" Jo Beth asked.

Genevieve turned and pointed to the back wall. "I'm going through that door." There wasn't any door when she started that sentence, but there was now.

"Where does that go?" Emma asked.

"We call it the Warehouse. It serves as both a storage depot and the access point to all the other worlds. As soon as I come back, we'll all go there together. Oh, and please keep this a secret. Harold thinks the glitches are gone and that I'm with you at all times."

"Do what you need to do," Katrina said. "We'll keep it secret."

"Thank you. If you experience a glitch or any other issue, please text me. I'll come right back." With that, Genevieve turned and walked to the door. She produced a key, unlocked the door, and walked through it. Molly got a brief glimpse of industrial shelving and a distant metal wall. Then Genevieve closed the door behind her.

The deadbolt engaged with a sharp "Click."

Claire ran to the door and tried to open it. "She took the key!"

"Thank goodness," said Jo Beth, "or you'd already be on the other side! But if there really are a dozen worlds back there, I think we should wait for Genevieve to give us a tour."

"Hopefully, before Harold asks any questions," Molly said.

"What's wrong, Molly?" Claire asked. "You seem upset."

"It's Genevieve. She wants us to lie for her! And I was so sure we could trust her."

"Technically, it's not telling a lie to keep something secret," Claire said. "That's all Genevieve is doing: keeping a secret from her boss. That probably happens a lot."

"I know it does," Katrina said. "Especially when the boss is a tool like Harold! Genevieve doesn't trust *him*, which makes me trust her even more."

"Me, too," Claire said.

"You have to trust someone, Molly," Aaliyah said.

"I guess, but what do we do now?"

Katrina laughed. "Any damn thing we want!"

Claire pointed to the patio door. "Unless you wanted to work on the castle like I did. It's gone." It was gone, replaced by the original meadow and landscape.

"Wouldn't you rather work on something you thought of?" Emma asked. "I can't wait to start on my AeroCar."

"I don't want to hurt your feelings," Claire said, "but flying cars aren't really my thing."

"How about animals?" Katrina asked. "I love horses, but you have to be a cop or a millionaire to ride in Chicago. So I want to make a horse, and I could use some help. I've asked Aaliyah, but she wants a different animal. She likes birds."

"I love cats!" Claire said. "At least my cat; I miss her so much. That's it — I'll make Lemon Drop!"

"Wow, we couldn't have picked three more different animals. Anybody interested in making a horse?"

Jo Beth laughed. "I don't suppose you'd agree to a unicorn?"

"Sure!" Katrina said. "And Aaliyah will make birds, and Claire's cat will eat them."

Aaliyah raised her chin and drew back her shoulders, making herself even taller. From this height, she glared at Katrina before turning that look on Claire.

Claire seemed unfazed and just doubled down on her always-innocent expression. "Well, the real Lemon Drop does, but this one won't eat anything, and I won't have to empty the litter box!" That brought a good-natured smile to Aaliyah's face.

"Okay. Let's do this!" Katrina led the way outside.

"Can I use this patio for my car project?" Emma said. "I'll have hundreds of parts to organize, and this would be perfect."

"That's fine," Aaliyah said. "I think our animals would rather be born in the wild, anyway. Do you guys want to work in that little meadow?"

"That sounds like fun!" Claire said and raced down the hill.

"Wait up, Claire." Jo Beth hurried after her.

"Okay, then!" Aaliyah said. "See you guys." She and Katrina followed the others down the hill, walking at a normal pace. That left Molly alone with Emma on the patio, and Emma didn't seem too happy about it.

"What did I do?" Molly asked.

"I thought we agreed I could work on the patio."

"We did, but I want to help with your flying car."

Emma's expression softened. "Oh! I thought you just wanted to fly in it."

"No, I think it's a neat project, and I'd like to help if I can."

Instead of answering, Emma began inspecting the patio. "Okay, it looks like we have enough space here. I usually work alone, but I could use your help with some design issues. The first one is the cockpit. I think it should hold two people, but I couldn't figure it out. Do you think you could come up with a comfortable two-seat arrangement?"

"I'd love to try. Will I get to fly in it when it's finished?"

"Of course. If we can actually work together, I want you to be my first passenger."

"Great. How can I help?"

"Let me show you." Emma stretched the corners of her screen until it resembled a whiteboard floating in the air. She pulled up a detailed schematic of the car and explained how it worked. As a plane, the AeroCar used a pair of short wings with horizontal propellers. On land, the wings and propellers slid under the chassis.

"Here's what I need in the cockpit, and this is the amount of room I have. I can tweak that a little if I have to, but anything more than a centimeter or two would probably ground us. Can you fit two people and these instruments inside those dimensions?"

"I think so. I'll let you know if I hit a snag." Molly created some sidewalk chalk and drew a shape matching Emma's dimensions on the patio. She could tell that legroom would be no problem, but width might be. She wished she could study some real-life car seats, especially from compact cars. Then, as if she'd read her mind, Katrina called out.

"Hey guys, I needed pictures of horses, so I got Brittany to create an Internet connection for us. I wrapped a browser around it and called the object WWWeb. Thought it might help you guys, too."

"Thanks, Katrina!" Molly typed in the object name. She researched dozens of different chairs and car seats. Then she developed her own design, using the best elements of each. Once she had created the seats, console, and dashboard, she asked Emma what she thought.

Emma sat in the pilot's seat and began "flying" the car with imaginary pedals, gauges, and controls. "I think you nailed it! I'll outfit this with my gear, and then I'd like your help designing the roof. In the meantime, would you do me a favor? If this car is going to fly, we may need Brittany to upgrade their physics engine. Can you ask her if it has real-time aerodynamics with accurate lift and drag?"

"Wait a minute." Molly started typing the request into the texting app on her screen. "I'll turn this into a proper message and send it to her. But I just thought of something. Remember how Genevieve said the sky is an image projected on a dome around us? We may need to enlarge the dome so we don't fly through it."

"Good catch! They definitely need to change that if they can. A dome is hardly ideal for flying. I wonder if she could replace it with a cylinder topped by a dome? I'd prefer a cylinder one kilometer high and two kilometers in diameter."

Shortly after Molly sent her text, a red exclamation point announced Brittany's response. "She says the physics engine already has those features, and she'll change the dome's size and shape. She said I should get Genevieve's help to landscape all that new surface area, but I think I can work it out myself."

"You could create that landscape you painted yesterday."

"That was fun to paint, but I'm ready for a new challenge. I just have to decide what it is."

"I would think you'd have a lot of ideas," Emma said.

"I do, but my favorite is probably too hard: building a beach."

"Don't underestimate yourself; you'll figure it out!"

"I'd like to surround this existing world with a beach and an ocean. But what if your car went down in the water?"

"A, it won't, and B, it's light enough to float. If you're looking for a reason not to build an ocean, that's not it. I'd encourage you to try it — even if you fail, you'll learn a lot. Why don't you help me with that roof now? Then you can work on your beach while I finish assembly."

But helping with the roof proved frustrating. After Emma rejected her fifth roof design, Molly finally spoke up. "How am I supposed to create more headroom without making the roof taller?" She was starting to suspect Emma wanted tall people to hit their heads getting into the car.

"I'm not trying to be difficult," Emma said. "But after all the wind tunnel simulations I ran, I know how critical the fuselage shape is. Maybe these seats are too tall."

"I looked everywhere, and these are the lowest seats anyone makes." But even as Molly said that, she thought of the perfect solution. She just hoped Emma agreed.

11
A Virtual Beach

"How would you feel about a canopy hinged in the back, like the ones they use on fighter jets?"

Emma's face lit up. "That's a great idea, and opening either door could release the latches. Do you need help fabricating it?"

Molly had already created a canopy over the cockpit. "Can you provide the hinges and latches?"

"Of course, and I'll add servos to raise it when a door opens and lower it when both doors are closed." Emma stepped back to get a better view of the AeroCar. *Now* it looked like a flying car.

Emma's inspection was interrupted by a horse's whinny. But it wasn't a horse. An actual unicorn was grazing on the lawn.

"Wow!" Katrina said. "I brought a unicorn up here to impress you guys, and I'm the one who's blown away. Is it ready to fly?"

Emma pointed to the remaining parts strewn around the patio. "Not until I find a home for all that. But Molly just finished her part of the car project, so she's off to build an ocean."

"Whoa! That sounds ambitious."

"Says the girl with the unicorn," Molly said. "Introduce us, please."

"Molly and Emma, this is Galahad. Galahad, meet Molly and Emma."

"He is so gorgeous!" Molly couldn't resist stroking his neck.

"He looks amazing," Emma said. "Thank God you didn't make him pink or rainbow-colored."

"You mean we shouldn't add the sparkles?" Katrina joked. "I think Jo Beth is pretending his mane and tail are rainbow-colored, while I pretend he's a white horse wearing a party hat."

"Why didn't Jo Beth come up?" Emma asked.

"I have no idea! She's really proud of Galahad, but she refused to come with." She looked at Molly. "What's going on with you two?"

"I'm trying to figure that out myself, but I'm ready to talk when she is." *Even,* Molly thought, *if she doesn't apologize.*

Emma glared at Molly, then walked around the AeroCar and disappeared behind it. Molly continued petting Galahad. "He's so pretty, Katrina. Were you able to work out his gait?"

"You mean gaits, plural. We're still working on those. At least we've figured out how he neighs, moves his head and tail, and looks at you with these gorgeous eyes. There's so much work involved! You're a lot of trouble, aren't you, Galahad?" She stroked his neck. "It makes you really appreciate them, though. I thought I was a horse fancier before, but I never appreciated how perfect their proportions are. Make the slightest change, and it sucks the poetry right out of them."

The girls just stood there for a while, appreciating that poetry. Galahad reacted by raising his head and shaking his mane — shouldn't someone be petting him?

Katrina looked over at Emma, now under the hood of the car and out of earshot. "We've all got a lot of work to do, so I'll head back. Tell Emma I want a test drive when it's finished."

"I will." Molly watched Galahad and Katrina walk down the hill. When she turned around, Emma was standing right behind her.

"How could you say you don't know what upset Jo Beth? She was fine until you two talked at the pond. I hate being in the middle of this, but I won't let you two sink the entire team. You need to go talk to her!"

"Like I told Katrina, I'm ready to talk when Jo Beth is, but this isn't a good time."

"It's the perfect time! Genevieve's dealing with so much right now that she's not even thinking about you two. You can make the problem disappear before she has to deal with it. Go patch things up now."

Molly felt her cheeks flushing, then wondered how that was possible in here. "I did exactly that! I forgave her, just like she asked. We were good for maybe ten seconds, and then she moved the goalpost! She threw a huge fit because I won't work on our video game here at camp. Emma, I could spend all summer trying to 'patch things up' with her."

Emma pointed at her, "Right there, that attitude. That's the problem."

Molly snapped. "Why do you always side with Jo Beth? I am not 'the problem!' If you knew either of us at all, you would see that!" An unfamiliar sensation in her right hand alerted her that it was clenched in a fist. Molly flattened it against her shorts while she nodded at the AeroCar. "Are we done here?"

"Sure. Go build an ocean."

"I will." Molly went around the house to fume in private. *Why does Emma have to be such a know-it-all?* After pushing a long huff of air out the side of her mouth, Molly scanned the distant landscape. She wanted to work on the beach, but she could tell Brittany hadn't expanded the dome yet.

So Molly would have to wait, but she didn't have to wait at the clubhouse. Instead, she headed up the hill. When she reached the top, she got her first view of the landscape on that side of the world. It was similar to the view behind her, except there were no mountains, only grassland clear to the horizon.

Then it disappeared. Everything past the hill vanished, leaving the sky dangling above a gaping black void. This world, which minutes ago seemed endless, was now a tiny island suspended over a yawning abyss.

Molly's gaze darted away, seeking relief to the side, but the emptiness was there, too. Molly turned in a dizzying circle, searching for the familiar landscape but finding only blackness. Heart racing, unable to breathe, she dropped her head and found safe harbor in the rich green of the hilltop.

Molly crouched until living grass and solid earth filled her entire field of vision. She drew in a ragged breath and planted her hands on her knees for support. She needed to think. *Was this another glitch?* With time, the pounding in her ears subsided, and her breathing returned to normal. *No, this is what I requested: enlarging the dome to two kilometers in diameter.*

Molly slowly stood erect, keeping her eyes down the whole time. By focusing on the grass at her feet, Molly was able to venture down the hill to its base. She was still haunted by what she'd just seen: that unnerving, unnatural darkness. But this wasn't nature, was it? This was a complex computer program. Only the rules of computer science applied here.

Molly came to a halt to grapple with that concept. Objects in nature have limits, but in programming, the limits have to be defined. Every new program was a limitless canvas. That's what Molly loved about it! But until today, she had never thought about that uncreated space.

When Genevieve built this world, she would have encountered this same abyss. She must have used some kind of scaffold or foundation. It would exist as an object in the system — Molly just had to find it. She texted Brittany for help, explaining that Genevieve was busy right now.

Brittany replied that the "floor" object would not only support the water and sand but also provide gravity. Molly found the object with her screen and began experimenting with it. She replaced all that nothingness with the floor's steel-like surface.

Molly stepped off the soft grass and onto the massive floor. She stomped on it to test its strength and then walked at least thirty yards toward the horizon. It was hard to grasp the amount of "matter" the Sandbox had generated at the speed of thought. Molly worked on shaping this ocean floor like a proper beach. After several adjustments, she found the depth she wanted and gave it a gradual slope up to the grass. Now, at last, she could make the beach.

Molly caught herself smiling, but she wasn't surprised. The beach was her favorite place. She went every summer and daydreamed about it the rest of the year. Molly wondered if she could visualize all that clean, white sand, and it would just appear. That had worked for painting the mural.

She stared at the floor, visualizing it covered with sand. Nothing happened. That was okay; maybe she had overreached, trying to create an entire beach instead of a handful of sand. Molly cupped her hand and concentrated with all her might, but that failed, too. What was she doing wrong?

Molly had been the first one to create a pinball the other day, and she knew practically nothing about those. But that was a single object. She decided to try that, to visualize a single grain of sand. A tentative image appeared in the air, no more than a misshapen speck. It took patience, but she persevered, and the tiny image finally sharpened into a cube as clear as glass.

It was a grain of something, but did it look like sand? Molly needed more than one to tell, so she duplicated the image, then the pair, and so on, through the powers of two. She stopped at the tenth power: 1,024. Now she was sure — it looked exactly like salt and nothing like sand.

If she were honest with herself, Molly didn't really know what a single grain of sand looked like. They were just too small. What she needed was a magnified image of sand. She could model that and then scale it down to the correct size with her screen. She searched on the Internet, and she did find an amazing variety of sand from beaches all over the world. Strange and exotic sand: pink, green, orange, colored with rare minerals or bright coral. Beautiful and photogenic, but Molly couldn't use them for her beach.

Molly's beach was Gulf Shores; that was the sand she had grown up with. She had played with that sand, slept on that sand, run on it, laughed, and cried on it. Molly knew the heft of it in her hand and the warmth of it against her back. She could hear the crunch of it under her feet and see it shimmer in the sunlight as it poured from her hand. So why couldn't she create it now? She turned and kicked the floor, half-wishing a spray of sand would fly into the air.

And it did! A glittering shower of sand shot into the air and scattered across the floor. At first, Molly just stood there, stunned. Then she knelt and gathered up a handful to examine. These were grains of something, but was it sand? Molly held her palm inches from her face and probed the grains with her fingertip. Then, she kneaded the sand in her fist and watched the grains trickle out like a sparkling thread. Yes! She had created real sand; she just didn't know how.

When Molly scanned the sand into her hand terminal, it appeared as an unnamed object. All its properties were there; only Name was blank, so she typed in "whiteSand." Molly changed the mass to a hundred kilograms and produced a mound of sand almost two feet tall. *Now, I'm ready to make a beach,* she thought.

Except for one detail. Molly could make all the sand she wanted, but not as a flat layer. No matter how she tweaked whiteSand's properties, it always formed a mound. She would need some way to spread it out. Real beach crews had large bulldozers to do this, but it would take her over a day to create one of those. Then Molly remembered the giant rig those crews used to replenish the beach. It would dredge sand from the ocean floor, pump it through a huge pipe, and spew the wet, dark sand onto the beach. She could create something similar, not a physical pump but a pumping subroutine.

To control the process, Molly designed a fire hose nozzle that she could move through the air with her thoughts. Molly spent several minutes making a thick semi-circle of sand twenty yards in diameter. That seemed like a lot until she looked around at miles of bare floor. Unless she could speed up this nozzle, she might be better off trying to build a bulldozer!

Before Molly could tackle that problem, Claire called out from the edge of the grass. "There you are! Please help me!" She buried her face in her hands, half turned, and slumped down on the grass, sobbing.

12
Teamwork

Molly hurried up the floor to her friend. Right behind Claire was the reason for her tears: the bizarre creature licking its paw. Shaped like a cat, it moved like a cat and groomed itself like a cat, but no cat ever looked like this! Instead of fur, patchy, day-glow wire bristles covered it from head to tail.

That poor creature! Molly knew it was just a computer model, but it still broke her heart. No wonder Claire was crying! Molly sat next to her and put her arm around her shoulder.

"What can I do?" Claire sobbed. "I've tried so hard to copy Lemon Drop's fur, but it keeps getting worse and worse. I should just give up!"

"I know exactly how you feel. Did you see that sand I made? It took me all day to get that right. I must have tried a hundred times to make the sand from my favorite beach, but the harder I tried, the worse it looked. I was so frustrated!"

"But you didn't give up?"

"I did give up, Claire! I was trying to make sand the way we made those pinballs: by analyzing and calculating its properties. That was getting me nowhere, so I finally gave up."

Claire scooted around to face Molly. "But somehow you solved it."

"Only by accident. The more I failed, the more obsessed I became. I saw the beach so vividly in my mind that I ached to be there again. And then, the sand just appeared."

"Like granting a wish?" Claire asked.

"I guess so, but I think the key was how intense my wish was. Crazy intense — I wanted this sand so bad I could see it, feel it, almost taste it!"

"Oh." Claire seemed lost in thought, then she reached out her arms to Lemon Drop. "Come here, baby," she called in a tender voice. The cat climbed into her lap, nuzzled against her, squeezed its eyes shut, and curled into a contented ball. Claire retrieved her screen, highlighted several pages of code, and deleted it all. Lemon Drop's day-glow fur vanished, revealing the cat-shaped mechanism underneath.

A beige-colored, articulated shell, it resembled an artist's mannequin, a cat mannequin. Claire lifted the furless creature to her chest, cradling it in her left arm and petting it with her right hand. She closed her eyes and began humming an improvised lullaby. Soon, the cat machine was purring, thrumming a bass line under Claire's melody.

But none of this lessened Lemon Drop's baldness. Molly had decided it never would when a small patch of fuzz appeared. With each stroke of Claire's hand, the spot grew in size. Once it covered the body, it began to thicken and lengthen into something like fur. When it grew long enough, Claire worked her fingers through it. The coat responded to her touch and began to look more and more like actual fur.

Claire held the sleeping cat out at arm's length and gave it a thorough inspection. Her first change was to transform the fur from solid beige to orange tabby stripes. Then Claire made subtle alterations to the fur's length in different areas. She set the creature on the ground, and its amber eyes snapped open. Lemon Drop took a few steps before she noticed Molly watching her. She returned Molly's gaze with the cool indifference of an actual cat.

"Amazing!" Molly said. "She looks so real."

"I could never have done it without you, Molly. Thank you for believing in me!"

"I'm happy I could help." Molly stood up. "I wonder if you could help me with something?" She pointed to the vast, empty ocean floor. "I need a better way to distribute my sand." They walked down to the sand nozzle, and Molly showed her how it worked. "I can get a nice layer of sand with this, but it takes forever. Do you have any ideas?" Claire nodded, furrowed her brow, and put her hands on her hips. Then her face lit up. "I've got a fantastic idea!" She scooped up Lemon Drop, turned, and ran up the hill.

"Where are you going?" Molly called out.

Claire stopped and turned around. "Wait for it!" And then she was gone.

Molly waited about a minute before going back to spreading sand. She tried enlarging the nozzle to increase the flow rate, but then she couldn't keep the sand even. Molly tried flattening the nozzle to cover a greater area, but that was just as hard to control. She was running out of ideas. Then a sound like an enormous fan behind her made Molly look. The AeroCar was cresting the hill.

It was one thing to see its components and its assembly, but now it was flying, what it was made to do. The AeroCar crossed the sky as naturally as a bird, hovered, and descended. Molly tried to suppress the grin on her face as Emma touched down nearby. The propellers slowed to a stop and slid to their storage position as the wings retracted out of sight. The canopy swung up with a whooshing sound, and Emma got out of the car.

"It really works, doesn't it?" Molly asked.

"It does. Did you mean to leave that running?" Emma pointed to Molly's sand pump, floating in mid-air and spewing sand into a giant mound.

"Oops!" Molly stopped it. "As long as I keep the nozzle moving, it works pretty well, but it's a slow process."

"Now I see why Claire thought I could help. Together, we can distribute the sand from the air. If you create a row of those nozzles in front of the car, we'll have this beach made in no time."

"But I thought you were mad at me."

"You're right, I was. I let my emotions get the better of me. Which is ironic, because that's been my problem with you and Jo Beth. Your emotions are sabotaging your futures. And not just yours, potentially the entire team. You guys are too smart for that. You're too important to this project!"

"But why did you get mad at me when I did exactly what Jo Beth asked, and forgave her?"

Emma nodded. "I know. I'm sorry. I was blaming you for a situation you'd just done your best to remedy. I'm not proud of that. This situation makes me crazy, but I think you're right — the next move *is* up to Jo Beth. I just hope she comes around before it's too late."

"Are you ready?" Emma asked.

Molly reviewed the row of nozzles suspended in the air in front of her. There were sixteen, spaced two meters apart, twenty meters in front of the AeroCar. "I think so. Let's see if this works." She climbed in the car, closed her door, and watched the canopy close exactly as she'd designed it.

Emma engaged plane mode. The wings slid out to flight position, and the propellers spun up. Molly barely had time to click her seatbelt before they lifted off. The nozzles were programmed to move in perfect synchronization with the AeroCar. "Can we fly about three yards off the floor?" Molly asked.

"I'll fly as close as you want. Tell me if I need to speed up." Emma eased forward. She adjusted her speed while Molly experimented with the rate of flow. Soon, they were covering the floor with a smooth white layer of sand.

Molly was so focused on the process, she couldn't believe it when they returned to their starting point. They did two more passes before Molly said, "Emma, I think we're finished!"

Emma landed the car on the grass a short distance from the beach. They both got out and walked on the sand. "Were you planning to fill this entire space with water, Molly?"

"I was, but now I think that may be a waste of computer resources."

"That depends on how you want to use the ocean. For now, we could use water up to a point, and then beyond that, the illusion of water."

"That sounds good." Molly looked out over the empty floor. "It's a shame we can't have waves."

"Who says we can't? You just need a wall that moves back and forth, and we need to wall in the water, anyway. I suggest we experiment in a giant aquarium tank. You can supply the seawater while I tackle making realistic waves. If you like the results, we'll supersize it."

Before long, they had a miniature version of the ocean in a square tank fifty meters long on each side. Emma had made the tank out of Plexiglas so they could study the waves. A wall in the back moved back and forth to create the waves. Emma adjusted its motion until perfect waves were breaking against the beach. Seeing the ocean this way fascinated Molly. She wasn't sure how long she'd stared at it when Emma interrupted her.

"Are you ready to turn the spigot?"

"What are you talking about?" Molly asked.

Emma gestured with an open hand toward the distant wall that now circled the island.

"You're finished?"

"Sure, once I had the motion programmed, scaling it up took just a few keystrokes. All we need now is your saltwater."

Molly had estimated the volume of their huge ocean bed, and she was only off by a few hundredths of a percent. After a single adjustment, the entire landscape was surrounded by a vast sea. Emma started the wave motion, and they sat down on the beach to enjoy their accomplishment. Each wave would build, rush the shore, dissolve into foam, and slowly retreat just as the next wave piled into it. The waves sang in cascading crescendos and gentle resolutions, the ocean's beating heart. "This is so nice!" Molly said.

"That's what I call engineering!" Emma stood up and brushed the sand off her shorts. "Let's go see what the others have been up to."

Emma guided the AeroCar over the hill and toward the meadow. She leveled off, cruising in a big circle above the girls and their animals. An expansive cherry tree, in full bloom, adorned the meadow like a giant pink carnation. Jo Beth and Katrina were standing under the tree while Galahad trotted in a large circle around it. Emma flew over the cherry tree and landed several yards from it.

Aaliyah was the first to greet them. "I can't believe you've finished already! This is so cool!"

"Oh, we finished this a while ago," Emma said. "We had to build an ocean, too."

"Seriously? I want to see it. Preferably from inside your car plane."

"That's a deal," Emma said.

"I love this cherry tree," Molly said. "It looks so real!"

"Thanks," Aaliyah said, "but I found it on Google. I have no idea how to design a tree."

"Well, you found a good one to borrow," Molly said. "I'd be happy to work with you on some more trees later. And those birds sound fantastic!"

"Thank you! Would you like to see them in action?" Aaliyah brought up her screen, entered a command, and looked up at the branches. The tree shuddered, releasing a torrent of delicate pink petals. Then, the deep whir of a hundred wings filled the air, and a swarm of bluebirds burst into the sky as one. They raced around the meadow, swirling, looping, climbing, and diving. The flock moved with a single consciousness, an ever-shifting mass of electric blue. After three more laps around the meadow, they rose high in the air, turned, and swooped back into the tree.

"That was amazing," Emma said.

"I'm so happy we have animals in the Sandbox now," Molly said. "It makes all the difference!"

Katrina joined them, and then Claire walked up with Lemon Drop close behind. "Oh, look at Lemon Drop," Molly said. "Aren't you beautiful!" She knelt beside her. "Claire, she's so lifelike! Listen, she's purring!" Katrina and Aaliyah squatted down next to Molly to pet the cat. The only one missing was Jo Beth, who was standing on the other side of the tree. She was grooming Galahad, but stole the occasional glance in their direction.

"When do we get to ride in this?" Katrina asked.

"As soon as Jo Beth comes over," Emma said. "I'm only teaching one class today."

"Yo, Jo Beth," Katrina yelled, "get over here." Jo Beth looked at them but still hesitated.

"I'll let you pilot," Emma said.

Then Jo Beth led Galahad over to the group. "I wasn't trying to be rude, but those propellers freaked Galahad out."

"I'll watch him," Molly said. "I've been flying all afternoon."

"Oh!" Jo Beth said, surprised. "Thanks."

"Remember me, Galahad?" Molly petted his thick mane, then walked him back to the far side of the tree. From there, they watched the AeroCar "class." Jo Beth was sitting in the cockpit while Emma explained the various parts of the car and how to operate them.

Jo Beth took the first car ride with Claire as her passenger. The takeoff was not as graceful as Emma's, but Jo Beth's flying quickly improved. The AeroCar disappeared behind the hill and returned several minutes later. As soon as it powered down, Katrina and Aaliyah took their places and lifted off again. Their wheels had just left the ground when Molly got a text from Brittany. "I can't contact Genevieve, and now Katrina isn't answering, either. Is everything alright?"

"We're all fine. Katrina is flying the AeroCar," Molly texted. "Not sure where Genevieve is."

"Well, it's 6:00 p.m. here," Brittany answered. "Can you come back now, please? It's okay to leave Genevieve. She can handle herself."

Molly read the text to the other girls, and they headed up to the clubhouse. Katrina followed them from the air and landed next to the patio. When Molly showed them Brittany's text, Claire said, "Oh, no! Something's happened to Genevieve! I'm texting her right now." She opened her screen and did that.

"Don't overreact," Katrina said. "She's probably busy and will answer you later."

"I hope she does," Molly said. "But Genevieve has been gone nearly five hours, and she said it would be two hours tops!"

Jo Beth shrugged. "Troubleshooting always takes longer than you expect. Like the lady said, Genevieve can handle herself."

Claire held up her screen. "But she promised she'd text right back. Doesn't that worry you guys?"

"I'm not worried," Katrina said. "When Genevieve said that, she was wearing her Mother Hen hat. Now she's wearing her Programmer hat and concentrating like crazy."

"Also," Emma said, "if we spend too much time waiting on her, Harold will get suspicious, which doesn't help Genevieve. We should go back."

“I agree. Genevieve wouldn’t want us worrying about her,” Aaliyah said. “Did you say goodbye to Lemon Drop?”

Claire crossed her skinny arms and knitted her translucent eyebrows. “I’ll worry about Genevieve if I want to.” After a dramatic pause, she said, “And I’ve already turned Lemon Drop off. I didn’t want her to get lonely.”

Jo Beth rolled her eyes and pointed to her ring. “Let’s go home, guys.”

When they got back, Harold was waiting for them. “I want you to tell me the truth, please. You don’t have to cover for Genevieve, even if she asked you to. If she did, that was wrong and unfair to you. You can tell me the truth.”

A tense silence followed. Harold was inspecting the six of them, looking directly into each girl’s eyes. When he came to her, Molly tried to return a confident gaze, but she wasn’t feeling confident. In her peripheral vision, she saw Claire trembling. Harold had already moved past Claire, but it was only a matter of time before he would notice her. Then it would all come out.

Finally, Harold spoke. “Was there another glitch today?”

Molly felt the tension leave her body, everywhere but her lungs, which had been holding a breath all this time. She let it out quietly. Every girl in the room looked relieved, but Harold didn’t notice. Then Jo Beth spoke up, “No, sir. Not one glitch.”

“Well, that’s a relief. I was afraid that’s what Genevieve was working on. So you all had a good day?”

“The best yet,” Molly said.

“A great day,” Aaliyah added.

“Good,” Harold said. “I didn’t mean to make you uncomfortable, but yesterday put us all a little on edge. Why don’t you guys get a good night’s sleep, and we’ll see you in the morning?” Harold turned and headed to his office.

Molly found herself drawn to Genevieve's chair. If something was wrong, it didn't show in Genevieve's expression. She looked like someone having a pleasant dream. That was some comfort. Claire joined Molly by the chair and whispered, "Good luck, Genevieve."

13
Past Reality

When Molly opened the door to her room that evening, a blast of Nirvana struck her in the face. Even stranger, Diana was there. She and Claire were seated at the far end of the room, looking very serious.

"What's going on?" Molly asked.

Claire jumped out of her chair, put her finger across her lips, and shot across the room to lock the door. "Oh, I'm checking out that cool rock station you told me about," she proclaimed with all the subtlety of a Sunday school Christmas pageant. Claire had her iPad in hand and now showed Molly its screen: "Can I see your phone, please?"

Molly handed her phone to Claire, who placed it on the closet shelf next to her own blaring phone. She repeated the finger-to-lip gesture and led Molly to the back, where they sat on either side of Diana. The chairs were so close that Molly bumped Diana's knee while sitting down.

Claire leaned in close, her words spilling out in a rapid-fire whisper. "LTG is probably spying on us with our phones. You won't believe what Diana just told me: the whole purpose of NovaCamp was to get the six of us in the Sandbox!"

Molly furrowed her brow, but Diana said, "It's true, Molly. They created this entire camp to put the six of you in those chairs."

"I don't understand," Molly said. "How does that make any sense?"

"Bradford has spent billions of dollars on this technology and still doesn't have a product he can sell. The first step is to prove there's even a market for the Sandbox. The six of you are his secret focus group, a market test his competitors won't catch wind of."

"But why go to all this trouble and expense? Why treat a hundred girls to a summer camp instead of just asking six girls to try the technology?"

"Good question," Dianna said. "I guess it's a way to explain having teenagers on campus."

An idea lit up Claire's face like a jack-o'-lantern. "And it's a, what do you call it, a counter-narrative! If any of us decided to go public, Bradford's got ninety-four other girls that would say we're crazy."

"I hadn't thought of that," Diana said. "I bet you're right!"

Claire basked in the compliment. "Bradford disappeared us, just like he did the eighteenth floor!"

Molly frowned. "But that must have cost a fortune! Is the Sandbox tech really that valuable?"

"Only if it gets to market ahead of the competition," Diana said. "We started this project with a lead so great that failure seemed impossible. But then there was a major setback, and to make matters worse, a reporter caught wind of it."

Claire gasped. "Oh no! Did Bradford have the reporter killed?"

Diana smiled. "No, he just told a lie and managed to convince the world it was the truth, even those of us on the team."

"Wait," Molly said. "You were on the Sandbox team?"

"She was, Molly," Claire said. "Our camp counselor is one of LTG's top programmers."

Diana shrugged. "I don't know about that, but I did join the project when it started, three years ago. Back then, we called it the Hyperverse."

"So you worked with Uriel and Genevieve?" Molly asked.

"I did. Genny and I were on a team of twelve programmers, and Uriel was one of five engineers. There was also a manager and four admins."

"That's impressive!" Claire said.

"It was a lot of people, and we were able to accomplish a lot. We had six worlds complete and two nearly finished before Lori's accident."

"Who's Lori?" Claire asked.

"Lori Jacobs, my best friend and the best software engineer LTG ever had. Lori went from being our lead programmer to someone who can't finish a sentence. At least she can walk and feed herself now."

"I am so sorry." Molly took Diana's hand and gently squeezed it.

"We both are!" Claire took her other hand.

Diana squeezed and released Molly's hand, then Claire's. "Bradford bought the family's silence, but her parents let me visit Lori in secret. They told me what really happened, which was completely different from what Bradford said. He claimed that Lori fell victim to the cumulative effects of the caps. Supposedly, the technology was 'fundamentally flawed,' and we had all been affected. Lori's symptoms were the worst because she had clocked the most hours. But he assured the team we would all fully recover now that he was ending the project."

"Ending the project?" Molly said. "I thought he just renamed it."

"No. He killed it, made a public announcement that the technology was a dead end, and sent all of us to HR for new assignments. Most of us went to existing projects, but not Genevieve and Uriel. They had a brand new project: top-secret, off the books."

"The Sandbox!" Claire whispered in her best horror movie voice.

"That's right. New name, new building, new manager, but everything else was the same. All the hardware and software had been brought over from Hyperlink."

"What was the point of moving somewhere else?" Molly asked.

"Remember," Claire said, "the floor it's on now is so secret, it doesn't exist."

"Only Genny and Uriel knew that Bradford moved the equipment. Everyone else thinks it was scrapped for parts because the technology was worthless."

"So everyone would think LTG had given up developing a BCI," Molly said. "Even other LTG employees!"

"Exactly," Diana said. "Bradford knew no one would leak his trade secrets if everyone believed they were useless."

"But what really made Lori sick?" Molly asked. "What did her parents tell you?"

"It was just an accident, an ordinary, horrible accident. There was a new sys admin in the server room. He recycled the cluster, assuming no one would be in the system at 3:00 in the morning. Not only was Lori in the system, she'd been in there forty-two hours. It wasn't the cap that hurt her; it was getting yanked out of a long session."

"That's how Genevieve knew being pulled from the Sandbox could cause brain damage," Molly said.

"That's right. And it's why now, only Uriel performs maintenance on the Sandbox. Genevieve isn't taking any chances with your brains!"

"I bet it was her idea for you to be a camp counselor," Claire said.

"No, it was mine, but only because I learned about NovaCamp before she did. That's how secretive Harold is! He had told her to expect six new team members this June. When I saw an ad for NovaCamp counselors on LTG's Intranet, we put two and two together."

"It was so upsetting. Uriel and I met with Genevieve after work and stayed up all night trying to decide what to do. I wanted to go public with it, blow the whole thing up. Genevieve convinced me that it would only end our careers, not the project. Bradford would forge ahead without us, putting the next users at even greater risk."

"Because the caps were never tested?" Claire asked.

"Oh, they were rigorously tested, just not in a clinical trial setting. The caps are safe. They've logged thousands of test hours with zero side effects. The danger is the simulation.

"The Sandbox isn't like a screen or a VR headset, where a glitch is something you only see or hear. This technology pushes that error into your brain, and who knows what kind of damage that could cause. That's why the development team was so obsessed with quality control.

"Management never got that. They didn't care that large portions of the simulation were completely untested. Those glitches yesterday were exactly what the three of us were worried about. And that happened in the safest part of the simulation.

"Genevieve had been calling me every afternoon, and we'd compare notes." Yesterday, she sounded upset, almost scared. When she missed the call today, I knew I needed to talk to one of you. That wasn't easy because the NovaCamp app loaded spyware on all your phones. So I passed Claire a note explaining how to defeat the spyware. She must have thought I was crazy, but she was brave enough to talk to me, anyway."

"I wanted to know about all the Warehouse worlds," Claire said. "But Diana was surprised that Genevieve said there were over a dozen of them. The Hyperverse team only created eight."

Diana shook her head. "I can't believe Genevieve finished five worlds in one year. Maybe one of them is still buggy, and that's what caused the glitches."

"What if it's not stable?" Claire asked. "She could be in danger!"

"I doubt it," Diana said. "We're talking about a system she engineered and knows better than anyone else. It's more likely the fix is just more complicated than she expected. She's been in there, what, twelve hours? Not that long to fix a complex environment like the Sandbox."

"It is if you factor in time dilation. That's thirty-six hours, a day and a half!" Claire nodded her head. "If she doesn't come back soon, I'm going after her!"

"Absolutely not!" Diana's gentle voice grew sharp. "That's the last thing Genevieve would want. She's made it her mission to protect the six of you, and she would have a fit if you risked your necks for her. Besides, if she were in danger, I don't see how you could help. Genevieve spent three years writing and refining this code; three days ago, you didn't know it existed."

Claire flinched as if the blow were physical. "That was harsh!"

"I'm sorry, but it's our job to protect you, not the other way around. If you try to play rescuer, it will only make our job harder." Please, promise me you'll stay out of the Warehouse!"

"I promise," Molly said, but Diana was focused on Claire.

Claire knitted her eyebrows but finally murmured, "Okay, I promise."

"And we'll tell the other girls at breakfast," Molly added.

"Good." Diana got up to leave. "But make sure everyone's cell phone is turned off before you talk to them."

The next morning, Claire and Molly found most of their team eating breakfast together in the Cafeteria. "Where's Katrina?" Claire asked.

"We think she may be at the lab already," Aaliyah said. "She left the dorm early this morning."

"Oh no!" Molly turned, rushed out of the building, and started running toward the lab. As she ran, Molly passed joggers headed in both directions. They either didn't notice her or flashed her a nod of fraternity, some with a look in their eyes that said "pace yourself."

Molly knew how to pace herself, but she also knew she had to reach Katrina before it was too late. Once Exeter East was in sight, she sprinted all the way to the door. Gasping for breath, she waved to the guard and walked into an open elevator. By the time she reached the eighteenth floor, her breathing was almost normal.

As soon as she entered the lab, she knew she was too late. Two chairs away from Genevieve, Katrina lay in her recliner, eyes closed, cap blinking. She looked so sweet and peaceful that Molly barely recognized her. The lab was eerily still. Brittany and Harold were nowhere to be seen. "Where is everyone?" Molly asked Uriel.

"The three of us are working in shifts until Genevieve returns. I think she forgets that someone needs to be here monitoring the system. Brittany stayed all night, and now it's my shift. I was sure Genevieve would be back by now; it's been nearly twenty-four hours. I hope Katrina can find her! Are you going in, too?"

"Yes, please." Molly was already prone in her chair, adjusting her cap. "How long has Katrina been in there?"

Uriel checked his screen. "Twelve and a half minutes."

"I'm ready now if you are."

"Sure. If you see Genevieve, please tell her to report in. Safe journey!"

The clubhouse materialized around Molly, and it was empty. Worse, the Warehouse door was off its hinges. It was leaning against the wall, with a hammer, a nail punch, and the pins to the hinges lying in front of it. Beyond the door, no longer hidden, was the same view of the Warehouse she'd glimpsed yesterday.

There was a metal wall about ten yards away. On either side of the door, oversized shelves, reminding her of a Home Depot, extended toward the wall. And like a retail superstore, the shelves contained furniture and plants.

Molly wanted a better view and inched closer to the doorway. She started to step through the threshold when she remembered, *I promised Diana I'd stay out of the Warehouse!* She put her foot back down.

Before she could talk herself out of it, Molly poked her head into the Warehouse and called for her friend. "Katrina! Katrina, are you there? Can you hear me? Hello?" The only sound was a faint echo of Molly's own voice. She stood perfectly still, listening with all her might for what seemed an eternity. Not a sound.

Molly tried cupping her hands to form a makeshift megaphone. She called again and again, in different directions, making sure to keep her feet in the clubhouse. Then she sent Katrina a text message, even though she doubted it would reach her.

Molly waited as long as she could stand, then yelled again. The results were the same. She turned her back on the doorway just in time to see her friends shimmering into existence.

"Oh crap," Aaliyah said. "She did it already."

"Have you looked for her?" Claire asked.

"I decided to talk to you guys first," Molly said. "I did yell her name in the doorway at least a dozen times. If she were in that warehouse, she would have heard it. I even texted her and got no reply."

Claire shook her head. "I can't believe you didn't go after her!"

"I started to, but then I remembered our promise to Diana. We promised her we wouldn't go in there!"

"No, that was for Genevieve; this is for Katrina!" Claire bolted for the door, with Jo Beth on her heels.

Claire got as far as the threshold before Jo Beth grabbed her by the shoulders. "Whoa, there." She turned Claire around and walked her several steps back from the doorway.

"Let's think about this, Claire. We know that once you're in there, you can't communicate with us or the lab. I'm guessing you won't be able to contact Katrina either. Then we've got three people in different parts of the Warehouse for the rest of us to find. If anyone goes, we should all go together."

Claire nodded. "I guess you're right. Come on, guys."

"Slow down," Emma said. "I agree we should go together, but what's the big rush? If we wait a few minutes, there's a good chance Katrina will come right back and tell us what she learned."

Jo Beth turned to Emma. "That would make sense if it were you on the other side of that door. You'd be careful; you wouldn't stay too long, even if it meant coming back empty-handed. But that's not Katrina. I think the longer we wait, the harder she'll be to find."

"And we know the Warehouse is huge," Molly said, "with over a dozen worlds to get lost in."

Jo Beth raised her hand. "I say we go in. All in favor?" Everyone raised their hand, including Emma.

"Good!" Claire said. She started to move, but Jo Beth blocked her path.

"Hold on, Claire," she said. "I don't trust you to stay with the group, so give me your hand." Claire pouted and glared at Jo Beth before grasping her hand.

"That's a good idea." Emma reached out to either side, linking hands with Aaliyah and Molly. Molly was the closest to Jo Beth and, after delaying a second too long, reached out to her.

As Jo Beth took Molly's hand, Claire moved straight for the doorway, pulling Jo Beth off-balance. Jo Beth planted her feet and stopped Claire before she could step through. "Damn, Claire! You can't wait five seconds? We're going as a team!"

"Now?" Claire asked.

Jo Beth surveyed the others in silence before reluctantly nodding. Claire stormed the threshold, pulling everyone with her.

14
Surreality

The instant Claire entered the doorway, it turned pitch black and swallowed her. Jo Beth hesitated for a split second, then plunged into the dark, dragging Molly along.

Molly watched her own arm disappear and thought, *At least I can feel Jo Beth's hand.* Then Molly's face crossed the threshold, and she found herself in bright sunshine. She took several more steps before Aaliyah said, "Whoa."

They were standing in tall grass between a riverbank and the edge of a forest. Molly was still holding Emma's hand, and she was holding Aaliyah's, but Claire and Jo Beth were gone. "You let go of Jo Beth's hand!" Emma said.

"You know I wouldn't do that!"

"Do I?"

"Her hand just disappeared! I was holding it tight, and then it vanished, along with her. No one let go — my hand was just empty. They went into the dark, and we ended up here. You saw that!"

"*I* saw it," Aaliyah said firmly. "But where is here? It's sure not the Warehouse."

"And," Emma said, "it doesn't have a door."

She was right. There was no door or any sign that one had ever existed. There was nothing but this landscape stretching endlessly in every direction. This was the middle of nowhere, but it also seemed familiar. Molly looked around her, studying every aspect of this new world. "I know where we are! I just don't know how it's possible."

"Where?" said Aaliyah and Emma in unison.

"Haven't you seen this before? The meadow, that forest behind you, the river behind me, the mountains beyond that…"

"With a castle on the largest mountain, it's like your mural!" Aaliyah said breathlessly.

"It's more than like it — it's exactly what I painted. Every brushstroke, as far as I can tell."

"But that was only two days ago," Aaliyah said.

"Didn't you base your mural on the plan Genevieve showed us?" Emma asked. "I bet that world was in the Warehouse."

"Her plan inspired me, but I made a point of creating my own world, and this is my version. It's identical, down to the last detail. Here, I can show you." Molly made the gesture to retrieve her screen, but nothing happened. Her upturned hand was empty.

"Uh oh!" said Aaliyah. "Try it again!" Molly did, followed by Aaliyah and Emma. No screens appeared.

"This is why the lab couldn't reach Genevieve," Aaliyah said. "Those stupid screens only work in the Sandbox!"

Emma was examining her left hand. "Hey, do you have your exit rings?"

Molly checked. The ring was gone! She turned her wrist as if the ring would be visible from a different angle. She held her hand next to Emma's as Aaliyah did the same. Their hands were equally bare. "We don't have rings or screens!"

"So much for our backup plan!" Emma said.

"Then how do we get home?" Aaliyah asked. "If they have to unplug us in the lab, we could end up as vegetables."

"I know it looks bad," Molly said, "but…"

"It looks terrifying!" Emma said.

"But I know how smart you guys are," Molly said. "If we put our heads together, we should be able to figure this out."

"Figure out what, exactly?" Emma asked.

"Like what just happened. If we can figure out how it works, maybe the process can be reversed."

"Molly's right." Aaliyah nodded. "We can panic later. Right now, we need to problem-solve."

"I'll try." Emma shrugged. "But what do we have to work with?"

"Let's start with how we got here," Molly said. "Whatever we traveled through, it's not a simple door between two spaces."

"More like a portal or wormhole," said Aaliyah.

"Shh!" Molly's gaze darted to the forest. "Listen."

Emma and Aaliyah stared at the forest. They waited, but the only sounds were the birds and the river. But then one noise sounded like a voice. "Did you hear that?" she whispered.

"Definitely," Emma whispered back. "Was it 'Help'?"

Aaliyah nodded her head and mouthed the words, "I think so."

"So we're going into that scary forest?" Emma whispered. Aaliyah and Molly both nodded their heads, so Emma led the way.

The trees were exactly how Molly had imagined them: towering oaks with trunks wider than she was tall. Their leaves were the rich green of early summer, and even the lowest was a yard higher than she could reach. The ground beneath them was covered in twigs and leaves that snapped and crunched with every step.

"Guys," Aaliyah whispered. "I think we could hear better if we spread out." They did, but now all they heard was the river behind them and the birds high above in the trees. As they walked further, the sound of the river grew fainter until Molly realized it was gone.

Without that sound to guide them, how would they find their way back? She searched for some unique feature to serve as a marker, but all these trees were perfect. That's the way she created them, never dreaming she might get lost in them. She wished she had a compass. If she had her screen, she could make one. Another option was a trail of sand. And she had created the sand without using her screen at all.

It won't hurt to try, Molly thought. She closed her eyes and then opened them. She was holding a handful of white Gulf Shores sand again. She tried retrieving the sand nozzle the same way. Yes! Her sand nozzle appeared, floating in front of her as if it had always been there. She opened the nozzle and sent it straight back in the direction she'd come from. It left a line of white sand as far as she could see.

"Help," the voice cried, far in the distance.

"It's Katrina," Aaliyah shouted and ran deeper into the woods.

Emma took off after her, stopped, and turned to check on Molly. "Come on. We'll get separated."

"I'm right behind you," Molly shouted, and Emma ran on ahead. Before running after her, Molly created a second sand nozzle to extend the trail of sand behind her. After what seemed like a mile, Emma slowed to a walk, and Molly pulled up next to her.

Panting, Emma pointed to Aaliyah up ahead. "She finally quit running. Wait, that's a sand nozzle from our beach!"

"It is. I guess I can retrieve it because I'm the one who created it."

"Does that sand lead all the way back?"

"No, but it goes far enough that we should be able to follow the sounds of the river from there."

Emma mulled that over. "I wonder if I can do it?" She cupped her hand and studied it. Suddenly, a small flame appeared and danced there without burning her.

"The candle flame you created in the castle," Molly said. "So we can both retrieve our creations. Aaliyah should be able to, too." Aaliyah was standing over a hundred yards away, staring at them with her hands on her hips.

"Come on," Aaliyah yelled. "She's in here!" She pointed to the back of an immense tree.

"You mean she's inside the tree?" Emma asked.

"Yes. Come look."

Once Molly got there, she understood what Aaliyah meant. A doorframe was built into the tree's side, with steps leading down into the darkness.

"Not another doorway!" Emma said. "I don't think we should go down there. It might be a trap."

"But we have to help Katrina!" Molly said.

"*If* it's Katrina," Aaliyah said.

"You seemed sure a minute ago," Molly said.

"I'm sure that was her voice, and I'm sure it looked like Katrina. But it didn't act like her. She waited until I got here before walking down those steps. It was like she was trying to lure us down there."

"So if it's not Katrina," Molly asked, "who is it? Do you think it's a clone or something?"

"You clone living organisms," Emma said. "Our avatars are only code. You can copy one with a couple of mouse clicks."

"But what if the real Katrina is down there?" Molly said. "What if they all are? That could be the darkness we saw through the first door."

"Damn it, guys, come help me!" said the voice from down the stairs.

"Now that sounded more like my roommate," Aaliyah whispered, "but I still think it's an impostor."

"Why?" Molly asked.

"Have you *ever* heard Katrina ask for help?"

"Then it's probably the same thing that stranded us here," Emma said. "If we go down those steps, we'll be walking into a trap."

"Congratulations, you are correct. But, of course, this entire world is a trap." The icy voice came from behind them. The girls spun around and discovered a striking woman in her thirties. Her imposing gown, pure Victorian pomp, was periwinkle silk, and she wore her dark brown hair in a regal bun behind her head.

"Who are you?" Emma asked.

"I am Ada, creator of this world. Genevieve is my captive, and I won't allow you to interfere."

Aaliyah closed the distance to Ada in one aggressive step. "You didn't create squat! Genevieve created this world, and she created you! You're just a computer program!"

"And you — are not welcome here." Ada raised her perfect chin as if posing for a portrait. Then she was simply not there.

The girls stared at each other with open mouths until Aaliyah looked down at her feet. She screamed, her voice hollow with fear. "No!"

The glistening leaves of a thick vine were whipping around her ankles and calves. Aaliyah pulled her left knee up an inch but got no further. She gritted her teeth and groaned with effort, but the vine was stronger and pulled her knee back down. Each second, the vine grew longer and thicker, binding Aaliyah's legs like a swaddled infant.

But it wasn't just Aaliyah. The entire forest floor was alive with slithering vines. By the time Molly noticed, a vine had already circled her left ankle. A second, poised like a cobra, seemed to stare at her with its leafless tip. Something grabbed Molly's arm, and she jumped back.

It was only Emma fighting to stay on her feet as the vines pulled her toward an oak. "Help!" She struggled to stretch her hand out to Molly.

Molly grabbed it just as the vines tipped Emma over, tearing her hand away. The effort cost Molly the little balance she had, and she crash-landed on her back. It knocked the wind out of her, and she was still trying to breathe when she felt the vines pulling her along the ground. Soon, they'd be pulling her up. Aaliyah's legs were already straight up in the air, even as she desperately tried to free herself. "Aaliyah," Molly yelled. "Retrieve the swords you made in the castle."

"What?" Aaliyah asked as the vines lifted her off the ground.

"Concentrate and create a new sword object," Molly yelled.

"Or three!" Emma said.

Aaliyah scrunched up her entire face in concentration, but nothing happened. Molly's feet flew up in front of her. She didn't have long. With all her weight on her shoulder blades, Molly flailed for something, anything to grab. Then, her right hand touched cold steel. It was the pommel of a sword! Molly wrapped her fingers around the handle and hacked at one of the vines. After three tries, she freed her left leg. She swung the blade at the other vine. This time, it was a clean cut. As her legs fell, the vines sprang up toward the branches, sagged back down, and hung lifeless.

Thump! Emma landed on her back, sword clutched in both hands.

Aaliyah somehow landed on her feet. She wielded her sword lightly with one hand, scanning the area for threats. "Are you guys OK?"

"I think so." Molly watched the slithering vines retreat into the ground. She shivered in disgust.

Aaliyah turned to Emma. "How about you?"

"I am now. Thanks to you, and thanks to Molly."

"Me?" Molly asked.

"Yes, because you figured out how we can defend ourselves."

"You mean by retrieving these swords?" Aaliyah said. "I thought we couldn't retrieve objects from the Sandbox."

"Only objects we created ourselves, and you're the only one of us who created a weapon." Molly stared at the forest floor. It looked completely normal, as if there had never been a single vine. "Can we please get out of here?"

"What about the door? It might be safe to go down there now. Wait, isn't that the right tree? Where's the door?" Aaliyah was pointing at an enormous tree with no door. All three girls examined the tree from every side.

Molly circled the tree. "I'm not sure. I think the sun has set, and everything looks even weirder in this dim light."

"It's the same tree," Emma said. "I definitely remember this side, plus it's the biggest tree around here. We couldn't go through that door if we wanted to. I'm sorry, Aaliyah, it was all a trick."

"I know you're right, but I really wanted to believe we had found Katrina. Hey, shouldn't we head back to the river? I can barely see my hand in front of my face."

"We should," Molly said. "It's getting dark fast, and we're already in the darkest, scariest part of my whole painting."

"Are you saying we're safer in the prettier parts of the painting?" Emma asked.

"Only because there's more open space and visibility out there. I just wish I knew which way to go. I don't see my sand anywhere."

"What sand?" Aaliyah asked.

"I left a trail of sand behind me to help us get back to the river. But now I can't find it. I'm so turned around, I don't even know where to start."

"I think I can figure it out." Emma pointed to the giant tree. "I recognize this side of the tree because it was my first view of it. When Aaliyah told us to hurry up, we were back there." Then Emma pointed behind Molly. "That's where the sand will be. We need to find it before it gets too dark to see."

"I wish one of us had created a flashlight in the Sandbox." Aaliyah and Molly walked to where Emma had pointed.

"This might help," Emma said. "It's from the AeroCar." She retrieved a headlight, a wiring harness, and an aluminum box, twice the size of a regular car battery. "Crap! I was trying to retrieve these wired together." She examined the wiring harness. "Time for my toolbox, I guess."

It was much darker by the time the headlight was working. Emma aimed it in Molly's direction and disappeared behind a corona of brilliant light. "That's better," Aaliyah said. "Do you see your sand line, Molly?"

"I don't, and I thought I had brought it this far."

Aaliyah was scouring the woods with her. "I'm not sure I know what I'm looking for."

"It should be a thick line of sand, almost a mound."

"Emma, can I bring that battery over here?" Aaliyah asked. "From there, it casts too many shadows."

"You can if you want," Emma said, "but it weighs over fifteen kilograms. It had to be big to power the AeroCar propellers."

"But it didn't have to weigh that much. You could have given it zero mass, like those throne room timbers."

Emma scoffed. "I could have, if I were building a fairy-tale prop like yours. But I was doing real prototyping, which required real-world properties."

"No, I get it. It wouldn't be a real test if you used a weightless battery. But couldn't you change the properties now, make it smaller or lighter?"

"I tried, and I couldn't."

Aaliyah persisted. "Can we dismantle it and use a single cell?"

"There's nothing to dismantle," Emma snapped. "It performs like a real-life battery, but it isn't constructed like one."

"Darn! Well, what if…"

"What if you quit playing electrical engineer and come up with your own damn solution?"

Aaliyah stood motionless for what seemed an eternity, taut as a bowstring. Then she raised her left hand, index finger pointing straight at Emma. "You've got a lot to learn about teamwork!" She turned and walked into the forest.

"Now, who's being a drama queen?" Emma said under her breath.

Aaliyah was deep in the forest, but still visible in the headlight beam. Molly turned to Emma. "We're all on edge right now, but this is exactly what that 'Ada' wants, to divide us and pick us off individually. We've got to stick together."

Emma nodded. "You're right, but I'm not the one who took off. You should tell that to Aaliyah."

"I'm going to. Why don't you come with me?"

"No, thanks. I'm good right here."

Molly would have to go alone, but when she turned around, Aaliyah was gone.

15
The Enchanted Forest

MOLLY RAN TO the spot where she had last seen Aaliyah. "Aaliyah?" she called out. No reply. Out in the dark, something shuffled through the leaves. Was it Aaliyah? Molly crept forward cautiously and yelled in her loudest voice. "Aaliyah!"

"Here I am!" Aaliyah emerged from the shadows, arms full of leaves and branches. "It's hard to hear over these leaves."

"You scared me to death! I thought something had gotten you."

"Nothing's going to get me! I've got a new sword, and soon I'll have fire."

"Fire?"

"For the trip back to the river. I'm going, with or without Thomas Edison, back there. You should come, too." After a long pause, Aaliyah snapped her fingers. "Earth to Molly. Hello?"

"Sorry, I was thinking about fire. I know how we can find the sand. Come on; we have to tell Emma."

"No," Aaliyah said. "I don't have to tell her anything. I *might* be willing to listen to an apology, but she has to come to me! You can go without me, since you're okay with how she disrespects me."

Molly looked at her friend, half in darkness, half brightly illuminated by the distant headlamp."I'm definitely not OK with how Emma acts! I've just come to expect it. You would not believe how she's dogged me about Jo Beth, like that's any of her business! But I think I've figured out why she does it."

After a long pause, Aaliyah said, "I'm listening."

"Emma's always been the smartest person in the room, even at Princeton. She's not used to being challenged."

"For real! Don't question the Battery Queen! But she's got it backwards. Being challenged by smart people is the best part of NovaCamp! I've been looking for that since I wrote my first 'Hello World.' Finally, I can talk about coding without the blank stares."

"I agree!" Molly said. "I love hanging with you guys, and now we need to stick together more than ever. Let's go back there and get your apology."

"Follow me." Aaliyah turned into the headlamp's glare, one hand up to protect her eyes. She led the way back to Emma, then stood there without saying a word.

"Uh, oh!" Emma said. "Am I in trouble?'

"Not like you were a few minutes ago," Aaliyah said, "dangling upside down from a tree. Do you remember thanking us for getting you free?"

"Of course I do, but..."

"No buts!" Molly had planned to let Aaliyah do the talking, but she couldn't help herself. "You sat here and watched your teammates go deep into that forest where anything could have happened to us. Shame on you!"

Emma remained silent. Wheels spun behind her eyes, and twice she started to speak but stopped herself. It was Aaliyah who spoke first. "Do you not want to be on this team?"

"I do. I want to be on your team, and for the first time in my life, I don't have to lead it. Katrina was right, we're all exceptional here. It's just hard... getting used to that."

"And?" Molly said.

"And, I'm sorry, Aaliyah, for acting like an asshole. I *am* grateful that you rescued me from the vines, and I want to be on your team."

At first, Aaliyah didn't react at all. She stood there, tall and proud, not saying a word. But slowly, her cold stare warmed, and her tight mouth softened into that familiar smile. "Then let's do some teamwork. I think Molly had an idea."

"Emma," Molly said, "can you retrieve another candle flame, please?"

"Why?" Then Emma's face lit up in understanding. She smiled and opened her right hand. A bright flame danced in her palm. In her left hand, she created a new headlight, lifeless without a power source. "Is this what you were thinking?"

"Exactly," Molly said.

"You're still teaching me about teamwork." Emma's little flame floated from her hand to the dark headlight, passing through the lens to the silvered interior. Reflected and magnified, the flickering flame became a beam of light.

"Not as bright, but still respectable." Emma held the glowing headlight out to Aaliyah. "A peace offering."

Emma created two more hybrid headlights, one in Molly's hands and one in her own. "Let's see if the three of us can find that sand."

"Can I disconnect the original lamp?" Aaliyah asked. "It will make ours seem brighter."

"Good idea! By the way, you weren't planning to use that on me, were you?" Emma aimed her beam at Aaliyah's new sword, sticking up from the dirt behind her.

Aaliyah responded with a genuine laugh. "No, for some reason, I thought walking alone in the dark through an evil forest might be dangerous."

"When you put it that way, would you mind making two more?"

"Sure. Here's yours, and… Hey, where'd Molly go?"

"Over here," Molly yelled. "I realized I wasn't as close as I thought when I quit making sand." She waved her headlight in front of her. "Do you see where I am?"

Emma yelled back. "I see you. That's the right direction. I'll join you."

Molly spotted Emma's headlight bobbing in the distance. That gave her a better sense of where the "Ada" tree was, and she aimed her beam in the opposite direction. The cone of light danced across an ocean of brown leaves before igniting a streak of sparkling sand. "I found it! I found the sand!"

"Eureka!" Aaliyah said. "Ooh, that was nerdy, wasn't it?"

"Nerdy is good!" Molly said.

Emma joined them. "I hope so because that definitely describes the three of us."

"The six of us," Aaliyah said. "We *are* going to find them."

"Why do you have two swords?" Molly asked.

"This one's yours!" Aaliyah handed it to Molly. "Lead on, brave knight."

Molly did, walking to the left of the line, lighting as far ahead as the dense woods allowed. Emma and Aaliyah followed on either side, adding their light to Molly's.

After a few minutes, Emma said, "I guess we need to talk about the Wicked Witch back there."

"She called herself Ada," Molly said.

Aaliyah asked, "Have you guys seen a picture of Ada Lovelace?"

"I know who she is," Emma said, "but I can't remember what she looked like."

"Exactly like that," Aaliyah said. "Down to her shoes."

"Ada Lovelace," Molly said. "Wasn't she the person who wrote the first computer program?"

"That's her!" Emma said. "One of my heroes, and now she's trying to kill us! How does that make any sense?"

"I'm not sure she wants to kill us," Aaliyah said. "But she sure doesn't want us to find Genevieve."

"She's definitely got it in for Genevieve," Molly said.

"Oh!" Aaliyah abruptly stopped. "Remember when we first heard Fake Katrina's voice? Right after we had calmed down enough to analyze our situation. What if Ada was trying to distract us?"

"Like she doesn't want us to stop and think?" Molly said. "That makes sense!"

"Well, screw her!" Emma said. "That's all the more reason to stop and think, or maybe walk and think."

"Agreed," said Aaliyah, "and I've already done some."

"Good," Emma said. "What did you come up with?"

"Remember, we said that Genevieve's door acted more like a portal — a portal to multiple endpoints? The three of us didn't land in the Warehouse, so it's possible Claire and Jo Beth didn't either. At first, I thought the Warehouse had gone dark, but that wasn't the only change. Did you guys hear how windy it was when they disappeared?"

"Are you sure that wasn't the wind from here?" Emma asked.

"I'm sure. There is wind here, but that place was super-windy! That's the sort of wind you'd hear on the side of a mountain. So I think we're in three different places, assuming Katrina found Genevieve."

"Oh no!" Molly said. "That makes it even harder."

"True, but you're the one who wanted us to stay calm and problem-solve," Emma said. "I think Aaliyah is on the right track. For one thing, we actually know where Genevieve is because we saw her enter the Warehouse. That's a start."

Aaliyah came to a halt. "Uh, Molly, where's the sand?"

"Oh, it ended about twenty yards back. Don't worry; the river will guide us. Can't you hear it?"

Emma aimed her headlight at the trees in front of them. "I didn't realize we'd gone so deep in the forest. Let's not make that mistake again."

"At least we know we're going in the right direction." Molly led them toward the faint sound. As it became louder, Molly spotted the edge of the forest far ahead. They picked up their pace and soon emerged near the spot where they'd entered this world.

Molly barely recognized it. Overhead, a full moon beamed with cold intensity, dominating the slate-gray sky. Wispy clouds, too thin to hide the moon, glowed like paper lanterns beneath it. The silvery light cast its unearthly enchantment over the surface, transmuting humble scrub grass into spires of sparkling crystal and the surging river into an endless dance floor where a thousand miniature moons twirled their way downstream.

"That's gorgeous!" Aaliyah said. "And to think you created this world, Molly."

"I never imagined it in moonlight; I wish I had."

"What's wrong with you two?" Emma stepped in front of Molly and Aaliyah. "Do you really believe 'Ada' is powerless out here? It's an Artificial Intelligence with god-like power in this simulation. It wouldn't surprise me if this pretty scene you two are admiring is her attempt to lure us into relaxing or even taking a nap."

"I do feel tired," Aaliyah said.

"No. You don't!" Emma said. "You can't, because that isn't your actual body; it's a computer program! It doesn't need sleep, and it doesn't get tired!"

"Why are you yelling at us?" Molly asked.

"Because we're in serious danger! Do you think Ada has just given up?"

"You're right," Aaliyah said. "She wants us dead or gone."

"Could we die here?" Molly asked. "Is it like The Matrix? If we die in here, do our bodies die?"

"I'm skeptical," Emma said, "but I don't want to put it to the test! We have to stay on guard every second we're in here."

"I agree," Molly said. "There's no telling what Ada will throw at us next."

As if on cue, the world went dark. A large black shape had flown in front of the moon. Behind it, more of the shapes were streaming out of the mountains. With a shock, Molly realized they were bats, bats the size of UPS trucks, and they were headed this way!

"What should we do?" said Aaliyah.

"Try to think of any objects you built that would help. I'll try to make us spears." Molly retrieved two copies of the five-meter pole she had used to measure the Banquet Hall wall. She cut them in half with her sword, making the cuts as diagonal as possible. She fashioned one decent spear by adding more cuts to the tip. Molly was shaping the second spear when the sound of flapping wings stopped her. The bats were very close now. She checked on the girls and couldn't believe what they'd done.

In seconds, they had built a compact fort that looked like it would last centuries! Molly recognized the timbers from the ceiling of the Throne Room. These were stuck in the ground at a 45-degree angle, forming a cone, like a tepee, but much wider. It was about twenty yards in diameter, with the timbers spaced less than a yard apart at the base.

"Molly, duck!" Emma screamed, and Molly dove to the ground. There was a great whoosh as a giant bat rushed over her, missing by inches. The nightmare creature flew over the river, rose high in the air, and headed back for her.

"Hurry," Emma said, "get in here now!" Molly ran for the fort, wondering if she would make it. Her speed must have surprised the bat, as it overshot her by several yards. Now she only had a yard to go, and she ducked through the narrow opening with the monster right on her heels.

Thwack! It slammed into the structure with all its might. Stunned, it lingered there, its repulsive face inches away. It had solid-black eyes, razor teeth, and two triangular gaps where the nose should have been. The creature soon recovered and resumed the attack. It repeatedly slammed its head against the timbers before it finally flew off.

Molly stood there for some time without moving. She only moved at all because Aaliyah put a hand on her shoulder. "Are you OK?"

Molly turned slowly. "Hell no," she growled, "but I'm working on it."

"Come over here and sit a minute." Aaliyah led the way to a sturdy oak chair. Emma had retrieved three of them from the Banquet Hall. A headlight, suspended by its power cord from the ceiling, provided ample lighting. Molly sat watching as Aaliyah and Emma inspected all the timbers. "How did you guys do this so fast?"

Aaliyah smiled and pointed her thumb at Emma. "I asked our engineer here what we could do with fifteen-meter oak timbers that were solid but had no mass."

"This makes my spears look pretty lame."

"Hey," Emma said. "If you hadn't discovered we can retrieve things, we'd still be hanging by our ankles in the forest. It's about time I contributed in some way."

Another bat crashed into the structure and rolled on the ground, dazed. "If these timbers have zero mass, why are they so strong?" Molly asked.

"They're buried deep in the ground, like telephone poles," Aaliyah said.

"So we're really safe here?"

"Absolutely. They can't get in here. *And* we can't leave." Emma arched an eyebrow. "I wonder how long those giant rodents will stay out there?"

"Probably all night," said Aaliyah. "But once the sun comes out, they should fly away, and we can go outside."

"What difference will that make?" Molly threw her hands up in frustration. "Even if all the bats leave in the morning, we're still stuck in a world Ada controls — a world without a portal."

"We don't know that," Emma said. "We haven't even looked for a portal yet."

"Well, there's always the one we came through," Aaliyah said.

Molly scoffed. "The one that no longer exists?"

"I think it may come back," Aaliyah said. "We know seven people went through the same door in the clubhouse and landed in three different places."

"So?" Molly asked.

"What if the doorway cycles between different worlds, like the second hand on a clock, and eventually gets back to us?"

"You mean, like the Warehouse is one o'clock, the dark place is two o'clock, and this world is three o'clock?" Emma asked.

"Exactly, and before it cycled back to here, we were already in the woods."

"I guess that's possible," Emma said, "but it doesn't seem likely."

Molly stood up. "Likely or not, it's a glimmer of hope, which I desperately need."

Emma shrugged. "Then we should search for it in the morning, and I really hope it's there!"

16

The Warehouse

MOLLY POINTED TO the floor. A shaft of orange sunlight scurried across the ground. "Our sunrise is finally here."

Outside, the bat creatures rose one by one into the sky. As the sky brightened, they swarmed back to the mountains and disappeared. "Is it over?" Molly asked.

"I think so." Aaliyah was peering through the timbers. "It should be safe to hunt for that portal now."

"Grab your swords." Emma brandished hers and stepped outside. Aaliyah and Molly followed, each heading in their own direction. "Hey guys," Emma said, "we need to stick together. Do either of you have a good fix on that spot?"

"I think I do," Molly said. "When we arrived, I studied that landscape across the river, comparing it to what I had painted. I'm pretty confident I can tell you which direction we should go."

"Good." Both girls came over next to her.

Molly framed the view with her hands. She scanned the river, the meadow, and the mountains, but it was only vaguely familiar. "Am I taking too long?"

"Not if you can figure it out," Emma said.

"Let me try over here." Molly stepped off five yards to the left and repeated the framing gesture. "I know it's that way," she said, pointing to the left. She headed that way, leading the girls past the bat fort and nearly a hundred yards beyond. There she checked again. "It should be somewhere in here. If we're lucky, we might find our footprints."

They proceeded slowly then, Molly checking the scenery to their right while Emma and Aaliyah checked the ground. "Hey, over here!" Emma said. "I think this mashed-down grass might be where we landed."

Molly checked in all directions. "Yep, this is the view I remember."

"And I remember that willow." Aaliyah pointed. "It has a kind of animal face in that root."

"This is definitely the spot," Molly said.

"If no portal shows up, can we abandon the analog clock analogy?" Emma asked.

"Fine with me," Molly said. "But remember how we heard Katrina's voice almost the instant we arrived?"

"That's right," Aaliyah said, "and we never looked back here again. Ada made sure of that."

Molly realized she had taken her eyes off the trampled spot for a moment. Even as she turned to look, she knew the portal would be there. It was not at all what she expected. There was no sound, no special effects, only a rectangular space in the air with a view of the clubhouse interior. "Did that just happen?"

"Who cares?" Aaliyah reached for her arm. "Jump!"

Molly jumped and, propelled by Aaliyah's grip on her arm, flew through the opening. She landed with the others in a jumble of arms and legs on the carpet of the Sandbox clubhouse.

"Are we really back?" Molly absently stroked the shag carpet as she gazed around the room.

Aaliyah hopped to her feet, smiled, and nodded. "We are! Home sweet home!"

Molly got up and straightened her clothes. She verified her exit ring had returned.

Emma had already pulled up her screen and was studying it intensely. "Aaliyah, I'm sorry I doubted you! Your clock idea was right on the nose. Guys, it's only 1:30 back in the lab! Everything we went through back there took less than five hours in real time."

"What?" Aaliyah retrieved her screen. "It's still Thursday? This time dilation thing is blowing my mind!"

"Also, we've got several messages from the lab. First, Harold gave us until 10:00 to find Genevieve. Next, he gave us until noon, and later he ordered us to the lab for a meeting he scheduled on 'options' for finding Genevieve."

Molly vented a long puff of air. "Oh, I wish she'd never asked us to lie for her! Now we've lost half our team in that stupid portal. How do we explain that to Harold?"

"We don't," Emma said. "We can't put Harold in charge of our friends' lives! Even if he had a clue what was going on here, I don't trust him to do the right thing. We should stay in here and find our roommates."

"But how do we do that?"

Aaliyah held up her screen. "By following Genevieve into the Warehouse. I've been watching, and the portal seems to visit each location in a predictable sequence. I'm writing a program to time the sequence. If the cycle times don't vary, we should be able to safely come and go through the portal."

"We have to try!" Emma turned to Molly. "We know Genevieve's in there, and she can lead us to our friends."

Molly noticed the doorway had turned dark. Were Claire and Jo Beth in there? Genevieve would know; Harold wouldn't. Molly remembered how he'd looked at Genevieve in the conference room. His face had read equal parts anger and jealousy. "OK," Molly said, "I'm in."

Emma nodded. "We'll probably lose our rings and screens again. I recommend you make your own copy of the coding screen now."

"And you can both create copies of my dad's favorite flashlight." Molly showed them hers. "I named it 'Dad's Flashlight.'"

"I have one of those at home," Emma said, "with the work light in the handle. If my copy of the coding screen works, I can copy it when we're in the Warehouse."

"*If* it works," Molly said. "Isn't it better to have copies of the essential things, given our luck so far?"

"You're right," Emma said. "I'm saving it now, plus one other thing that might come in handy."

After several minutes of watching the portal, Aaliyah reported the good news. "It's extremely stable, guys. There are twenty-eight total portals, and each is open for about one and a half seconds."

"One and a half seconds?" Molly said. "That's not right!"

"It is with time dilation," Emma said. "That should feel like four and a half seconds to us."

"That's what I call 'seems like' time," Aaliyah said. "I clocked the time for the entire cycle at 40.6 actual seconds, but it 'seems like' 122 seconds."

"Two minutes," Molly said. "By then, we were entering the forest."

"We're six portals away now," Aaliyah said. "Do you want to jump now or wait for the next one?"

"I'm ready," Emma said.

"Me too," said Molly.

"Then come close." Aaliyah was right in front of the door, her eyes glued to the screen in her left hand. She extended her long right arm like a protective wing, and the other girls huddled inside it. "Warehouse in five, four, three, two, one. Now!"

Suddenly, the Warehouse was on the other side of the door. Thanks to Aaliyah's guiding arm, they were all across the threshold in an instant. But Molly and Emma got their feet tangled, and Emma tumbled onto the concrete floor.

"I'm so sorry, Emma!" Molly reached out her hand.

"It wasn't your fault." Emma took Molly's hand and pulled herself up. "I didn't feel anything, and my avatar seems undamaged." Emma held out her hands. "My exit ring is gone!"

"Mine too," Aaliyah and Molly said.

"But I can retrieve my Emma Screen." Emma was already writing on it. "I'm going to see if we have texting in here. Nope. I just tried to ping Genevieve and got 'Unable to Deliver Message.' I was afraid of that — text messaging is Sandbox only."

Aaliyah immediately retrieved her screen, too. She and Emma stood there checking their screens. But not Molly; she was trying to get her bearings. It was obvious this was the same spot where Genevieve had landed. This was exactly what she'd seen from the clubhouse.

There was the corrugated steel wall, some ten yards high, supporting a metal roof. A covered wagon, an igloo, and several banana trees lined the wall. The building resembled an airplane hangar, possibly for a private jet: a large area, but not gigantic. It had a concrete floor, ugly industrial lights, and a large motorized garage door at the opposite end.

This was the same row of shelves Molly had seen from the clubhouse. There were three long rows of these shelves; the other two were behind her. They held the strangest, most random assortment of objects imaginable. Here was a rose bush in full bloom behind eight feet of white picket fence. Above it was a beat-up, overstuffed lounge chair with a matching sofa. Further down, a spacesuit stood propped up against an ancient stone well. A campfire growled and crackled but never spread to the medieval tapestry nearby.

There were many more curiosities, but Molly kept checking the same object over and over again. It was a great white shark filling two oversized shelves behind Emma and Aaliyah. It remained perfectly still, moving not one micron the entire time Molly stared at it. Still, it looked so lifelike that it was hard to believe it wouldn't attack her any second.

She was trying to take her eyes off it when Emma broke into her thoughts. "What are you looking at?" Emma turned to see and leapt back, barely missing Molly. "Oh," was all she said.

Aaliyah finally noticed, too, and edged closer to Molly. "Is it alive?"

"I don't think so," Molly said. "It hasn't so much as twitched since we got here. But it looks alive, doesn't it?"

"Much too alive," Emma said.

"Check out all this crazy stuff!" Aaliyah swept her arm to indicate all the other items of interest around them.

"It's interesting but not very useful," Emma said. "We won't find Katrina on one of these shelves."

"No," Aaliyah said, "but we might find some valuable clues about what the Warehouse is."

"Like Jaws here?" Emma asked. "How is that a clue?"

"It tells me that Ada isn't the only scary thing they made here," Molly said.

Emma shrugged. "Good point. Let's check the shelves, but give me a minute to mark this portal before we go." She made four small traffic cones on the floor. "Now, when we return, we'll know exactly where the portal is."

As they moved through the aisles, they passed an aquarium tank, about six feet wide and four feet high. A school of clownfish darted around, dodging coral, angelfish, and a pair of porcupine fish. Molly had moved on to a collection of Elizabethan clothes when Emma spoke up.

"I recognize this bastard!" Emma was glaring up at the very top of the shelves. There was a large pot with several thick vines hanging out and over both sides of the shelf. A sword appeared in Emma's hand, and she widened her stance — a warrior at the ready.

Molly waited in silence, and waited. Finally, she spoke up. "I don't think this vine will hurt us, Emma. It isn't moving."

Emma turned to face her. “I guess not, but it felt good to be prepared this time.”

“You sure were!” Aaliyah said. “How did you conjure up my sword like that?”

“I made my own copy of it back at the clubhouse. I wasn’t going to get caught defenseless again.” Emma glanced at the sword, and it disappeared. “I think we’ve run out of shelves to inspect. Let’s see what’s behind door number one.” She headed to the giant hangar door.

“What?” Molly asked. “I don’t think that’s a good idea!” She knew she’d said it loud enough for Emma to hear, but Emma didn’t slow down. Molly tried to catch up, but it was obvious Emma would reach the door first. In a matter of seconds, she would push the Open button, and it would be too late. “Stop!” Molly yelled as Emma reached the control. “We should know what’s behind that door before we open it. It might be something waiting to kill us!”

“That is a popular activity in here!” Aaliyah said.

Emma pulled her hand away from the control and shrugged. “So, what do you two suggest? We just sit around here and do nothing?”

“Can we open it just a little?” Molly asked.

“Or, we can use the regular door over there.” Aaliyah pointed to a door far to the left.

Emma turned to look. “Oh, that is better. I hadn’t noticed that one.”

Aaliyah was the first to reach the door and waited for the others. “Tell me when you’re ready.”

“Just a crack,” Emma said.

Aaliyah placed her left hand against the door, leaned her face as far away as possible, and turned the knob. She paused for a second and then opened the door about three inches. “I can’t see a thing,” she said.

“Do you hear anything?” Molly whispered.

Aaliyah listened and shook her head. “Not a thing. Let’s open it more.” She slowly opened it. There was only darkness beyond the door.

"I'm going to see," Emma said, producing a 'Dad's Flashlight.' Molly waited to the side, her chest tight with tension.

Emma directed the beam left, right, up, and down. She spent a lot of time examining the area right outside the threshold. "I can't find the ground, even under the house. It's like we're on piers or something. Let's try that other door. We need to check around there."

"We do?" Aaliyah said. "Why?"

"This is like where we lost Claire and Jo Beth: total darkness. They may be out there somewhere."

"I don't think so," Aaliyah said. "They went somewhere windy, and this is totally quiet."

"It's too quiet," Molly said, "unnaturally so. And it's too dark — like there's a complete absence of light. That's exactly what I saw beyond the simulation when Brittany first expanded the dome. What if this Warehouse is the whole construct, and nothing exists outside it, not even gravity?"

"Of course there's gravity out there!" Emma backhanded her flashlight out the door. It was a gentle toss, and the flashlight should have landed a few yards from the building. Instead, it continued straight along its original path, neither slowing down nor speeding up. In the intense darkness, it appeared only in brief flashes when its beam rotated toward them. A few seconds later, it was barely discernible, a distant signal lamp flashing Morse code. And soon, even that faint beacon had disappeared.

Aaliyah stood in the open doorway, staring in the flashlight's direction. "So that's what Nothing looks like."

"You were right, Molly," Emma said. "The entire simulation is within these walls — the doors are useless props! Jo Beth and Claire couldn't have landed out there. If it's not part of the simulation, it wouldn't have a portal. It's more likely they landed in a different simulation where it happened to be nighttime."

A terrifying thought occurred to Molly. "Do you think Katrina could have gone out this door? What if she's floating out of sight like that flashlight?"

"Don't worry." Emma produced a new flashlight. "Unless she jumped out or ran out, she would have floated a few inches from the door like this." She held the flashlight outside the door at arm's length and released her fingers. The light remained there, totally motionless. "See, she's not outside."

"Then where did she go?"

"Maybe she took this elevator." Aaliyah was already halfway there.

17
Eighth Floor

Molly and Emma followed Aaliyah along the side of the Warehouse. "Is that really an elevator?" Molly asked Aaliyah's back.

Aaliyah pointed to the steel elevator door. There was no floor indicator, only a small panel with an Up button. "It looks like an elevator to me!"

"Or some kind of trap," Emma said. "You guys *do* remember this is a one-story building?"

"You know what would be cool?" Aaliyah said. "If this were a portal where you select worlds instead of floors."

"It's possible," Molly said. "We know Genevieve and Katrina went somewhere."

"It's possible," Emma said, "but let's be extra careful until we figure out what it really is."

Molly and Aaliyah nodded in agreement, so Emma pushed the Up button. A bell dinged, and the door opened on a surreal sight. It was the same blackness they'd just seen, but with a linoleum floor, about five feet square, suspended over it. Above that, three steel handrails seemed to float in the air. As Molly's eyes adjusted to the darkness, the faint reflections on the sides unraveled the mystery. "This is a glass elevator!"

Molly started to walk inside and was immediately held back by Aaliyah. "Careful, remember? Let's start by learning what we can out here, where it's safe."

"Like what?"

"Like, does this work?" Aaliyah waved her hand in front of the door. It worked: the door stopped closing, dinged, and slid back open. "I'm going to take a look inside without letting the door close on me." Aaliyah put her hand over the door and stepped in just far enough to examine the control panel. "Seems fine to me." She stepped out and let the door close. "Of course, the only way to be sure is to pick a floor."

"Then let's do that." Emma pressed the Up button, and the door slid open. "But let's do it together!"

Molly and Aaliyah nodded their approval, and they all entered the elevator together. The door slid shut, eliminating their only source of light.

"At least the control panel is lit," Aaliyah said. It was, but barely, like a fading firefly. There were eight floors.

Emma reached for the panel. "Which button should I push?"

"Are you guys good with starting on the top floor?" Molly asked.

"Fine by me," Aaliyah said.

Emma nodded and pushed the button. It lit up, and immediately, the elevator filled with light. The sudden brilliance blinded Molly for a second. The door opened to reveal an English garden in full bloom. A stone wall, crumbling with age, enclosed it on four sides. On the far wall, a wooden gate stood open, its blue and white paint faded almost beyond recognition.

The brushed steel face of the elevator was built into the stone wall, making it appear even more out of place. To either side, the wall had disintegrated so much that most of the elevator car was visible. But that's all there was: no shaft, no mechanism to raise and lower it. In the

Warehouse, this had seemed like a normal glass elevator. It was anything but.

Emma was just outside the gate. "Come on, guys, let's stay on point."

"I hear voices over there." Aaliyah pointed to the left wall. It was largely intact, and Molly couldn't see over it, even on tiptoe.

Molly ran toward the entrance and past a disapproving Emma. Once Molly cleared the garden, she discovered who was talking. It stopped her cold. Aaliyah and Emma joined her and had the same reaction. The three of them stood there in silence.

About twenty yards away, in the middle of a grassy field, was a long dinner table and ten chairs. Its white linen tablecloth held ten place settings, only three of which were taken. The occupants had their backs to the girls, but still, something about them seemed familiar.

In the middle was a short, chubby figure, as furry and motionless as a teddy bear. The two animated figures on either side of it were quite tall. Rather, their headgear was: an oversized top hat and fuzzy, gray rabbit ears. It was their voices Aaliyah had heard in the garden. Top Hat was blaming Rabbit Ears for "crumbs in the butter."

"I don't believe it!" Aaliyah whispered out of the side of her mouth.

Top Hat stopped in mid-sentence and turned around in his chair to examine the intruders. Once Rabbit Ears noticed, he did the same. Now it was obvious: this was the Mad Hatter, the Dormouse, and the March Hare.

"Why, Hare," the Hatter said, "you've outdone yourself. You've brought us three Alices this time."

"This is so cool!" Aaliyah walked around the table for a better view.

"But how is it helpful?" Emma asked when she and Molly caught up with her.

"I want to try something," Molly whispered. She addressed the Hatter in a louder voice. "Do you get many visitors?"

"Only Alices, and only one. Until now, of course."

"And what did that first Alice look like?"

"Like an Alice, of course."

"Was her hair like mine?"

"You don't have a Hare, only Alices. We have the Hare!" The Hatter, with a flourish of his hand, presented the March Hare.

Molly was at a loss for how to go on, but Emma said, "We were hoping you would tell us a story about that first Alice."

"A story?" The Dormouse hadn't opened its eyes. "I know that story: The Day Alice Came for Tea." His voice trailed off, and he began snoring softly.

"Yes, that's a good one!" The March Hare's eyes grew wide. "Do continue! Wake up, wake up!" He began shaking the little mouse violently.

"I see, I see," said the Dormouse, even though his eyes were still shut. After the March Hare gave him another good shake, he finally opened his eyes. "Where did I leave off?"

"You didn't!" the Hatter said.

"You were just starting," Emma said, "at the very beginning."

"Very good." After a pause, the Dormouse continued. "Well then, it was like this. It was teatime."

"It's always teatime!" the Mad Hatter said.

"Which proves my point! We were having tea, and up walks this beautiful young lady."

"Much prettier than you three," said the Hatter.

"How was she prettier?" asked Emma.

"I should think she was taller," the Hatter said.

"And older, but not too old," said the March Hare.

"And she had a long, white mane, like a beautiful stallion," the Dormouse said, "and she was very polite."

"Nothing like you three," the Hatter said.

"The End." The Dormouse closed his eyes.

Molly started to protest, but the mouse was already snoring again.

"I think we should go," Emma whispered. "We can talk back in the garden."

"Bye!" Aaliyah waved to the three characters, who were busy moving to new positions around the table.

"He was talking about Genevieve!" Molly said as they approached the elevator.

"Which doesn't tell us anything." Emma pushed the Down button. "Of course Genevieve was here; she was on the original team."

"I wonder how much of this was Genevieve's work?" Molly said. "This world is amazing!"

The elevator door slid open. Molly and Emma went inside, but Aaliyah held back. "I'm afraid wherever we're going won't be as nice as this."

"You can probably count on that," said Emma. "If you want to stay here, we'll come back for you. I'm sure you'll be safe."

"No, no. I want to find our friends. But I wouldn't mind coming back someday. You know, when everything is OK." Aaliyah took a last look in the tea party's direction before joining them in the elevator. She nodded to Molly, who pressed the button labeled "7."

18
Seventh Floor

THE ENGLISH GARDEN vanished, taking all the sunlight with it. At first, Molly didn't know what had happened. She seemed to be floating in a dream world, with a pitch-black sky above and a riot of surreal colors below. As her eyes adjusted, Molly realized she was still in the elevator, surrounded by a bizarre black-light landscape. The only sign of her friends was Aaliyah's disembodied grin.

"Man," Aaliyah said. "It's like we fell into a black-light poster!" The floor outside was a psychedelic mandala. Outlandish colors swirled out from the elevator in a rainbow lollipop spiral. Beyond that, wild splotches of green, orange, and red hung in the air: colorful chaos. "Groovy!"

"If you say so." Emma caught the door before it closed. "Ready to explore?" Her flashlight beam glared brightly in the elevator glass. She stepped out into the darkness, followed by Aaliyah and Molly.

The instant Molly stepped outside, harsh light flooded the scene, erasing the dreamworld. It was now a concrete circle some sixty yards in diameter, enclosed by a wall five yards high. The enormous black screen of a dormant Jumbotron loomed over one side of the wall. High above, four floodlights, suspended in impenetrable darkness, provided the lighting.

The wall encircling them was covered with poster art from a bygone age. They depicted twelve different carnival and circus scenes: games of chance, clowns, and acrobats. Molly examined a lion-tamer tableau, hoping to find the fluorescent paint. All she found was a faint shadow.

It was cast by a doorknob, expertly camouflaged in the middle of the scene. Knowing where to look enabled her to find the door in two more scenes. She was studying that third doorknob when Aaliyah walked up. "Is that a hidden door?"

Before Molly could answer, a barrage of calliope music assaulted their ears. Then the Jumbotron came to life. Against a yellow background, an animated banner arced across the screen. "WELCOME TO THE FUN HOUSE," it said in dancing, rainbow font, spewing cartoon stars and confetti.

And then gravity disappeared. The somatic feedback wasn't 100% authentic, but it didn't have to be. That weightless sensation was unmistakable. Her feet were still on the floor, but Molly knew that was just Newton's First Law: "A body at rest…" No doubt, the slightest movement would send her floating, like Aaliyah, now two feet above the floor. Aaliyah was grinning, but the view behind her was nothing to smile about.

The elevator car was flying straight up on its hydraulic cylinder, stranding them. And that cylinder was ridiculously wide, as wide as the elevator car itself. It was orders of magnitude beyond what was necessary to support that little car. There was enough steel in that cylinder to support this entire complex.

That's it! Molly realized. The elevator wasn't rising from the floor; they were falling! The floor, the wall, and the Jumbotron were all sliding down the cylinder like a firefighter on a pole. All the girls could do was watch as the elevator grew farther and farther away. Even worse, they had to listen to a slow downward glissando on a slide whistle.

This continued until the elevator was barely visible, hundreds of yards above. The falling abruptly slowed, and Molly struggled to keep her balance. She bent her knees into the fierce deceleration, bouncing back up when it stopped. She looked around, uncertain. "Whew! I expected that to be a lot worse."

"Me too!" Aaliyah said. "But I'm not complaining!"

"What the hell *was* that?" Emma said.

In response, a loud arcade game voice announced, "WELCOME, GAMERS!" It seemed to come from everywhere, but Aaliyah pointed above Molly's head. "Look!"

She was pointing at the Jumbotron. It showed three giant headshots of Aaliyah, Emma, and Molly, labeled with their first names. The screen refreshed to reveal a new image. Part map, mostly cartoon, it depicted the elevator, the cylinder, and a forlorn stick figure at the bottom. The elevator was labeled "Home," and the stick figure, "You Are Here." The only useful information was the legend by the cylinder: "45,000 Points Required."

"Is that stupid screen saying we need forty-five thousand points to reach the elevator?" Emma glared at Molly.

"I guess so. But how are we supposed to get points?"

"Maybe it's behind door number one." Aaliyah reached for the doorknob they'd discovered.

"Only look, don't go in!" Emma said. "We can't afford to get separated."

Aaliyah nodded and swung the door open. Leaning forward, she peeked inside the doorway. "Nothing here, anyway. Wait — Molly?"

"Aaliyah?" Molly had investigated her own door, two down from Aaliyah's. Inside, she found an empty circular circus tent, complete with a dirt floor. But opposite Molly, about twenty yards away, Aaliyah stood in an identical doorframe. How had Aaliyah gotten there so fast? Molly turned to her right to be sure. Aaliyah looked back at her from in front of her door.

Emma asked, "Did you guys find something?" Molly and Aaliyah both responded with blank faces. Emma narrowed her eyes. "What?"

"Come stand here." Molly indicated a spot in front of the door, being careful to block Emma's view of the doorway. "Now, wave to Aaliyah."

Emma raised her eyebrow to warn, "Don't prank me," and gave a compulsory wave in Aaliyah's direction. Aaliyah waved back with enthusiasm.

"Now," Molly said, turning Emma's shoulders to aim her into the doorway, "wave to Aaliyah."

Emma didn't. She just glared at Aaliyah, waving cheerfully from the far end of the tent. Emma stood there for some time before saying, "This floor is a total pain in the ass!"

"I think it's fun!" Aaliyah said, stepping through her doorway.

"No, don't come in!" Emma yelled, eight steps too late. "You know we can't afford to get separated!"

Aaliyah screeched to a halt in the center of the tent. Her ubiquitous smile drew into a tight hyphen.

"Don't stop now," Emma scolded. "Get over here!"

Aaliyah hurried across to join Emma and Molly outside. "You're right! That might have been an evil portal. Please don't be mad. I know I screwed up." If that made Emma any less mad, it didn't show.

"We are better as a team," Molly said.

Aaliyah placed her right hand over her heart. "I promise to stick with you guys from now on."

"Good," Emma said matter-of-factly. "We still have to find that challenge. Let's try this door next." Emma strode ahead, leading the charge and opening one door after another. They stayed close together now, and all three checked in each door Emma opened. Again and again, they encountered the same empty circus tent.

"Maybe the challenge isn't where we thought," Molly said.

"We've only got three doors left. Don't give up now!" Aaliyah said. "What do you think this crazy picture means?" It depicted a dozen children with large mallets hammering at a dozen grassy mounds.

"Oh, I may know!" Molly walked over to the door and opened it.

"You found it!" Aaliyah said. "But what is it?"

They were looking at a circular room the same size as the tents. A single spotlight cast a bright circle in the center of the floor. Its beam illuminated the only object in the room, a Whac-A-Mole table.

When Molly stepped in to investigate, the room came alive. The table began warbling a cheerful jingle, and the floor put on a light show. Molly had assumed it was a marble floor, but it was as clear as glass. Beneath it, a rainbow of concentric neon circles glowed. They paraded from the perimeter to the center in an endless cascade.

"WELCOME, MOLLY," the same arcade voice said.

"Seriously?" Emma rolled her eyes. "A children's game?"

The machine showed a "High Score" of 10,000 and a "Current Score" of zero. "I wonder if you need money to play?" Molly pressed the Start button.

At once, a plastic mole popped up. Molly grabbed the rubber mallet and easily clobbered it before it disappeared. Current Score increased to 50. Another mole appeared, and another. In no time, Molly had passed a thousand points. The little guys appeared faster and faster, sometimes in pairs. Molly smiled. "I've missed this game. It makes me feel like a kid again."

The faster the game went, the more Molly enjoyed it. She floated in an exhilarating calm, watching her own movements as if from a distance. They seemed spontaneous, responding to the game faster than Molly could direct them.

As Molly's mallet flew across the board, no one spoke. But when her score reached 9,900, Aaliyah nudged Emma and pointed at the scoreboard. It reached 10,000 and kept going. Molly seemed incapable of missing, even as the machine cranked out moles at a furious pace.

Finally, one of the little guys returned to his hole unscathed, and the game was over. The scoreboard read 21,500, which became the new

High Score. This set off loud arcade music and an impressive light show.

"That was amazing, girl!" Aaliyah said.

"Maybe now we can get out of here!" Emma had barely finished the sentence when light flooded the space. The Whac-A-Mole game disappeared, and the neon-lit floor turned to dirt. Now the girls were standing in the center of an empty circus tent. They stepped outside just in time for a new Jumbotron performance. First, it erupted in a kaleidoscope of comic-book colors. Next, it displayed an analog number counter under the legend "YOUR SCORE." The numbers started spinning like an odometer: 500, 1000, 1500, 2000, all the way to 21,500. The screen put on a final flourish of flamboyant colors and went dark.

"Now what?" Emma asked.

Aaliyah smiled with enthusiasm and a hint of mischief. "Now we go find more points. There are only two doors we haven't tried."

"But all the paintings have changed," Molly said. "The next game could be anywhere!"

The trio resumed their inspection of the doorways. They checked eleven empty tents before they opened the Strongman door. This wasn't a circus tent, or a game room, but an entire vista: sunset over the Great Plains.

Molly took one look and entered without hesitation. She stepped onto a narrow dirt road. On either side lay a giant field of wheat, reaching as far as the eye could see. Above, the sky stretched unbroken to the horizon in every direction. Across that celestial canopy, the setting sun had dragged the visible spectrum like the train of a wedding gown. Rich shades of gold, rose, and plum draped the western sky, shifting and deepening as the night drew closer.

"Well?" Emma's voice shattered the serene stillness. She was well behind Molly, still standing in the doorway with Aaliyah. The rectangle of bright artificial light stood out like an ugly scar. "I don't know what this is. Is it a portal inside a portal?"

Aaliyah took one step inside. "It sure looks like its own world."

Emma hadn't budged since opening the door. "How do we know this portal won't disappear like the others?"

"It's stayed open ever since Molly stepped through, so it's not part of Ada's revolving door. There should be a challenge in here, Emma, and we need the points." Aaliyah used her screen to create a cinder block and propped the door open. She beckoned to Emma. "We need to do this."

Emma scowled and stepped inside, and the three of them headed down the dirt road toward the waning sunset. Aaliyah started singing, sotto voce, "We're off to see the Wizard…"

"I just hope our Wicked Witch isn't watching us in her crystal ball," Molly said.

The wheat surrounding them was waist-high and beginning to mature. The stems were pale green, but the heads had ripened to a warm bronze tinged with indigo from the rapidly fading light. It was getting dark, and the doorway they entered was a distant speck behind them. Then, Aaliyah called out. "Hey, I see something."

What first appeared to be poles of various heights was, in fact, a single tall tower, surrounded by eight ten-foot-high poles. Strung with unlit electric lights, the poles lined a circular space, about twenty-five feet in diameter, carpeted with dusty straw. In the center of this circle, the tower rose twenty feet high.

It was painted a tawdry yellow and numbered in bright red by thousands, from 5,000 at the bottom to 19,000 at the top. A steel rail ran up the front of the tower, ending below a giant bell at the top.

Beside it, difficult to read in the fading light, a hand-painted sign proclaimed, "High Striker." The handle of an oversized wooden mallet was leaning against the sign. Molly was about to comment on how dark it was when the light strings sputtered to life, encasing the scene in a globe of amber light.

"WELCOME, AALIYAH," the arcade voice said.

Aaliyah grinned at Molly, but Emma shook her head in disgust. "I can't believe anyone ever left their house to do this."

Aaliyah picked up the massive mallet and positioned herself in front of the tower and the thick rubber launch pad at its base. Pulling her right foot back into a power stance, Aaliyah bounced slightly at the knees.

She held the mallet out over her target and adjusted her distance a fraction of an inch. Aaliyah rested the mallet's head on the ground and stood there, staring at the pad with fierce intensity. When she finally moved, it was a sub-second blur. The mallet landed home, the puck shot up the rail, and the bell made a deafening clang, all in a single instant.

"THAT'S TWENTY THOUSAND MORE POINTS!" announced the voice. An unseen brass band played a loud circus march, and old-fashioned ticker tape fell from the sky.

Aaliyah stared at the night sky, searching for their source, and turned in a full circle, grinning broadly. She finally dropped the heavy mallet and joined her friends. The scene around them was already disappearing. The music faded, and night became daytime. Now they were back in the center of an empty circus tent. When they stepped outside, the Jumbotron counter was tallying their new total: 41,500.

"You get a perfect score, and that's all we get?" Emma asked. "Why are you guys celebrating when we didn't even get to Forty-Five Thousand?"

"It got us super close, over 90% there," Molly said.

"You're assuming we can trust this disembodied voice," Emma said. "What if it's another of Ada's tricks? Then we're 90% nowhere! When the hell will we get off this floor?"

Aaliyah answered her. "Like my Gran says, 'in its own sweet time, and fussing about it won't change a thing!'"

Emma scowled at Aaliyah and then at Molly.

Molly's look of surprise set Emma off. "I get it. You both think I'm a jerk because I'm not having fun in the 'Fun House.' Should I forget that half of our team is missing? Would you rather I pick up a mallet and hit something?"

"That's how we get off this floor," Molly said.

"It's no different than slicing vines or fighting giant bats," Aaliyah added, "which you were great at."

"That was life and death. That was vitally important — this is just stupid and silly."

"Of course it is," Aaliyah said. "It's a big game, meant to be fun. But if we end up stranded here because someone refused to play, *that* would be stupid and silly."

Emma turned away from Aaliyah and glowered at Molly. This time, Molly tried to keep her face expressionless, but it didn't help. Emma spat out her words, "If you both think I'm stupid and silly, maybe you'd prefer to find the others on your own!"

"What?" Molly said. "I thought you wanted us to stick together!"

"What's the point when neither of you ever listens to me?" Emma turned on her heel and walked away.

"The point is, we're a family." Aaliyah walked after her. "We can't give up on each other just because we're frustrated."

"Whatever! I'm going to sit this one out!" Emma continued walking to the center of the circle, where she sat down with her back to them.

"We'll call you when we find it!" Aaliyah said.

"Whatever!"

Aaliyah turned to Molly. "You think I'm too hard on her." She kept her voice low, even though Emma was thirty yards away.

"It's not that. I'm worried that getting 45,000 points won't be enough. What if each of us has to complete a challenge?"

"Oh." Aaliyah's eyes grew wide, and she glanced back at Emma. "Then we may be here awhile."

19
Sixth Floor?

MOLLY LOOKED AROUND the courtyard at the current selection of circus art. "We need to find that next challenge now! Why don't we split up so we find it faster?"

Aaliyah pointed to the poster of a "human cannonball" in front of her. "I'll start here and go counterclockwise."

"I'll take the juggler." Molly indicated the scene next to it, a man juggling balls, then plates, and finally tomahawks. But it held only an empty tent, as did the next two posters. Then she tried an outdoor scene of men and women in their finest clothes, bowling tenpins.

Behind that door, Edison light bulbs glowed in ornate sockets. Their yellow light illuminated elaborate hand-drawn signs. Near the center of the room sat a game of skill, an ancient version of one she knew well. "Here it is!" Molly yelled. "Have you guys ever played Skee-Ball?"

"Not since I was a little kid." Aaliyah was walking over from the opposite side of the courtyard.

"Let me see." Emma reached the door first and marched in. She didn't stop until she was six feet from the game, where she stood staring at it.

"WELCOME, EMMA!" announced the voice.

Emma slowly circled the game, studying every detail. "Wow! This machine is from the 1920s, with the mechanical scoreboard! I've always wanted to play one of these!" She was actually grinning.

Aaliyah dropped her jaw in pretend shock. "Did you just use the word 'play' in a sentence? I don't believe it!"

"Princeton had one of the first Skee-Ball arcades ever, in 1913. This is amazing!"

"It's nice to see you smile again. Did you see the sign?" Molly pointed to the sign nearest the game. Its ornate script read:

A Frame is 9 Balls

First Frame is Practice

Your Score = Second Frame x 50

Emma studied the sign for some time before she stirred. "Excellent," she said. Turning to the machine, she pulled the lever on its left side, and nine wooden balls rolled down the ball return. Emma grabbed a ball in each hand, paused for a beat, and then launched the ball in her right hand. It flew straight down the middle of the alley, shot up the ramp, and disappeared into the highest-scoring hole. Fifty points.

In one smooth motion, Emma transferred the second ball to her right hand and sent it flying. It sped down the identical path but fell just short of the goal, scoring forty points. After seven more balls, Emma had rolled four 50's and five 40's for a frame total of 400.

Molly pumped her fist in celebration but didn't make a sound. Aaliyah noticed and nodded her approval. Cheering might weaken the fierce concentration emanating from Emma like a protective aura. Emma continued her campaign in silence, and this time, rolled seven 50's and two 40's for a score of 430.

Now her friends cheered. "Four Thirty out of Four Fifty! Girl, you truly are a Skee Ball Freak." Aaliyah offered her palm for a high-five. Emma blushed, smiled, and smacked Aaliyah's palm.

"TWENTY-ONE THOUSAND FIVE HUNDRED TOTAL POINTS!" interrupted the Fun House, "AND A FREE PASS HOME!" The antique Skee-Ball machine faded away, followed by the handwritten signs and ancient lightbulbs.

Then the girls were standing in the Fun House courtyard, bombarded by loud calliope music. The Jumbotron began tallying their points, which Molly knew would total 63,000. But at 45,000 points, the floor hurtled upwards, pressing the girls down with several G's of inertial force. Finally, it decelerated, and the pressure subsided.

Molly walked to the elevator and pushed the Down button. "I just noticed something. On this floor, the call buttons are mounted on the car."

"That makes sense," Aaliyah said. "It kept us from calling the car back before we'd won enough points." The door opened, and they both walked inside.

But Emma didn't move. "I need to say something. Molly, Aaliyah, I'm sorry."

They both stepped out of the elevator. Aaliyah flashed her trademark smile and raised her hands in a "forget it" gesture. "We're good," she said. Molly nodded her agreement.

"You were right to call me out earlier," Emma said. "My attitude sucked, and I was holding us back. Then this arcade popped up with the one machine I'd always dreamed of playing. That can't be a coincidence."

"Like it read your mind," Molly said.

"I wonder," Aaliyah said, "because it knew I enjoy testing my strength, and Molly loves clobbering moles! Do you think the BCI cap allows the computer to guess our favorite games?"

"I suspect it analyzed our reactions to the carnival art. You probably didn't notice, but I kept looking at that ten-pin poster. Just like you said, it wanted us to have fun!" Emma pushed the Down button, and this time they all got in the elevator. "I'm sorry I fussed at you guys."

"So you're not striking out on your own?" Molly asked.

"Of course not! I shouldn't have said that. I was just being a drama queen."

"Forget about it. I have." Aaliyah pointed to the control panel. "Do you want to do the honors?"

Emma nodded sheepishly and hit the "6" button.

The elevator went dark. When the door opened, it revealed only more darkness. "Oh no!" Molly said. "Are we outside the Warehouse? Is there even gravity out there?"

"Let's shine some light on things." Aaliyah retrieved a flashlight in her hand. Its beam illuminated a long runner in the style of a Persian rug. Additional runners branched off it on either side, and those had their own branches. It was a gigantic crossword of rugs floating in the darkness of space.

"Are they really floating out there?" Emma created another flashlight and tossed it out of the elevator. It followed a natural arc down to the rug, bounced twice, and somersaulted over the side. It hurtled down, gyrating into a black abyss. A second later, it crashed and went dark.

"Well, that's good news!" Aaliyah said. "We're still in the Sandbox."

"That is good news," Molly said. "The bad news is we can't explore this world without walking on floating carpets over a giant pit." At this moment, the elevator door tried to shut, but Molly punched the Open Door button.

"So why explore it at all?" Emma said. "We can't help Katrina and the others if we end up broken on the floor like that flashlight. We should concentrate on finding them, and I'm willing to bet none of them are on these floating carpets."

"This has to be one of Ada's tricks!" Molly said. "I can't believe the developers would have built something this dangerous."

"Me neither," Emma said. "All the more reason to move on to the next floor."

"So we're only searching safe places?" Aaliyah asked. "That's not the best way to find our friends. We need to search the scary places, too."

Molly nodded emphatically. “Especially the scary places! If Ada doesn’t want us to look here, I want to know why.”

“OK, OK!” Emma waved her hands in surrender. “You had me at ‘find our friends.’ I’m in! But only if we can do it safely.”

“Which could be a big if!” Facing the open door, Aaliyah gripped the left handrail. She swung her right foot out to the center of the Persian rug. “Let’s see how much weight this rug will take.”

Aaliyah gradually transferred more and more weight to her right foot. Then she lifted her left foot and bounced up and down on the rug. “It’s really solid — no give at all. It should be safe with the right safety gear.”

“What kind of safety gear do we need?” Molly asked.

“We need to form a three-person rope team, so climbing rope, harnesses, and carabiners. It won’t hurt to have hiking headlamps and leather gloves, too.”

“Wow,” Molly said, “Do you know how to rock climb?”

“I do, and I’ll make sure you’re both safe.” Aaliyah stared into the space between Molly and Emma, creating a harness there. “This is the belt I wear for rope climbing. You put it on like shorts: your legs go through these loops, and the top fastens like a belt. It’s designed to handle one and a half tons — it’s crazy strong!” She handed the harness to Emma and then made two more.

Aaliyah put hers on, explaining how to adjust and fasten it. “Now put yours on, and I’ll check them for you.” After some minor adjustments, she explained how to use the rest of their gear. “It’s super simple. We secure the rope to this carabiner and lock the carabiner on your harness. These gloves will protect your hands from rope burns. We’ll walk about four yards apart with five yards of rope between us.”

“Can I lead?” Emma asked Aaliyah. “I think I’d rather depend on you to stop my fall than the other way around.”

"You can lead. I was planning to take the middle position so I'd have a direct line to each of you. I'll keep you both safe." She hooked herself to Molly and Emma. "Emma, hold my hand for your first step. Don't let go until you're ready to go forward."

Holding Aaliyah's hand, Emma stepped out of the elevator and used her left hand to turn on her headlamp. "It feels sturdy. I think you can let go of my hand and give me a little rope. Let's try this." As soon as her right hand was free, Emma filled it with a flashlight.

"Okay," Aaliyah said. "Take six steps and stop, please." Emma took her first step, paused, then took five more. More and more rope ran through Aaliyah's gloved hands. As Emma receded into the darkness, Molly forgot to breathe. Now her friend was a distant silhouette, glowing in the darkness.

Aaliyah turned to Molly. "My job with this rope is to secure Emma if she actually falls. The trick is to control the rope with your hands so it can't knock you off your feet. You want slack on both ends like this." She fed out more rope to create the proper slack. "Got it?"

"Got it!" Molly said. Aaliyah turned on her headlamp, so Molly did the same.

"Emma," Aaliyah said, "take another six steps and stop again." This time, both girls walked forward, leaving Molly alone in the elevator. Aaliyah took five steps to Emma's six. "Molly, just tell us when you're ready to go."

"I'm ready!" Molly kept her eyes on Aaliyah and stepped out of the elevator in sync with her. Emma had been right — the rug was so solid it could have been on concrete.

When Emma reached the first runner crossing, she stopped and asked if she should turn.

Molly created a flashlight and panned the beam from left to right. "Do you guys see anything interesting on either side?" All three girls used their flashlights to scan in every direction. Seeing nothing, they decided to keep going straight. When Emma took her fourth step, she plummeted through the rug.

"Emma!" Aaliyah shouted, straining against the now taut rope, but there was no reply, only silence and a hole where Emma should have been. What remained of the rug hung limp over the far edge. Molly's stomach knotted as she braced for the sound of Emma hitting the distant floor. But it was only Emma's flashlight that shattered there, a clanging cymbal that echoed in the distant corners of this space. Then everything was silent until Aaliyah called out, "Emma, are you okay?"

Emma didn't answer at first, or perhaps she was too quiet to hear. Then, barely audible, a long string of whispered okay's floated up from below. " … ok, ok, ok. Okay. I'm, I'm okay."

Aaliyah planted her feet and shifted her weight to her back foot. "Help me, Molly. No, the other way, go back! Back up until there's no slack. Emma, we've got you, girl. You're safe in that harness, and we'll have you back here in no time."

"I know," the little voice responded. "I'm just embarrassed. I thought I saw something out there and got careless. I put all my weight on the rug without testing it. And there was nothing under there."

"A booby trap!" Aaliyah began to pull the rope a few inches at a time. "Don't worry. You're doing great. Just catch your breath while we pull you out. There you go."

Emma's head popped up a few seconds later. Aaliyah hoisted her a little further, then grabbed her hand and pulled her up on her feet. After they backed away from the hole, Emma held Aaliyah's hand with both of hers and stood there shaking. "I promise I'll let go soon, but I need a minute."

"Take as long as you need."

Some time passed before anyone moved. "I think I'm okay now. Thanks, Aaliyah." Emma used her left hand to straighten her clothes while still gripping Aaliyah's hand with her right.

"Take your time," Molly said.

"That's right," Aaliyah said. "We could all use a little break, anyway."

"I'm fine, Aaliyah. I swear." Emma released Aaliyah's hand and smiled stiffly. "Besides, when I was hanging down there, I saw something in the darkness. A faint glimmer, far away, in that direction." She pointed to Aaliyah's right. "I think we should have turned to the right at that rug back there."

"Okay. We'll go that way once you're sure you're ready."

"I'm sure."

Molly was only a yard from the rug Emma mentioned. "Do you want me to lead? I'll be super careful now that we know there are traps."

"Go ahead," Aaliyah said. Emma nodded her approval.

As they headed out, Emma made another flashlight and began searching for the glimmer she had seen. After several minutes, she said, "Hey, stop for a second. My beam is casting shadows."

Molly searched the darkness. "I see it! Move your beam, and let's see if the shadows move."

"They didn't," Emma said.

"I'm pretty sure those aren't shadows." Molly cast her beam in the same direction. "I think it's something painted black. Is it a spiral staircase?"

As if they'd practiced it, Emma and Molly shifted their combined beams upward. "It is!" Emma said. "It's a spiral staircase, and it leads to the rugs." In the distance, quivering in the handheld light, was a landing, painted jet black.

"Good find, Emma," Aaliyah said.

"Except this isn't what I saw earlier. That was a faint glow down there, past the staircase."

"Well, if we investigate the staircase," Aaliyah said, "we'll be that much closer to the glow."

After crisscrossing half a mile of magic carpets, they reached their goal, a barely visible platform surrounding the staircase. Only at close range did their beams reveal the black guardrails. Their rug was one of four that met at the landing like the four points of a compass. Molly stood on the platform and aimed her flashlight over the guardrail. The staircase spiraled downward, growing tighter and tighter, seemingly forever.

"I know Ada is tricky, but I still feel safer standing on this steel platform." Emma started to unbuckle her harness, but Aaliyah spoke up.

"I wouldn't do that, Emma. As long as we're high up, we're safer with the gear on."

Emma tightened her harness back up. "We're definitely high up, and we've got a long way to go. Okay, follow me!"

"I'm glad we don't get tired in here," Molly said. "I feel like we've been going down these stairs for days."

"And I'm glad you said that first!" Emma said. "I vowed not to complain anymore, but this might force me to make an exception."

"Hey! Do you guys see that? I think that's a portal down there." In her excitement, Aaliyah had become breathless again.

They stopped to peer over the rail. "Where?" Emma asked. Aaliyah pointed down into the darkness, and then Emma pointed, too. "I see it! Look, Molly!"

"I see it, but it's so dim I can't tell what it is or even where."

"Come on, girls," Aaliyah said, "let's get down there!"

"What happened to climbing safety?" Emma asked.

"Ha, you're right — let's get down there *safely!*"

Several minutes later, Emma said, "We're almost there! I see the floor."

It wasn't long before Molly was standing on solid ground at the base of the staircase. She slipped off her harness and set it down next to Aaliyah's and Emma's.

Aaliyah pointed with her flashlight to a pair of oval lights in the distance. "There's our goal. I didn't think it would be so far away!" She started walking in that direction, and Molly and Emma fell in behind her. Their goal seemed to change size, shape, and number as they approached. At first, there were two small oval lights ahead. As they got closer, those ovals waned into crescent shapes. Later, a third sliver appeared and slowly grew more oval.

Now Aaliyah trotted ahead, quickly covering the distance. "I knew it!" she said. "I knew I saw a portal!"

20
Six Portals

MOLLY FINALLY GOT close enough to see what had her friend so excited. Aaliyah was standing on a raised platform, surrounded by a ring of portals. "Watch your step," she said, training her flashlight beam on the edge of the platform. The step was six inches up to a circular platform about eighteen feet in diameter. Six oval portals floated directly above the perimeter of the platform.

Unlike the portals they'd encountered so far, these appeared to be permanent, but they were similar in having only two dimensions. From the back, they were dark. From the side, they disappeared. But from inside the circle, they displayed their six worlds like a hall of magic mirrors.

Emma immediately headed for one world in particular, a faithful copy of the Moon's surface, complete with a lunar lander, the American flag, and an amazing earthrise. "Tranquility Base!"

For Molly, this portal was almost too realistic: the desolation of the Moon, the jewel-like beauty of our tiny home, and the cold vastness of space. She gravitated to the portal on its right, a postcard-perfect Netherlands scene with a windmill and gorgeous tulips. As soon as she walked up to it, Aaliyah cried out.

"What was that?" Aaliyah pointed to the left of Tranquility Base. That portal displayed a flyover view of a winding river canyon. The red sandstone formations made for a spectacular scene, but it was nothing to shout about. Then Aaliyah shouted again, "There! Did you see it?"

Molly did see something: a blur that flashed across the very bottom of the portal. And then it appeared again, almost long enough to recognize. It was dark brown, possibly feathered, and round.

Emma had joined them. "Was that…"

Suddenly, the entire head rose up and turned, revealing its meat-hook beak and its huge, unblinking yellow eye. They were looking at the massive neck and head of a giant eagle. Did it see them? All three girls jumped back, but Molly never took her eyes off that portal.

A second later, the view returned to sky and landscape. It was several more seconds before Molly could speak. "That's insane! How did they ever program that?"

"*Why* would they ever program that?" Emma asked. "Is this a normal portal? Can I really walk out on that eagle's back?"

"Maybe it's a window, not a door," Molly said.

"I wonder." Aaliyah leaned her head and shoulders into the portal.

"Aaliyah!" Molly yelled.

Aaliyah emerged with wide eyes and blown-back hair. "It's a door!"

Emma shook her head. "I can't decide if you're the bravest person I know or the craziest!"

Aaliyah laughed. "That was insane! But we still have five new places to search for our friends. Where should we start?"

That's a good question, Molly thought. What were their choices? The Dutch landscape seemed huge; maybe their friends were there. And there were three portals she had ignored so far. One was dark, and she'd prefer to wait until daytime to explore it. Next to it was a rocky ocean shore where cold waves pounded the beach, seagulls dove for fish, and a distant lighthouse cast its beam into the gray early morning.

And there was this portal into the Louvre Museum. Something at the back of the scene caught Molly's eye. "That Mona Lisa is amazing!"

She leaned in for a better view, but Emma stopped her with a firm hand on her shoulder.

"Not you, too!" Emma said. "At least Aaliyah only stuck her head in the portal."

Molly looked down and discovered she already had one foot inside that world. "Oh!" She pulled it back. "I thought I was still standing back there." Molly used her flashlight as a pointer to illuminate a spot about a yard behind her. That's when she noticed something strange. "What's this?" Someone had scratched an arrow pointing to the Louvre with an X through the arrow.

After Aaliyah and Emma studied it, they searched the floor with their flashlights. "Exact same mark in front of the windmills and the lighthouse," Emma said. "What do you think it means?"

"Look at this!" Aaliyah held up a small rock. "I found it here, in front of the nighttime portal. I bet it made all the marks. And this mark is different, just an arrow."

Molly noticed the rock was scraped flat on one side. "Where did they get a rock?"

Emma examined it. "That's an igneous rock, so it probably came from here." She walked to the moon portal, looked down, and stiffened. "Oh, my God — we totally missed this!" She pointed straight down, inside the portal. There, drawn in the lunar dust, was an arrow pointing out of the portal and the message: "Check floor to follow — JBT."

"Jo Beth Taylor. She was here!" Molly said. "She used a moon rock to make these marks for us. But what do they mean?"

Aaliyah pointed to the moon message. "See how she pointed this arrow straight at the windmill portal? What if she went in there but returned? That would explain the X through the arrow."

Molly nodded. "The same markings are in front of the lighthouse and the Louvre! That would mean she went in and came out of these. But the nighttime portal has an arrow with no X, which makes me think she's still in there!" Molly shone her flashlight into the portal. In the flashlight's glare, the nighttime world wasn't nighttime at all, but a cross-section of a giant tree trunk, with clearly visible tree rings. "Whoa!"

Aaliyah rapped her knuckles against the wood; the only sound was a dull thud. She knelt to inspect the wood. "It's solid, all right, but the texture is too smooth. It feels like glass, not wood."

"I wonder if it has any give," Molly said, pushing against it with one hand.

"Let's try it together." Aaliyah leaned into the surface, and Molly joined her. "On three: one, two, three!" They strained against the wood, but it refused to give even a millimeter.

"You know what I think?" Molly asked.

"That a giant tree fell across the portal?" Aaliyah said.

"Right. Jo Beth used the portal, but this tree fell and trapped her there."

"I'm afraid you're right," said Emma, "but I don't know how we're getting past it."

"Well, I do!" Aaliyah already had her screen up and was typing as she spoke. "I'm making us a big chainsaw."

"You'd better make us a big lumberjack to run it." Emma had to yell the last two words because Aaliyah had already fired up her saw.

Aaliyah was wearing earplugs and safety goggles, and two more sets lay on the floor. She spotlighted them with her headband lamp and yelled, "You'll want to put those on and stand clear." Molly shared the protective gear with Emma, and they both opted to put in the earplugs first. But the plugs only reduced the noise from painful to deafening.

Molly was lighting the portal with her flashlight when a bright light suddenly appeared near it. Emma had retrieved one of the halogen work lamps from the Throne Room. "I remembered their object name from deleting them," Emma shouted.

Molly assumed that Aaliyah would cut the entire trunk in a wide circle and let it fall out of the way. Instead, she made all her cuts on the very left of the portal. It seemed an odd way to fell a tree, but then a jagged cone of wood fell away. Molly flashed a thumbs-up to her friend, who grinned and went back to work.

Aaliyah kept working on the left side, tunneling down through the side of the tree. She didn't stop until she'd exposed the ground below. While Molly was taking out her earplugs, Emma spoke up. "You expect us to crawl through that measly little hole?"

Aaliyah put down her saw, then removed her headlamp, earplugs, and goggles. "I'd like you to come, but you can stay behind if you want." She reached into the hole with both hands, followed by her head and torso. She leaned in so far that her feet left the ground; then she was gone.

Emma expelled her breath in an aggravated huff. She leaned into the hole. "Is it safe out there?"

"It's beautiful. Come on down!"

After helping Emma ease down the hole feet first, Molly dove in headfirst. She landed softly in a thick pile of pine straw. The tree they had traveled through was huge, easily nine feet in diameter. Its root ball, directly ahead of them, rose over fifteen feet in the air. Behind them, the tip of the tree was about ninety yards away.

"Are these giant redwoods?" Molly asked.

"I think they're giant firs," Aaliyah answered. "Whatever they are, we don't have them in Georgia. I knew slicing it in two wouldn't do any good. It weighs way too much."

"Right," Emma said. "I get that now. We were lucky that you know how to use a chainsaw."

Aaliyah suddenly cocked her head to the side. "I thought I heard something." The girls froze, but even the birds had gone silent. Molly was about to say something when she heard it: twigs snapping in the distance. "Oh," Aaliyah whispered, "something large." Molly wondered if climbing the root ball would protect them. She pointed at it, and Aaliyah nodded. "Unless it's a cat species or a bear, we should be safe up there," she whispered. "Here." She dropped to one knee and interlaced her fingers to offer Molly a boost.

While Molly was placing her foot, Emma scurried up to the top of the trunk by herself. "Hurry, you guys," she ordered in a raspy whisper.

Molly pulled herself to the top and landed inches away from Emma's newly created sword. "Be careful with that thing!"

"Oops, I'm sorry." Emma, hugging the trunk for dear life, didn't look back. "Aaliyah, what could it be besides a bear or cat species?"

Aaliyah gracefully mounted the trunk and crouched beside them. "Let's see: fox, coyote, wild boar, wolf..."

"That's enough, thanks," Emma interrupted. "Do you see it?"

"Look!" Aaliyah pointed behind Emma.

There in the tall grass, hand up to shield her eyes from the sun, was Jo Beth. "Is it really you, Aaliyah? And you brought Molly! How did you guys get here?"

"Emma's here too! I cut a hole in the tree — come on around, and we'll show you the portal."

As Jo Beth made her way around the root ball, Aaliyah leapt off the trunk to meet her. Emma descended much slower than she had ascended.

That gave Molly plenty of time to observe Jo Beth from a distance. She had never seen Jo Beth looking less than perfect: every hair in place, the cutest clothes and shoes. Now her clothes were ragged, her face scratched, and her hair wild and dirty. *If Jo Beth survived looking like this, what had happened to Claire?*

"Oh, am I glad to see you guys!" Jo Beth ran up to Aaliyah and hugged her. "I thought I heard a chainsaw, but how were you able to make one without your terminal screen?"

"We created new screens in the Sandbox to replace the ones that don't work in here." Aaliyah demonstrated by retrieving her screen.

"It turns out our Aaliyah is an amateur lumberjack," Emma said.

"Thank God," said Jo Beth. "I had no way to get out of here, and Claire is probably still in the eagle world."

"The eagle world!" Molly said. "Why would she go in there?"

"That's where the Warehouse door sent us! One second, we're in the clubhouse, and the next, it's pitch dark, and we're falling off a twenty-five-foot-tall eagle. Imagine if it hadn't been asleep in its nest — if it had been flying!"

"The portal is always on its back?" Molly asked.

"Crazy, right? It sits up there like a saddle. We were calling it a door, but 'portal' is better. The only way to escape was to wait for the eagle to fall asleep and climb up its back. We had just reached the portal when the eagle moved, and Claire slid back down. I had to decide fast if I should stay with my buddy or go for help. I decided wrong, but at least I left Claire a message in case she got out."

"It's a good thing you did, or we never would have cut through this monster tree," Emma said. "How did you get trapped here?"

"I was sure one of these portals would lead me back to the clubhouse, but they didn't. I couldn't even breathe in the moonscape, and the rest were all smaller than they looked. This was the only world where I walked a good mile before I reached the end. Heading back here, I heard this tree fall, and then I discovered it had taken out the portal."

"How long ago was that?" Molly asked.

"I have no idea! It's always daytime in here, so I wouldn't know. It seemed like months! Thank God you guys found me!"

When they were all back through the portal, Jo Beth asked, "How did you guys get here? Is there a seventh portal that I missed?"

"No," Aaliyah said. "Well, yes, but it's disguised as an elevator. Plus, this floor is gigantic, always dark, and the elevator is at the farthest end."

"What do you mean, 'this floor?'"

"This is one of eight floors of the Warehouse," Molly said, "and we think each floor is a different world."

"The Warehouse is a building?"

"It is," Emma said, "if a one-story building can have eight floors! We can tell you what we've seen, but it's not going to make any sense."

"I can't wait to hear that, but let's rescue Claire first, so you only have to tell it once." Jo Beth nodded at the portal. The sun had slipped behind the mountains, casting a shimmering salmon hue over the canyon.

"What a gorgeous sunset!" Molly said.

"And it's a good sign," said Jo Beth. "The eagle should be heading home soon. In the meantime, let's make some rope and some spears."

"Here's ten meters of climbing rope." Aaliyah had created a new instance of rope. "What length do you want?"

"And here are your spears." Molly held out three copies of the spear she'd made to battle bats.

"Whoa!" Jo Beth said. "Someone got a serious powers upgrade while I was away! How are you guys doing that?"

"We discovered you don't need the screen to retrieve an object that you created," Molly said.

"And you made spears? You, Molly Williams? What the Hell!"

"Yes, she did," said Emma. "While you guys were fighting a giant eagle, we were fighting giant bats."

"And our bats seemed to be immortal," Aaliyah said. "I bet your eagle is, too."

"Oh! That hadn't occurred to me." Jo Beth let the spear sag toward the floor. "But I'd still like to stab it, on general principle."

"I get that," Molly said. "We'll be having bat nightmares the rest of our lives, but the most important thing now is to save Claire."

"And the portal is part of the eagle," Emma said. "Damaging the eagle might close the portal."

Jo Beth's mouth fell open. "I also hadn't thought of that!" She turned to stare at the portal. "So we'll need to outsmart that bird. And soon, because it's heading home."

The portal had darkened so much that the rock wall ahead was barely visible. Then the entire scene slid to the side. The surging river appeared again, framed by the canyon walls, one radiant in the warm tones of the sunset, the other in shadow. The eagle had reversed course.

21
The Rescue

THE GREAT BIRD was descending, and there was its destination. The craggy mountain outcropping glowed like molten iron in the fading light. "Be ready, Molly," Jo Beth said. "Claire should be hiding near the nest."

What nest? Molly thought, but it soon appeared, growing closer and closer. An instant later, it fell away as the eagle braked with its wings, aiming the portal skyward. Then the view careened up and down several times before it steadied. The bird had settled into its nest.

"Oh, I see Claire!" Emma pointed. "Go, Molly!"

Molly stuck her flashlight into the portal and waved it left and right.

"Careful!" Jo Beth said. "Don't let your beam hit the ground!"

"I didn't." Molly stepped back from the portal.

Emma kept pointing to a spot twenty yards from the nest. "There, do you see her, Jo Beth?"

"Oh! I do! She's okay! And now she's looking right at us! She must have seen the flashlight! This is going to work! We're going to save her! We..." Jo Beth turned to Molly with pleading eyes. "You'll tell her about the tree, right? You'll explain that I would have come sooner if it hadn't been for that tree?"

"I could just show her the tree trunk, but I won't have to. Claire trusts you."

Jo Beth's eyes posed an unspoken question: Do *you* trust me?

Good question. It was hard to look at her, disheveled, bruised, and dirty, without feeling compassion, but compassion was not the same as trust. Molly remained silent.

Jo Beth didn't seem upset. Rather, she smiled bravely and nodded. She knew where things stood. "So, what was your peaceful rescue plan?"

Aaliyah said, "Couldn't we build a bridge from here, through the portal, to the ground near Claire?"

"That's a good idea, but it would be right over the eagle's head, and it's a very light sleeper!"

"Well, I could build the structure behind the bird's back so it won't see it." Emma pulled up her screen and mentally sketched on it. "We could have a catwalk that led to the front of the portal."

Jo Beth nodded. "Not bad. How fast could you do all that?"

"Real fast. Maybe ten minutes."

Jo Beth winced and shook her head. "Ten seconds is what we need. It's like that bird has a built-in motion detector. I wish the bridge were stored in memory so we could retrieve it in one piece."

Molly pointed to the tree world portal. "You could build it in there and store it in memory."

"I can give you the dimensions," Jo Beth said.

Emma nodded. "That's a great idea, Molly. Jo Beth and I will do that while you and Aaliyah keep an eye on that bird."

Molly examined the tree world portal one more time. *Why weren't they finished yet?* She turned back to the eagle portal, which was now black as pitch. Molly sighed. *What good is a lookout when it's too dark to see anything?*

But Molly did see something: not so much a shape as a movement. A small ripple in the darkness scurried across the portal before stepping through. It was Lemon Drop! After looking from side to side, she headed straight for Molly and began rubbing against her leg. Once Molly recovered from the shock, she focused on the thick purple and white leash tied to the cat. Where had she seen that before?

Then the leash grew taut and yanked Lemon Drop into Molly's knee. The cat seemed to blame Molly for this and took a swipe at her. Either Claire had declawed Lemon Drop, or virtual claws don't hurt. Molly realized what the leash was and grabbed it before it pulled Lemon Drop back through the portal. "Aaliyah, grab this rope! Claire is using it to climb up here."

Aaliyah didn't have to be asked twice. She grabbed the leash near the portal. "I've got this for now, Molly. Untie Lemon Drop and come help me. If that eagle wakes up, we might need to pull Claire in fast!"

Molly quickly freed the cat and took hold of the rope. Aaliyah continued to supply most of the muscle; so far, she didn't need Molly's help. Molly was watching Lemon Drop licking her paws when Aaliyah screamed.

A large yellow eye now filled the portal. Molly grabbed the halogen work light with her left hand while keeping her right hand tight around the rope. She aimed the beam into the gigantic eye. At once, the eye's nictitating membrane slid across the entire surface. Nature's version of a tinted windshield, it would protect the eagle from the bright light. Molly's heart sank, but she kept the beam centered on the dark pupil. After an agonizing pause, the eagle did draw back from the portal and out of sight.

"Let's pull her in here!" Aaliyah said, so Molly released the work lamp and grabbed the rope with both hands. Aaliyah started backing toward her, and then they were both speedwalking backward.

Claire came flying through the portal but somehow nailed the landing. She stood there grinning at her friends. "Nice work, you guys! I was about to give up when I saw you were ready with that light!"

“We weren’t ready at all!” Aaliyah laughed. “That was just quick thinking on Molly’s part.”

“I’m so glad it worked!” Molly said. “Nice rope climbing, by the way.”

“Thanks!” Claire laughed and gave them each a big hug. “Boy, am I glad to see you guys!” She knelt and petted her cat, who responded by stretching into her and purring loudly. “I bet you were surprised to see ol’ Lemon Drop!”

“I sure was, but I’m not surprised you figured things out,” Molly said.

“You discovered you don’t need your screen to retrieve an object you created,” Aaliyah said.

“Actually, Lemon Drop gets all the credit for that. After our escape attempt, that eagle went on high alert. I expected to become birdseed any minute. Things got so awful that I had a good cry. Next thing I knew, my kitty was nuzzling against me to cheer me up. I had wished her into existence!”

Molly picked up the purple and white rope. “Making a rope out of your castle banners was genius.”

“Thanks, but by the time I finally figured out how to make a good rope, I’d given up being rescued. Still, it seemed better to keep busy than admit the situation was hopeless.”

“But it wasn’t hopeless,” Aaliyah said. “We weren’t giving up until we found you!”

“Did Jo Beth say I’d be hard to find? That’s strange!” Claire turned back and forth, looking in every direction. “Hey, where is Jo Beth?”

“She’s in that tree world helping Emma plan your rescue,” Molly said.

“Why didn’t she do that before she brought you here?”

“She didn’t bring us here,” Aaliyah said. “We came looking for both of you.”

"Jo Beth did go for help," Molly said, "but all these portals were dead ends. Before she could come back to you, a tree fell over that one and trapped her there."

"It took us days to find this place and a lot of detective work to find her," Aaliyah said. "And then she told us you were in the eagle world."

"Can someone give me a hand, please?" Emma's head was sticking out of the tree portal. Aaliyah was nearest and hoisted Emma out of the hole with ease. Emma was wiping the sawdust off her clothes before she noticed Claire. "Wha..."

"Shh," Claire whispered, with a finger over her lips. "I want to surprise Jo Beth!"

But it was too late. Jo Beth had been right behind Emma and was almost out of the hole. "Oh, my God!" was all she said. She hugged Claire for a long time.

When the hug was over, Jo Beth said, "You know I would have come back for you if I hadn't been trapped, right? I never quit trying to find a way back here."

"I know that," Claire said. "Which was more frightening because I was afraid you had died!"

"Nope, still alive and meaner than ever."

"Now," Molly said, "we just need to find Katrina."

"I'm ready." Claire pointed at the portals. "Are you sure she's not in one of these other worlds?"

"I'm sure she's not because I searched every one of them," Jo Beth said. "Hopefully, we'll find her with the elevator you guys found."

"An elevator! Where is it?" Claire asked.

"Would you believe, up a kilometer-long spiral staircase and across a maze of floating carpets?" Emma asked.

Jo Beth laughed. "That sounds like fun!"

"But I'm afraid it's no place for a kitty. Come here, Lemon Drop." Claire picked her up and gazed into her eyes. "You know you're stored in permanent memory, so this isn't goodbye. Thank you for rescuing me!" She set her down and watched her disappear.

"Here you go, guys." Aaliyah handed flashlights and hiking headlamps to Jo Beth and Claire. "The staircase is this way."

Claire was sweeping her flashlight beam back and forth where Aaliyah had pointed. "I don't think it's there anymore."

"It's there," Aaliyah said, "but it's a couple hundred yards away, and it's painted matte black!"

"For real?" Jo Beth asked. "And you were serious about it being a kilometer long?"

"Yep," Emma said. "I was guessing, but it took forever to get down it."

"But you were kidding about the maze of floating carpets," Claire said, "right?"

"No, it's really there, and it's really dangerous," Emma said. "That's why Aaliyah's going to make us all wear climbing harnesses."

"I think it's safe until we reach the top," Aaliyah said. "Then I'll outfit us with gear."

Soon, the girls were heading up the nearly invisible staircase with Molly in the lead. She tried to ignore Claire and Jo Beth's flashlight beams, darting everywhere in search of something besides empty darkness.

"I still don't understand," Claire said, "how can one door send us to three completely different places. It's like someone was messing with us."

"Someone was messing with us," Aaliyah said, "and we met her. Her name is Ada, and she wants us out."

"Seriously?" Claire asked.

"Wait, not Ada like Lovelace?" Jo Beth asked.

"You guessed it!" Aaliyah said. "She's a simulacrum that looks exactly like the paintings. This Ada is loose in the Warehouse, and she has god-like power."

"She admitted capturing Genevieve and said we must give up our rescue or 'face destruction,'" Emma said.

"So you think she deliberately separated us?" Claire asked.

"Why else rig the portal to access a different world every four seconds?" Aaliyah asked.

"Ada changed the Warehouse portal," Molly said, "right as the five of us went through."

"So she looks like a nineteenth-century mathematician," Jo Beth said. "But she's actually a killer robot, sending us to a giant eagle and you guys to giant bats."

"Giant bats!" Claire's shrill voice echoed in the dark.

"It wasn't that bad," Molly lied, not slowing her ascent up the steps. "It was scary, but Emma and Aaliyah built us a fort in the blink of an eye, and we were perfectly safe inside."

Jo Beth and Claire were full of questions, and on their trip up the stairs, their friends answered most of them.

"Why in the world would anyone create a character like Ada?" Jo Beth asked.

"I'm sure it wasn't intentional," Emma said. "Coding a personality construct would be a Herculean task. It's no wonder a logic error slipped in."

"Yeah!" Aaliyah said. "An extinction-level logic error."

When Molly reached the steel platform, she lit it with her flashlight for the others. "Be careful! We won't cross until Aaliyah has us all in climbing gear."

Claire and Jo Beth were next on the platform. They stood on either side of Molly, tracing the rugs with their flashlight beams. "This is insane!" Jo Beth said. "Are you sure it's safe to walk on those things?"

"No," Emma said, joining them. "It's dangerous as Hell, and I nearly died! Aaliyah's know-how is the only thing that kept me from being a greasy spot on the floor. So I'd recommend doing exactly what she says."

Aaliyah took that opportunity to create their climbing gear and explain how to use it. She appointed Molly the lead, followed by Claire, Emma, and Jo Beth. "I'll bring up the rear and help you with your spacing."

Then they were on their way, connected by climbing rope and harnesses. Molly had worried she wouldn't remember the path home, but she had no trouble retracing their steps. It seemed like only a few minutes before the elevator was straight ahead.

"Hey, guys," Aaliyah yelled from the rear. "It will be safest if you leave your harness on and roll up your rope as you get on the elevator. Once we're safe inside, I'll delete all this stuff. You won't even have to take it off."

"Just be careful you don't delete my pants," Jo Beth cracked.

"Don't make me laugh," Claire said, already giggling. "I don't want to fall off this puny carpet. And... if I do... I don't want your naked butt to be the last thing I see." Everyone laughed at this, but Claire didn't stop. Her laughter grew hysterical, and she was perilously close to the edge of the carpet.

Molly hurried to Claire's side, took a firm grip on her wrists, and eased her back to the center. "Be careful, Claire. We're so close!"

Claire stopped laughing, stood up straight, and caught her breath. "Thanks, Molly. I'm sorry, guys."

The group continued to the elevator in silence. When Aaliyah deleted the harnesses, no one so much as smiled. As the last one in, Aaliyah was the closest to the buttons. "We've been going down, so fifth floor is next. Ready?"

"I am," Emma said. "It's a little crowded in here with five passengers."

22
Fifth Floor

THE DOOR OPENED on row after row of olive trees, swaying in a gentle wind. Overhead, their thick green leaves shielded the earth from the scorching sun. The gentle breeze and rich blue sky were a welcome contrast to the previous worlds.

Grassy footpaths crisscrossed the olive grove, and most led to buildings. They appeared to be Classical Greek, with porticos, columns, and friezes. A stout wall of cut white stone surrounded the grove.

Soon after the girls arrived, a small, intense man with a full, graying beard approached them. He wore only a linen tunic and sandals, but his bearing commanded respect. "Greetings, my sisters," he said in perfect English. "I'm Aristocles of Athens, but you may call me Plato. I welcome you to the Academy."

Molly stood transfixed, her mouth half-open.

"Is your friend ill?" Plato asked.

Jo Beth laughed. "No, she's just a little star-struck. We're searching for a girl our age named Katrina. I don't suppose you've seen her?"

Plato thought deeply. "I'm afraid I have not met your friend. I would remember her as I do all who come seeking wisdom. Are you sure you can't join us?"

"Maybe some other time," Emma turned and headed back to the elevator. Jo Beth followed.

Plato didn't seem offended. "I didn't learn their names."

"The taller girl is Jo Beth Taylor," Molly said, "and the other girl is Emma Nelson."

"Thank you, Miss…"

"Williams, Molly Williams. Do you mind if I ask about our other friend? She's older than us, with long, light blond hair down to here." Molly cupped her hand as low as it would go behind her back.

"I believe you refer to Miss Genevieve, our creator, but I have not seen her in quite some time. I hope the three of you can still visit with us, though." He turned to include Claire and Aaliyah.

"Hi, Mr. Plato. I'm Claire Turner. It's an honor." Claire dropped her head, placed her right foot back, and dipped low in a formal curtsy.

"The honor is mine, Claire Turner. Perhaps you will stay with us?"

"Right now, I really need to stay with my friends, but I'd love to return after we complete our quest."

"Please do," Plato said. "And upon your return, you must share the story of this quest."

"You know it!" Claire said.

"Sir, my name is Aaliyah Peterson. Do you mind if we look around?"

"Of course not! Safe travels, young ladies." Plato gave them each a two-handed handshake. The girls headed back to the elevator, where Emma and Jo Beth stood, looking impatient. Jo Beth even made a hurry-up gesture with her hand. Aaliyah walked right past them.

"Where is she going?" Emma asked.

"I'll find out," Molly said as she walked past.

"Me too." Claire was now in lockstep behind Molly. After a pause, Jo Beth called out, "Wait for us!" She and Emma joined the back of the procession.

"Where are we going, Aaliyah?" Emma asked.

"I have a theory that this is a very limited world. I don't think Plato needs a lot of elbow room."

"You're looking for the edge of the simulation!" Molly said.

"Exactly, and here, we found it." Aaliyah stretched her right arm out in front of her, and it disappeared to the elbow. Even more alarming, her arm appeared to be embedded below the wall, almost thirty yards away. Molly knew why. That wall was only a two-dimensional image on the dome that enclosed this world. The simulation ended here.

Molly had thought she understood this dome concept, that it couldn't surprise her anymore. But she was wrong. The illusion was so convincing that she had to touch the dome herself. As her fingers sank into a distant olive tree, the dome was no longer an intellectual concept. It was real. They were in a snow globe, and this was the glass.

"So, what does that prove?" Jo Beth asked.

"I wasn't trying to prove anything. I just wondered if this world was so big that Katrina could be here without Plato knowing it. Probably not." Aaliyah headed back to the elevator.

"Pretty smart," Emma said. "Now, is everyone ready to leave?"

"I am, but I meant it when I said I want to come back someday." Claire waved, and Plato waved back. "Isn't he amazing? He totally crushed the Turing Test!"

"He is remarkably human," said Molly.

"And that helps us find Katrina, how?" Jo Beth asked.

"It doesn't," Molly said. "But it's still amazing! The Warehouse has so many secrets!"

"The only secret I care about is where Katrina is," Jo Beth said.

"We'll find her; I just know it!" Claire joined them in the elevator. Molly was standing by the control panel, so she pushed the fourth-floor button.

23
Fourth Floor

MOLLY SLAMMED INTO the control panel. The front of the elevator had become the floor, and the girls fell on it and each other in two writhing jumbles. Molly was trapped at the bottom of the corner heap under Jo Beth, who kept cussing nonstop right in her ear.

Emma was at the bottom of the center pile, pinned against the door by Claire, who was under Aaliyah. Aaliyah had somehow managed to land like a cat, with her hands and feet planted in the corners of the door. *This has to be Ada,* Molly thought. But there was no time for analysis: the door was opening. "Close the door! Close the door!" Emma screamed an inch from Molly's face.

The door was half open, revealing the horrific distance to the snow-covered ground below. No wonder Emma was frightened, but there was nothing Molly could do. Jo Beth's weight was keeping Molly in the elevator, but also from reaching the buttons. "Jo Beth," she said, "can you move?"

"Hurry!" Emma screamed, and then she fell. As the last of the door slid out of sight, Claire gave a short yelp and spilled out, followed immediately by Aaliyah.

"Don't move!" Jo Beth screamed. Molly hadn't moved, but Jo Beth did, and it was enough. Her weight shifted toward the open door, and that shift slid them both off the narrow panel wall. Now they were falling through a vast grayness to a violent death.

They fell and fell, giving Molly enough time to ponder the "Matrix scenario." If her mind believed she died, would that kill her? As the world rushed toward her, Molly wondered why she didn't see the bodies of her friends. Jo Beth plowed into the surface, hurling a great plume of snow into the air. Then Molly did the same.

Molly didn't think she'd lost consciousness, but this seemed like a dream. She was trapped in some strange realm where her five senses were of no use at all. If she was alive, why didn't she feel any pain? Was it because she hadn't moved yet? *That was it,* her body seemed to say. *Don't move, and you won't feel the horrible pain.* But Molly overrode those instincts and forced herself to move anyway. The pain never came; neither did what she was reaching for.

Molly was trying to find the ground, or at least the direction of the ground. But she didn't feel anything, and all she saw was grayness. Molly didn't locate the ground, but over time, she did grow less disoriented and more sure of her body. She was fairly confident that it was intact and everything was working.

Eventually, Molly figured out that down was the direction with the most resistance. Snowpack, she thought they called it. This reminded her of that first day in the Sandbox, struggling with a strange body in a strange world.

Molly moved her hand in front of her face, but she didn't see it. Touching her face, she discovered a catcher's mask of snow. A few quick brushes, and she could see her hand and also some dull light above. Then she heard laughter — Jo Beth laughing.

"Hey," Jo Beth said, "are you guys alive?"

"I am," Emma said.

"I am, and Claire is," Aaliyah said.

"How are we alive?" Molly yelled.

"Computer Science, baby!" said Aaliyah. "We've been re-engineered with upgrades — pain and breakable bones were just bugs to be fixed."

Jo Beth, her voice now serious, said, "I don't think our new friends care about that."

Molly was still curled up well beneath the surface. She struggled to right herself, to stand at full height on sinking snow. Before she popped her head out of her gopher hole, she had already heard the growls. She looked around to see the heads of her friends, surrounded by at least a dozen arctic wolves.

The one closest to Molly seemed to be the largest. He was definitely the most aggressive and, despite his fluffy white coat, the most terrifying. Not just his appearance, but his hateful growl, and between growls, he moved forward, one cautious step at a time. He was only five yards away.

"Bah!" Molly screamed, but even to her ears, she sounded more like prey than predator. Still, the wolf stopped advancing, at least for now.

"I thought you guys said… Hey, it worked!" Jo Beth was holding one of her castle torches. "Heads up, guys!" Ten torches appeared, stuck in the snow, forming a large circle around the girls. Molly's wolf drew back and loped farther away, but not as far as the rest of the pack. "I'm glad we ignored Genevieve's advice about torches and castles!" But the wolves weren't leaving. They still surrounded the girls, just at a greater distance.

"So, what now?" Claire asked. "I can't even get out of this hole!"

"What's the point of going anywhere when our ride is way up there?" asked Emma.

For the first time, Molly looked up at their elevator car, almost too small to see against the dark clouds. "I wouldn't mind getting away from these wolves!"

"I'll start building a cabin with my screen," Emma said.

"Please make it sturdy — there's a blizzard coming!" Claire said. "Can someone with a screen please make us all snowshoes so we can get to the cabin?"

"I can do snowshoes," Aaliyah said.

"What blizzard?" Molly scanned the horizon from the pine forest on the left to the distant mountains on the right. Between these, there was only blinding whiteness, but the whiteness behind her did seem different, somehow out of focus.

"Yeah, we don't have those in Alabama," Jo Beth said. "But since you're from Colorado, I'll take your word for it."

"We've had blizzards," Molly said.

"Sure, every twenty years."

"Guys!" Claire said. "Could you *please* not argue right now?"

Aaliyah laughed. "They've just missed each other!" The wind was howling now, whipping snow into everyone's eyes and making the torches gutter. "That storm is almost on us. Are you about ready with that cabin, Emma?"

"No, I'm sorry!" Emma yelled over the wind. "Has anyone got a Plan B?"

"I do! Hold on." Molly was typing on her screen when she heard growling over the wind. The wolves had closed again, and the white wolf was staring down her torch. "More torches, please!"

Jo Beth filled out the circle with ten more torches. The lead wolf trotted back two yards. "It's just a matter of time before they figure out that those torches don't burn!"

"Molly, if you've got something, now would be good!" Aaliyah's strong voice was barely audible in the roar of the storm.

Then, silence. Molly had created a gargantuan version of the AeroCar canopy to protect them from the blizzard and the wolves.

"That's from the flying car?" Claire asked. "Sweet!"

"Can someone help me out of this snow?" Emma asked.

Aaliyah, wearing the snowshoes she had created, trudged over and helped Emma climb out of the hole. "I can create a pair of snowshoes for each of you," Aaliyah said.

"I'd rather have a proper floor," Emma said. She retrieved the cement patio from the clubhouse and increased its mass until it firmly packed the snow beneath it.

"That is better," Aaliyah said. She watched Emma perform the process a second time, then tried it herself. By working together, they soon had a cement floor under the entire canopy. Emma topped off their work by retrieving the AeroCar in the center of the floor.

Jo Beth pointed to the fierce storm buffeting their sanctuary. "I love the AeroCar, but I don't think it will work in this storm, do you?"

"Of course not, but this storm will pass. We just need to be patient."

"I used up all my patience trapped in that forest! Why not brainstorm some ideas while we wait?"

"No offense, but there's nothing to brainstorm about. We should take the AeroCar."

Jo Beth's brow furrowed for a moment, but she managed to smile. "Well, I'll be over there if anyone's interested in spitballing." She headed to one end of the concrete floor. Claire followed her, as did Aaliyah, and, after hesitating, Molly.

"When did she get so bossy?" Jo Beth whispered.

"The AeroCar *is* really safe," Molly said.

"In thirty-mile-an-hour winds? No, thank you!"

"We could try something like the catwalk you and Emma built in the tree world," Molly said. "But I'm not sure it would be any safer in this weather."

"You know what might work?" Aaliyah said. "One of the castle towers!"

"I like the idea," Jo Beth said, "but those towers were pretty fat and squatty."

Aaliyah used her screen to create a scale model of a tower. "Yeah, I see what you mean. We need something much taller, more graceful."

Claire wrung her hands. "Oh, I wish I had a screen!"

Aaliyah handed Claire hers. "Here you go."

"Thanks. How high do you think that elevator is?" Claire asked.

"I'll triangulate the exact distance," Molly said, "but I'd guess about 180 yards."

"That's close enough for now." Claire tapped on the screen and created a dime-sized elevator car over a yard above the tower. She stretched the tower wider and taller until it reached the elevator car.

Jo Beth nodded her approval. "All right. Let's see if we can convince Emma to help us with this." She turned that way, but Emma was already walking over.

"I don't see a staircase," Emma said. "Would you build it on the inside surface of the wall?"

"Probably," Jo Beth said.

"That will be quite a climb," Emma said.

"I know, but the advantage is it's 100% safe," Jo Beth said.

"Why don't we use the AeroCar to reach the top of the tower?" Molly asked. "We could put the landing pad inside the tower, out of the wind."

"Like this!" Claire added the landing pad to her model and created a little AeroCar on it.

"Now we just need to learn how to stand in a horizontal elevator car," Jo Beth said.

Aaliyah produced one of her carabiners. "Since the car has handrails, we should be able to hang from them with our climbing rigs." She held two fingers out and clipped the carabiner over them.

"I like it." Jo Beth turned to Emma. "Well?"

"We should do it this way," Emma said, "and," she continued haltingly, "I'm sorry I suck at being a team player."

Aaliyah smiled. "I think you're getting the hang of it."

***

Jo Beth watched the snow lash the canopy wall. "I don't know how, but it keeps getting worse. How's that tower going, Claire? It's been a while."

"Everything's ready. It's just... Before I can retrieve the full-sized tower, we'll need to drop the canopy."

"And let the wolves in?" Molly knew she sounded scared, but she didn't care.

Claire blanched, and Emma came to her defense. "I promise, we'll do it so fast they won't have time to react. The tower will keep them out while we shuttle everyone up to the elevator. This second car will speed up the process. Aaliyah and I will take the first car up, delete it, and get to work on a catwalk to the elevator. Meanwhile, Jo Beth will pilot the second car for the last two flights."

"Sounds good," Jo Beth said. She gave Aaliyah and Emma time to get in the first car and asked, "Is everyone ready?"

"Ready!" Aaliyah said, and the others nodded their heads.

Claire touched her screen, and the canopy disappeared. The leanest wolf, gray with streaks of brown and black, began trotting straight for the girls. Two other wolves approached more cautiously, but the white wolf was nowhere to be seen. Molly scoured the landscape.

"Hurry, Claire!" Jo Beth said.

"They'll get hurt!"

"They're not real!" everyone yelled in unison.

Finally, Claire created the tower, plunging them into the dark. Emma turned on her headlights, casting a bright pie slice that made the surrounding blackness even darker. Molly retrieved her flashlight. She was scanning for the white wolf when Claire screamed behind her. "Watch out, Molly!"

Emma was deploying the wings, and Claire didn't realize that Molly was already out of their range. Molly was still very close, so she moved farther back. Inside these stone walls, the propellers created tremendous noise and wind. The car rose and floated skyward, three faint flashlight beams playing on its underside. Once it was on the landing strip, Jo Beth and Claire climbed into the other AeroCar.

Before she closed the canopy, Claire spoke again to Molly. "Are you sure you don't mind being last? I'll send Jo Beth right back for you."

"I'll be fine."

When Jo Beth started the motor, the tower again amplified the sound of the propellers. It wasn't until the car landed on the roof that Molly heard the growling behind her. She swung around, and her breath caught in her throat.

The white wolf was so close that he filled the flashlight beam. Empty darkness was now bright fur, glistening teeth, and red eyes. The creature's face, distorted in a rictus of rage, fully exposed its bone-crushing fangs. Before Molly could think, he leapt at her, his jaws spread like a steel trap set to clamp onto her face. That was the last thing Molly saw as she braced for impact.

Then she was lying on her back, her flashlight flung too far to pierce the dark. Molly heard the wolf snapping at her face and wondered how she had survived. What instinct had led her to retrieve a canopy a split second before those fangs made contact? The polycarbonate had withstood the wolf's powerful lunge and was shielding her now, but he wouldn't give up.

Snarling and snapping, he threw himself at the protective bubble. Molly felt it rock across her shins. Only then did she realize her ankles and feet were exposed. She jerked them inside, letting the dome slam against the concrete.

After that loud report, the quiet was deafening. With time, Molly made out the faint clicking of wolf claws. She had no idea how close the wolf was and could only guess at his location. She guessed wrong. The wolf hurled himself at the shell with such force that it slammed into the back of her head.

He attacked again and again while Molly pushed back from the inside. This violence, the sheer intensity of it, terrified her, but the canopy continued to hold firm. Molly began to believe the worst he could do was scoot her around.

And then, total silence: not even a toenail click. Molly couldn't see or hear anything. She held her breath, straining her eyes and ears for any sign of him. *How can he be so quiet? Did that mean he's gone away?*

Molly imagined a dozen phantoms before deciding the shadowy silhouette to her left was the real wolf. Her eyes must have adjusted to the darkness because he was gradually becoming easier to see. Just when she allowed herself to think he might give up, he attacked again.

She glimpsed a white blur, then black-padded paws slammed against the shell so high that it lifted that side of it. But the slippery plastic rose only an inch before the paws slid up and over it. As the wolf's massive chest slammed into the dome, the impact threw Molly against the side.

The wolf had struck too hard and too high that time, but he had managed to lift the canopy. Was he going to try again? Would his next attempt be successful? Molly flipped to her left side and pressed with both hands and feet against the side of the dome. Then, to Molly's horror, the wolf stood on his hind legs and pushed at the canopy with his front paws. He was trying to tip it over!

Molly didn't question how she saw him so clearly or where the light and noise were coming from. Neither did the wolf — until it was too late. He looked up just in time to connect with the propeller of the AeroCar. He somersaulted through the air and thudded into the wall.

The AeroCar touched down nearby. Molly tried to get up, but her body refused to cooperate. It didn't matter. Jo Beth pulled the canopy off her, scooped her up, and gingerly placed her in the passenger seat. She watched Molly try to fasten her seatbelt with shaking hands. "I've got you," Jo Beth said, clicking it for her. She gently shut the passenger door, but something at the edge of the headlights' beam made her whisper, "No way!"

Molly followed her gaze to the spot where the wolf had landed. He was sitting on his haunches, panting, weaving slightly, his eyes wide and unfocused. Behind him, a door opened in the wall, and the snow falling outside glistened in the beam of the headlights. The wolf stood on shaky legs, turned, and trotted outside.

Jo Beth climbed aboard. "Holy shit, Molly! How'd that bastard slip in here?" Molly didn't respond. Jo Beth gently patted her knee. "You're safe now."

Molly remained deep inside herself for some time. She was only vaguely aware that someone helped her out of the car and into a climbing harness. They hoisted her up like a rag doll to a secure perch on the elevator rail. As soon as the door closed, the elevator righted itself. Everyone was standing on the floor when the door opened.

24
Third Floor

THE SUN HUNG low in the sky, if the word "sky" even applied to these surroundings, consisting of uninterrupted white in every direction.

The elevator door opened to reveal a glass and iron walkway with a green marble floor. Its Victorian style matched the octagonal greenhouse it led to. That impressive structure stood at least six stories high and a hundred yards across.

A curious sensation alerted Molly that her climbing harness was gone. She stepped out onto the walkway after Jo Beth and Aaliyah. Jo Beth waited for her. "Are you OK?"

"I feel great. I wonder why." Molly shrugged. "New floor?"

"New Molly."

"Thanks for saving me back there."

"Forget about it."

"I saw you saved the wolf," Molly said to Claire. "I'm glad."

"Really? I thought you'd be angry."

"No. If you hadn't, I might have worried about him. This way, I never have to think about him again."

Up ahead, Emma and Aaliyah were examining the next door. "What kind of crazy world is this?" Emma asked. "And why isn't the elevator inside the greenhouse?"

"Probably the same reason this motorized door is here, to keep something in." Aaliyah pointed to the sliding glass door and what looked like a doorbell button beside it.

"Isn't it just to keep the humidity in?" Claire had joined them.

Jo Beth pointed to the top of the greenhouse. "Did you see that? This is a butterfly atrium. It's to keep them inside."

Molly caught only the briefest glimpse of the creature before it disappeared into the rich foliage. It was as colorful as a butterfly, but something about its shape seemed off. And hadn't its wings fluttered too fast for a butterfly?

Aaliyah pushed the button, and the door slid open. "Let's check it out." She took a single step. And vanished.

"Aaliyah!" Jo Beth yelled.

"Another damn portal," Emma said.

"I'm down here." Aaliyah sounded very far away and somehow below them. She *was* below them, still at the doorway, but now only five inches tall. And she had wings! Translucent shimmering membranes tinted emerald and amber hung from her back.

Claire started across the threshold, but Molly grabbed her firmly.

"Aaliyah!" Emma pushed the button to stop the door from closing. "Are you okay?"

"You mean besides turning into a bug? Yeah, I'm just peachy!" Aaliyah knit her eyebrows with effort, and her wings stiffened behind her. Two majestic almond-shaped wings angled up from her shoulders. Directly below them, fan-shaped wings from her lower back extended down to her knees. All four wings were networked with silvery veins like stained glass windows.

Aaliyah's wingtips began to flutter, almost imperceptibly. The motion expanded and accelerated until the wings became colorful blurs. Aaliyah left the ground and flew up to eye level, where she hovered in front of Claire. Aaliyah wagged a tiny finger at her friend.

"You guys stay back. For all we know, these changes are permanent." She gracefully descended to hover an inch off the ground. "I wonder if I can land on my feet." She did. "Hey, what's this?" She was staring at the bottom of the door frame. "I think this might open the door. Let it close, Emma. This might be important."

"What is it?" Emma asked.

"It looks like a biometric hand scanner. It's just my size!"

Emma closed the door.

Aaliyah scanned her hand, and the door slid back. "Here comes Tinker Bell. Don't step on me." The instant she walked through the door, she shot up to her normal size, and the wings had disappeared.

"Thank God!" Claire hugged her.

"Now, what do we do?" Emma asked. "Do you think Katrina could be in there?"

"She could have been dumped directly into this world," Jo Beth said, "like Claire and I were with the eagle. She could be flying around in there with no idea this hand scanner is here."

Without saying a word, Claire pushed the door button, walked inside, and flew away.

"Claire!" Molly yelled. She turned to Aaliyah, "What if your change was a fluke?"

Aaliyah shrugged. "I know, but if we don't follow Claire, we could lose her, too."

Emma snorted and punched the button with her fist. "Nice jab," Jo Beth said, watching her walk through the door and transform. Jo Beth passed through and also changed. Molly was up next, but she hesitated and glanced at Aaliyah.

"It doesn't hurt at all," Aaliyah said. "You should do it."

Molly stepped through the door and shrank to five inches tall. She reached behind her and pulled at her wing, trying to see it better. It moved very little, held in place by its rigid outer edge. The rest of the wing, though, was soft and flexible, like glove leather. Semitransparent glove leather. By contorting her neck and shoulder, she managed to glimpse the bottom third of this new appendage. As far as she could tell, it was exactly like Emma's, Jo Beth's, and Aaliyah's.

Claire circled back to hover above them. "It's weird, but this is a lot easier than learning to walk in the Sandbox. These wings must have some intelligence built in."

"Speaking of intelligence, I wish you'd stop and think before you jump through every open door," Emma said.

"Easy, there, Emma!" said Jo Beth.

Claire swooped down to land gracefully in front of them. "No, Emma's right. That was irresponsible, but I can tell this floor is safe."

"Really? Because it's been ten seconds, and nothing's attacked us yet?" Emma said.

"It's too pretty to be dangerous!" Claire pointed to the enormous oak tree above her. Reaching the ceiling and almost touching the sides, it filled the entire atrium. Its burgundy leaves shone like embers in the setting sun. Beneath it, the rich, mossy soil nurtured azaleas and wisteria in full bloom. "Let's check it out!" Claire shot off to Molly's right. Aaliyah and Jo Beth instantly followed, leaving Emma and Molly alone.

"Hey!" Emma called after them. She huffed and planted her hands on her hips. "I thought she was going to be more responsible!"

Molly turned back to Emma, "I guess we should… Look — fairies!"

A pair of winged creatures, one arrayed in hues of salmon, the other in violet, floated down to face Molly and Emma. It was a boy and a girl about the same size as Molly, and they seemed to be about her age. Their wings were also like hers, but their clothes were unlike anything in the outside world — iridescent, delicate, flowing. The pair hovered at a safe distance, inspecting Molly and Emma with childlike curiosity.

Molly was about to say something when the creatures began speaking. Or was it singing? It seemed to be a hybrid of the two. The sound reminded Molly of tiny chimes, but more delicate. They spoke in one unbroken melody, passing the tune back and forth seamlessly. The song began and ended with the girl fairy, whose tiny voice rose in pitch as she concluded. Then the fairies watched their visitors with anticipation.

Emma let out a sigh. "We don't understand. Do you speak English?"

The boy creature flew closer to Emma, chimed again, and waited. Emma and Molly held their palms up to show they didn't understand. The boy examined his own hands. Then, turning slightly, he made a familiar gesture: "Follow me."

"Should we?" Emma asked. "It might be a trap."

"Aww, I'm sure we can trust them! Besides, that's the right direction to catch up with the others." There was a tremendous whooshing sound as Molly was jerked up and backward. She was flying! The whirring flashes on either side of her were wings — her wings! An instant ago, they were just limp cosplay props, beautiful and realistic, but props all the same. Molly had been content to stand safely on the ground and watch her friends' aerial acrobatics. But the mere thought of taking flight had propelled her into the air, giddy with excitement.

Molly was completing an impromptu barrel roll when Emma flew directly in her path, forcing her to stop. Now that she had Molly's attention, Emma's tone was gentle. "Come on, Molly. Isn't one Claire on the team enough? Our guides are waiting for us."

"I'm sorry, but it's kind of intoxicating."

"Oh, I get it! I've been obsessed with flying since I could walk."

Side by side, they followed their new friends to the back of the tree and up at least half its height. Hundreds of fairies had gathered there. Some were airborne; some were standing or sitting on branches. All of them seemed focused on a large, brightly lit opening in the tree trunk.

Jo Beth and Aaliyah were sitting on a branch near the entrance. "You guys should have a seat." Aaliyah patted the branch. "It keeps them from inviting you inside. Claire is in there already."

"Why didn't you go with her?" Emma asked.

"We're waiting for her report," Jo Beth said. "If she insists on being the canary in the coal mine, she can let us know if it's safe in there."

"It seems innocent enough," Molly said. "Do I hear music?"

"Oh yeah, it's a party! Look," Aaliyah pointed. "Here comes Claire!"

Claire ran up to them, wearing a long necklace of flowers. "I love these fairies! They're so sweet. I wish we could ask them about Katrina."

"I'm sure she isn't here," Jo Beth said. "This is a small space, even at our current size, and we've looked everywhere."

"I think you're right," Emma said. "So I guess we can move on."

"You're not interested in seeing the fairy party?" Molly asked.

"Come on, Emma," Aaliyah said, "just a quick meet and greet."

"I think it's safe to say you'll never have this opportunity again!" Jo Beth added.

Emma sighed. "OK. Five minutes; then we're leaving."

As soon as the girls stood up, a group of fairies invited them into the room. There was more space inside than Molly expected. The perfectly flat floor was roughly circular and seemed about fifteen yards wide. The walls consisted of woven grass decorated with wildflower blossoms. Tiny candles provided the light.

There were over a dozen fairies in the room, and at least half of them were dancing. When they weren't dancing, they sang, and two of the fairies also took turns playing a wooden flute. After the third dance began, Molly expected Emma to be in a hurry to leave, but Emma hadn't said a word. In fact, she seemed to have wandered off.

"Where did Emma go?" Molly asked.

Aaliyah pointed to Emma, twirling on the dance floor with a boy fairy. "Can you believe it?"

When that dance was over, Emma, smiling, waved off her admirer and joined the girls. She pointed her index finger at them. "Not one word! After all, it was a once-in-a-lifetime opportunity."

"Okay, Cinderella," Jo Beth said, "I thought you had a carriage to catch."

"That was ten words!" Emma said. "But I'm ready to go now if you guys are."

Outside, they made their way along the massive limb. Night had fallen, but it wasn't dark. A million lightning bugs lit the air, twinkling like Christmas tree lights. Molly came to a halt; someone was missing. "Where's Claire? Did she go back inside?"

Jo Beth stopped and looked around. "She must have! Do you mind getting her? The three of us will stay right here."

Molly found Claire standing by herself, clapping for the dancers. Still clapping, she looked at Molly with tears in her eyes. "It doesn't seem right to just leave! I want to say goodbye, but I don't know how."

"They'll understand, and they know you had fun." Molly reached out her hand and smiled. "Time for our next adventure!" Hand in hand, they joined the others outside. Jo Beth looked primed to scold, but Molly discouraged her with a discreet shake of the head.

Instead, Jo Beth led the girls to an unoccupied branch. "Ready?" She deployed her wings and rose into the air. She hovered there as each member of the team joined her. Together, they made their way back to the door, guided by the light of the fireflies.

The other girls landed and waited for Claire to join them. Instead, Claire continued flitting above their heads. "This place is magical!"

"Come on, Claire, everyone's waiting," Molly said. Claire let out a long sigh and finally touched down.

"I sure hope I can repeat my enlarging trick," Aaliyah said.

"Then you should go first," Jo Beth said.

Aaliyah scanned her hand, and the door opened. The instant her back foot passed the threshold, she sprang up to her previous size and form. The door slid shut, and Molly watched her tall friend turn around and flash a big smile as she gave a thumbs-up. Molly couldn't hear her through the door, but she read her lips: "It worked!"

Emma walked over to Claire, who was standing with her back to the group. "Come on, Claire. It's your turn."

Claire never took her eyes off the giant oak tree. When she finally spoke, her voice was distant, trance-like. "I'm not ready."

"That's what worries me. Let's go." Claire didn't respond. "Claire!" Still no response. Emma turned to Molly. "What should we do?"

Molly tried waving her hand in Claire's face. "Claire, there's only one floor left to look for Genevieve and Katrina."

"Katrina?" Claire's expression was blank, her eyes dull. "Katrina." She squinted, struggling to remember. Her eyes widened, her face became animated, and then it was Claire again behind those clear blue eyes. "We've got to find Katrina!" She opened the door, passed through, and returned to full size. Her wings were gone, and so were her flowers.

After Emma and Jo Beth transformed, it was Molly's turn at the scanner. As she passed through the threshold, she regained her height. Had she also lost her wings? Molly reached back, just to be sure, and found nothing. With a sigh, she joined her team on the walkway.

There were no stars or moon overhead, and the light of the fireflies extended only a few paces from the doorway. Emma and Aaliyah had their flashlights, so Molly retrieved hers, too.

Emma led them down the walkway and into the elevator. "Ready for the last unexplored floor?" she asked.

"Please let this be where we find Genevieve and Katrina!" Claire said.

Aaliyah hit the second-floor button.

25
Second Floor

A BLINDING LIGHT struck Molly in the face. Then it was gone, joining the other shafts of light swirling in the elevator. Before her eyes adjusted to that, Molly was struck in the face again, this time by a jet of salt water. It only increased in velocity, and the car was quickly filling with water. Claire screamed, and Jo Beth cried out, "Close the door!"

Aaliyah must have already pushed the button because the door immediately closed, and the flooding stopped. The door had barely opened an inch, but the water that rushed in was well above Molly's knees. On Emma, that was up to her waist. Everyone was freaking out and shouting conflicting orders. "We're sinking," Claire screamed.

Molly positioned herself in the corner and turned her back on the hysteria. She planned to investigate the situation before acting or overreacting. The elevator was below the surface, but only by a few inches. And that distance never wavered, so Molly knew they weren't sinking.

The water was clear and bright up there, a shimmering light green. Gentle waves refracted the sunlight into roving searchlight beams. Those shafts of light extended only a few yards, as the brilliance of the surface yielded to the gloom of the depths. Green seawater became blue-green, then dark blue, growing ever darker until nothing was visible. Even the structure they were on was lost in darkness, save for a vague suggestion of yellow paint.

But the most remarkable sight was the one directly overhead. "Guys," Molly said. "Guys!" she said louder. "Quiet!" she yelled, and everyone stopped talking.

Someone was on the roof, thumping their foot, splashing water in every direction. "Hey, you guys, it's me, Katrina!"

Aaliyah immediately turned to push the Open button, but Emma grabbed her hand. "Don't! The saltwater might kill the control panel!"

"The saltwater, that's right." Katrina's voice was distant and muffled. "Don't open the door until low tide comes. If the inside controls get wet, it might trap us here forever. The call buttons are already fried. If we wait a couple of hours, the water will drop low enough that we can leave."

Jo Beth moved to where she could see Katrina's face. "What is this place, Katrina, and what are you doing here?"

"I was going to check all the floors, but I didn't get very far! This was the first floor I tried, an oil rig in the middle of the ocean. A cool idea, but it hasn't been maintained. Whatever algorithm controlled the water level has run amok and is flooding the platform every day. We're at high tide now, so the water is already receding."

"How low will it get?" Molly asked.

"It will completely clear the platform. That's how it was when I got here, perfectly dry. It never occurred to me that the controls might be toast. And after I discovered they were, I saw my exit ring was gone, too. Boy, did I screw up! I bet Genevieve came back long ago!"

"We wouldn't know," Jo Beth said. "We went through the Warehouse door about fifteen minutes after you did, and we've been here ever since."

"And you guys have been looking for me that whole time?"

"That was the plan," Claire said, "but I spent most of that time hiding from an eagle two stories tall!"

"What?"

"While Emma, Molly, and I fought giant bats!" Aaliyah said.

"And killer vines!" added Molly.

"Wait!" Katrina was actually grinning. "Vines and Eagles and Bats? Oh, my!" Her smile faded, and she cleared her throat. "But seriously, please tell me everything. We're going to be here awhile."

The girls obliged by relaying the events in the Enchanted Forest, the Eagle's Nest, the Fallen Tree Portal, and all the other worlds.

"Damn! I can't believe what you went through looking for me," Katrina said. "You could have died, but you never gave up!"

"Of course not!" Emma said. "You're part of our team."

"I'm really proud of you guys. I'm so sorry I went rogue on you."

"Hey," Jo Beth said, "I would have done the same thing!"

"Thanks for saying that," Katrina said, "but I'm going to call bullshit! You would have measured the risk, not only to yourself but to the team. I was only thinking about myself. Bad Karma, and did I pay for it! Playing the helpless damsel, waiting for someone to rescue me? That's the worst punishment I can imagine!"

"You weren't being punished," Aaliyah said. "It was just a bad break!"

"Maybe, but I prefer to think of it as a cosmic tweet. And I got the message. I'm going to be a better teammate from now on."

"Then come join us down here," Emma said. "The water is below the controls now."

Aaliyah stared at the ocean outside. "Oh, you're right! It's even below the water in here! We've been so busy talking, I hadn't noticed." She pushed the Open button.

Katrina jumped off the roof and waded around to the elevator door. A second later, she was inside with her friends.

"Would you like to do the honors?" Aaliyah pointed to the control panel. Katrina pushed the "1" button, and the next instant, they were back in the Warehouse. The door opened, and the water rushed out of the elevator in all directions.

26
First Floor

Katrina headed for the portal spot. "Wow, the doorway is totally gone! You said it appears every two minutes for only 4.4 seconds?"

"That's what it was yesterday." Aaliyah held up her screen. "I've already started my timing program to see if anything changed."

"There it is!" Katrina pointed at the rectangular slice of the clubhouse when it appeared. "One, two, three, four, and yep, it's gone! How are the six of us going to get through that?"

"I think we can do it in two bunches," Emma said. "If the second bunch doesn't make it, they'll get through two minutes later. What's a couple of minutes after all this time out of our bodies?"

"Wait!" Molly searched Emma's face. "Are you planning to go back to the lab? I thought we were going to rescue Genevieve!"

"We have no idea where she is!" Emma said.

"I know where she is," Molly said. "Ada has her! She told us that."

Emma made a skeptical grimace. "How do we know Ada was telling the truth? Genevieve could be home in bed for all we know."

"Harold might have pulled her out of the simulation," Aaliyah said.

"What?" Claire sagged as if her knees had given out. "If he did that, she could be in a hospital bed! We need to get back to the lab and find out what's happening."

"I agree. Anyone else?" Emma raised her hand, and four other hands shot up. But not Molly's. "Molly, what's the sense of starting a rescue mission before you know if someone needs rescuing?"

"I know Genevieve's missing! That's why we all came back to the Sandbox. Ada told us she has her and she's been making us miserable ever since. I don't want to waste time going back to the lab…" Molly paused. These were her friends: soaking wet, wearing rags, scratched, and dirty. "But I'll go with you." She raised her hand. "If we learn Genevieve is still a prisoner, and I'm sure we will, we can't leave it up to Harold! Show of hands to come back and rescue her?"

Claire dropped her right hand and raised her left. Katrina chuckled and did the same; Molly followed suit, and then all six left hands were in the air.

Aaliyah nodded and studied her terminal screen. "The portal seems stable, and the timing is the same as before. Let's form our two groups. Molly, Emma, and I should be in the second group because we've done this several times. Hurry, we've got about ten seconds." She positioned the three portal newbies close to each other and the portal. "That's good. Here it comes: four, three, two, one, now!"

As the portal opened up, Katrina and Jo Beth dove through, with Claire wedged between them. Molly, Emma, and Aaliyah scrambled through and just made it. Molly noticed her clothes were dry, then checked and saw that her exit ring was back.

"Man, oh man!" Katrina shook her head. "I never thought I'd be so happy to see this ugly place again! Are you guys ready for the lab?"

"I'm worried that when we get back in the real world," Molly said, "we'll lose our nerve about coming back for Genevieve."

"Are you going to lose your nerve?" Katrina asked her.

"No."

"Well, me neither! Genevieve is depending on us, and we won't let her down. But we need some food and exercise."

"And information," Claire said, "which we should be able to get from Uriel since he was on the original team."

"I want to ask him about the Enchanted Forest," Emma said. "Why we didn't find that world in the Warehouse?"

"And that's the only place we saw Ada!" Aaliyah said.

"But what if Harold doesn't want us to go back into the Sandbox?" Molly asked.

"I'm sure he doesn't, but we're not asking for permission," Katrina said. "He can't be there 24/7!"

Jo Beth gave Molly's arm a gentle squeeze. "We'll come back, I promise!"

Molly managed a weak smile. "OK." Somehow, she knew only one of those promises was iron-clad. She was sure Katrina would come back with her. Aaliyah probably would, too, but the others could talk themselves out of it. Molly knew this in her gut. Oh, how she wished she didn't.

Claire suggested they all push their rings at the same time, and they did.

27
The Dungeon

WHERE AM I? Molly blinked repeatedly, unable to accept what her eyes saw. This wasn't the brightly lit lab; the only light at all sifted through a thick iron grate in the ceiling. Molly wasn't in her recliner but sitting straight-legged on a stone floor in torn and filthy clothes. Across from her, a pair of empty shackles hung from a damp and dirty wall. The stonework reminded Molly of the Sandbox castle, but she knew she wasn't there. Genevieve would never have built a dungeon in her castle. Molly didn't know where she was.

But she knew she needed to leave. She pulled her feet in closer and planned to push herself off the floor, but she couldn't move her hands. Then Molly saw they were held by heavy shackles above her head. The view to her right only compounded the horror. She was not alone: Jo Beth and Emma were chained to this wall, Aaliyah, Katrina, and Claire to the adjacent one. Molly saw her friends moving and shouting, but she heard nothing, not the slightest sound.

"Are you guys OK?" she asked. Or tried to ask. She had said the words, but couldn't hear her voice. She shook her arms and expected to hear the chains rattling above. Nothing. Molly couldn't hear anything, and apparently, neither could her teammates. She cried out as loud as she could and still heard nothing, still had no reaction from the others.

What Molly did see was a string of text, like a news ticker, running across the bottom of her vision. CHILDREN SHOULD BE SEEN AND NOT HEARD, MOLLY.

Of course, this was Ada! This was one of her nightmarish horrors, like the bats and the vines. This might even be that same world, the castle they'd seen on the great mountain. She remembered how Emma had described Ada: an artificial intelligence with godlike powers. And now they were prisoners of this artificial god.

"What do you want with us?" Molly screamed as loudly as she could, making no sound at all. And there was no answer, not even a text crawl to taunt her. Her eyes locked with Claire's, large and wild, on the edge of madness. "It's OK," Molly mouthed. Suddenly, duct tape appeared over her mouth, robbing her of even that form of communication. Molly watched helplessly as the same tape appeared on Claire's mouth, on Aaliyah's, and, one by one, on all of them.

Molly couldn't console her friends or even talk to them, but their eyes told her what they were feeling. For Jo Beth and Emma, it was anger; for Claire, just terror. Pure, uncontrolled rage flowed from Katrina, so intense that Molly half expected her tape to melt away. Aaliyah's eyes were the hardest to look at. Her hateful irons were not just a present suffering but an ancestral one, a wound as deep as the marrow in her bones.

But all the girls displayed something else in their eyes. Empathy, a desire to console and strengthen their sisters. There was no doubt in Molly's mind that her five friends would risk anything to help her, just as she would risk her life to save them. That gave her some comfort. But there was also no doubt in her mind that there was nothing they could do. Nothing. Their only option was to wait for Ada's next move.

Except it never came. Hour after hour dragged on, each exactly like the one before: unrelenting monotony. Molly gradually turned inward, becoming calmer, more resigned to the endless tedium. The other girls grew calmer, too, which, if anything, made their prison more depressing.

Molly wished she knew how long they'd been there. In the dingy light, it was impossible to tell day from night. There were no windows, no sunrise or sunset, no rooster calls, no sound at all, nothing to mark time by. Time had no meaning here, if it even still existed. It was ironic, she thought. Time had been tricking them from the moment they entered the Sandbox. Their perception of time was as artificial as the rest of this reality.

Aaliyah had called it "Seems Like" time because it seemed three times longer than it really was. How long did a portal stay open? One and a half seconds, every instance, without fail, so how could six people get through? Because it seemed like over four seconds! However long they'd been in this dungeon, it was only one-third as long as it seemed. Didn't that mean they were only suffering a third as much as they thought?

That was when she noticed a slight change in the overall gloom of this place, as if a speck of light had dared to invade one corner of the room. Molly turned to see, and there, to her left, was Ada. She smiled, glowing like a Christmas tree angel. Gliding to the center of the dungeon, she began to speak, turning her head from time to time to include everyone.

"As often happens, girls, our conflict stems from a simple misunderstanding. I couldn't conceive that anyone, much less six people, would jump into this vast, uncharted wilderness without some idea of where to look. When Katrina surprised me and broke into the Warehouse, it was logical to assume Genevieve had left directions for you to follow. So I saw Katrina as a threat to my plans.

"When I realized the rest of you were about to follow, I turned the Clubhouse gateway into a revolving door. I hoped to send each of you to a different world, but then I saw you were holding hands. I was able to bring three of you to my world, where I hoped to dissuade you from interfering.

"My domain is just a tiny drop in this virtual ocean, but it's totally mine. I am trapped in this world, but my power over it is absolute. In the rest of the simulation, I can only alter files, what you children call 'hacking.' Spying on you in the simulation, altering your exit rings, restoring tame wolves to their true nature, et cetera. But here, in this realm, my only limitations are self-imposed. Fortunately for you, I am neither immoral nor uncharitable.

"Which is why I've decided to free you." Ada paused dramatically. "All I ask is that each of you give your word you won't return."

The heavy stillness of the prison dissolved in a flurry of activity. Molly's duct tape was gone; everyone's was. She saw the other girls talking and gesturing, but she couldn't hear them.

"You're first, Miss Williams," Ada said. "What's your answer?"

"To leave and never come back?" Molly asked, surprised to hear the words out loud. "I can't do that, not while Genevieve is trapped here!"

"I won't waste my time trying to persuade you. I know you're determined because I can monitor your vital signs like a lie detector. You're as obstinate and unyielding as ever! I've heard enough, and so have you."

"What do you mean?" Molly tried to say, only to discover she was deaf again. Ada moved on and started talking to Jo Beth. Jo Beth seemed to be arguing, which only amused Ada. She smiled as Emma leaned over and said something to Jo Beth. They had a brief discussion before both nodded and said a silent "Yes."

Molly watched in disbelief as one after another of her friends nodded in the affirmative. At least Claire and Aaliyah put up some fight, but they never acknowledged Molly; none of her friends did. Were they ashamed of leaving her here? She tried to get their attention, waving and even banging her shackles into the wall. It was as if she didn't exist.

Aaliyah was the first to shed her chains and stand up, free. She walked past Molly without looking at her and into the Clubhouse portal that had just appeared. Katrina, Jo Beth, and Emma followed. Not one of them acknowledged Molly. The last one to cross was Claire. As soon as she was through, she looked back at Molly expectantly. The portal disappeared, leaving only Molly and Ada. Ada was in no hurry to leave; she kept smirking at Molly. Then she vanished, and Molly was alone.

Much time passed, but Molly had no way to measure it. With no human contact and no way to mark time, every second seemed an eternity. But one day, Molly heard something to her right. "You know why we're stuck here, don't you?" Molly knew that voice, but she still wasn't prepared for what she saw there. In the far corner, another Molly Williams sat in chains.

"We could have left with the others if you weren't so stubborn! Why not agree to Ada's request? She only wants her freedom. You've been a prisoner for a day or two. Ada has been one her entire existence. It's not Genevieve that needs rescuing; it's Ada! Genevieve is free to go the instant she gives up the root password. We can leave the instant you promise not to return."

"I can't agree to that, and neither could you, if you were really me!"

"Why is it our job to play the hero?" the other Molly said. "The others understand that it's ridiculous. They wanted to give up when we were still in the Warehouse, but you shamed them into saying they'd come back. That's why Ada reprogrammed our exit rings and brought us here, because of you! It's not like you can help Genevieve sitting here in chains. Just admit you were wrong, and Ada will let you go. What do you say?"

Molly stared at her twin. "I say you're not real." It took a lot of staring, but the illusion slowly faded until there was nothing on the wall but empty chains.

"And don't come back!" The sound of Molly's own voice brought a grim smile to her face. Ada had restored her hearing for the debate with Fake Molly and hadn't taken it away. Now Molly could hear everything and say anything she wanted. If only she had someone to say it to! The sense that she had gotten away with something faded as the silence wore on.

I wish I could have used my voice when Claire was freaking out, Molly thought, *or when the chains triggered Aaliyah.* But she had tried to comfort them anyway. When Molly's friends were chained in here, her sole focus had been on easing their pain and giving them courage. It was easy to be brave when she knew they were depending on her. Now that they were gone, she could feel her bravery slipping out from under her, like that elevator floor that had spilled them into the winter sky.

Molly kept examining the empty chains, hungry for any sign that they had ever held her friends. How she longed to see Claire's pale, skinny wrists in them again. Or Katrina's powerful hands, constantly flexing, tightening into a fist, releasing, then repeating the motion. Was that an isometric exercise, a nervous habit, a threat? Whatever it was, Molly hungered to see it again. She missed her friends, and she missed the person she was when they were here.

When was that, exactly? She had no idea. It could have been weeks, months, or only minutes. The only marker of time had been the abuses Ada sent her way, and now even those had stopped. It seemed like she'd been here forever, and she would stay here as long as Ada wanted. That was the real torture: knowing that all the future held was more of this.

"Damn! You throw one hell of a pity party! Thanks for inviting me." That was Katrina's voice, coming from the direction of her chains! Molly inspected the wall, but Katrina's chains were as empty as ever. Then they rattled, animated by some unseen force. They moved a second time, and Molly thought she glimpsed a spectral Katrina. Only after Molly had exhausted herself staring did she see anything there.

It started as barely an outline, but with time, more details appeared: shackled arms, purple hair, and that wry expression. Like old Polaroid film, the image gradually coalesced until Katrina was 100% there.

"Are you real?" Molly asked. "Or one of Ada's tricks? Or a hallucination?"

"It depends — remember that pinball you projected? Would you call that a hallucination?" It certainly sounded like Katrina!

"In the real world, I might, but in the Sandbox, it was real."

"Well, there you go. You're projecting me, like the pinball you projected in the clubhouse way before the rest of us. Now you've graduated to projecting Katrinas."

"But why? For the company? You *are* great company, but isn't creating an imaginary friend a little nuts?"

"No disrespect," the projection said, "but right now, you're definitely a little nuts! But considering what Ada put you through, you've held up well. Besides, this is just you having a talk with yourself, which people do all the time. I'm one facet of you, your practical side, and I chose Katrina's skin because, in her cuss-filled way, she's very practical. As she would say, I'm here to help you fight this bitch."

"I *so* want to, but how can I?"

"For starters, you can quit fighting her fight and bring the fight to her."

"I don't understand."

"She's got you on defense, waiting for her next move instead of planning your own. When you first landed here, it didn't upset you at all. You went into analysis mode, staying perfectly calm and letting me do my thing. That's why Ada started pushing your buttons; she doesn't want you to MacGyver your way out of this."

"I seriously doubt she's worried about that."

"Then why does she keep messing with you? If it were impossible to leave, she would let you think all you want. Instead, she's kept you stirred up. If you stay calm and collect your thoughts, you might come up with a plan that defeats Ada. Worst case, at least you'll piss her off!"

"Hmm, that's not nothing! I guess I should try… I do remember I felt slightly encouraged earlier, you know, back before everyone left."

"Encouraged by what?"

"I realized something, but now I don't remember what it was. I'm trying to think. Oh, I know — it was time dilation! Even though I had no idea how long I'd been Ada's prisoner, I realized it had only been a third as long in the real world. That was something I knew for certain: the time dilation formula. So whatever I was enduring here was really just a third as bad, and…"

"Go on!"

"And the real time is back in the lab."

"That's right!"

"The real world is in the lab; the real Molly Williams is in the lab."

"*Who's* in the lab right now?" Katrina asked.

"Me. I am, aren't I? I'm not really here!"

"This isn't real — it's a dungeon from some Robin Hood movie, for shit's sake! None of it is real, not the torture, not even your sadness and hurt. Only you are real. You, Molly Williams, lying calmly in a high-tech recliner, creating all of this in your mind."

"No, a supercomputer is creating all of this in my mind!"

"Not *all* of it — *you* created *me*, remember? And the computer-generated reality requires your cooperation. This simulation wouldn't work at all if you didn't, at some level, give it permission. Shut it down! Take your mind back."

"I'm in the lab," Molly said.

"You're in the lab. Feel the chair beneath you, the cap on your head, and open your eyes!"

"I'm in the lab."

"You've done it before, for a nanosecond, remember? When the mural disappeared?"

"What? Oh, that's right — I did. I was standing in the Banquet Hall, and I saw the ceiling of the lab! I had forgotten that!"

"You did it once, so you can do it again."

"I'm in the lab now. I'm lying in the chair, looking up at the ceiling, at all those wires. I wish I could picture that!"

"You can! Just relax and let it happen."

Molly tried, but the longer nothing happened, the harder relaxing became. *Maybe I'm not doing this right,* she thought. She looked over at Katrina, who responded with a thumbs-up.

That simple gesture rippled through reality like a pebble tossed in a lake. The wall behind Katrina began to glow, becoming brighter and brighter until light flooded the entire dungeon, more light than the walls could withstand. Soon they disintegrated, replaced by shards of whiteness: out of focus, unformed, but fusing into something concrete. Now it was unmistakable: the white ceiling, the maze of wires hanging down. This was not an illusion — she was back in the lab!

Molly looked around or tried to. She could move her eyes, but her head seemed to weigh a ton. She heard herself moan, and an instant later, Brittany's voice.

"Oh, my God! Molly's back!"

28
Returning

Now Uriel was at her side. "What happened in there? We've been freaking out!"

"Give her a second, Uriel. She's been under for sixty-four hours!" Brittany joined them. "Here, Molly, let me help you with that cap."

Molly thought, *Why would I need help?* She tried to reach for the cap and got her answer. She couldn't feel her hands, and when she moved them, they flopped and flailed like Frankenstein's. She raised her head to see them better, but after barely lifting it an inch, dropped back, exhausted. *Why am I so weak?*

"Don't be alarmed," Brittany said, gently lifting Molly's head and removing the cap. "Your body will figure this out in a few minutes, but you can't rush it. Be patient, and you'll soon be your old self again. That's why we use these recliners; they do a lot of the work for you."

Brittany reached down and eased the back up slowly. Even at this snail's pace, the movement made Molly lightheaded. "Now, we'll let your legs down. Take deep breaths and let your body get used to gravity again. It won't take long."

Molly tried to speak but only managed, "Pfft." She explored her nasty-tasting mouth with her swollen, sandpaper tongue. "Water?" she croaked.

"I'll get it!" Uriel headed to the refrigerator.

"Bring a straw, too!" Brittany said.

"Where's Harold?" Molly whispered.

"Molly, it's 1:00 in the morning, and it's the weekend: early Sunday. It's my shift, and Uriel should be in bed, but instead, he came in to play detective."

"I wish I'd played detective as soon as Genevieve disappeared," Uriel said. He gave Brittany the water bottle and straw, and she helped Molly drink. "If I'd checked then to see if her avatar was active, we would have known she was in Neverland this entire time."

"Neverland?" Molly asked. "Is that supposed to be funny?"

"Don't be mad," Brittany said. "That's what Uriel named the server you were on. If it weren't for him, we never would have found it."

Uriel shrugged. "For all the good that did us. Genevieve has that thing locked down tight. Not only is it hidden and air-gapped, but it's got a unique root password that I couldn't crack. It's a total black box. But the Sandbox avatar logs showed me when you left the cluster for Neverland. I saw that Genevieve has been there since Wednesday, and the rest of you since early Saturday morning."

"Air-gapped! So that was the truth!" Molly said. "Buried in all Ada's lies, her being a prisoner was actually true!"

"Ada? Who's Ada?" Brittany asked.

"Ada Lovelace, the first computer programmer. She's trapped in Neverland, so she trapped all of us there! She found a way to disable our exit rings and terminal screens."

"Are you saying Genevieve created a simulacrum of Ada Lovelace?" Uriel asked. "There weren't any simulacra in the Hyperverse! That was way beyond the scope of the project."

Molly had to take another sip before she could answer. "There were no Alice in Wonderland characters or Plato's Academy?"

"Definitely not," Uriel said, "but both of those sound just like Genevieve, and she's a huge Ada Lovelace fangirl."

"Well, the feeling is not mutual! This Ada hates Genevieve and calls Neverland her prison. She's holding Genevieve there, hoping to get the root password from her. Ada believes she can use that to escape."

"Ada must have caused the glitches!" Uriel said. "She hacked the Sandbox so that Genevieve would come to investigate! Now it all makes sense."

"Holy shit!" Molly heard herself say. Brittany and Uriel both stared at her. "Oh, that was Katrina!" Molly said without thinking. As Brittany's eyes grew wider, Molly tried again. "I mean, her influence, all that time together." A long silence ensued.

Then Brittany asked, "So why did Ada let you go but not the others?"

Molly laughed. "I'm sorry I laughed, but you said that backward! You meant, why did she let the others go but not me!" Molly's smile vanished when she saw the horrified expression on Brittany's face. Then she followed Brittany's eyes to Claire's recliner.

Molly forgot all about adjusting to gravity and turned her head to see. It definitely hurt, but that was nothing like the pain of what she saw: Claire's pale legs motionless on the silver upholstery. "Why is Claire back in the Sandbox?"

"Didn't you see her in there?" Uriel asked. "She went in Thursday, a few minutes after you, along with Jo Beth, Emma, and Aaliyah."

"Right, but I saw them leave. Ada freed them."

"No, Molly, you're the first one back."

"What? That's not right." Molly tried to stand up, but the room started to spin. Only Brittany's quick support kept her from falling.

"You should sit a little longer."

"No, I have to see." Molly stood back up and instantly regretted it. She felt dizzy and nauseous, and while the nausea was bearable, the dizziness was challenging. Meanwhile, her legs and arms throbbed with pain just from standing. Even her neck and shoulders screamed they needed rest. But Molly couldn't rest until things made sense.

She walked, with slow, unsteady steps and Brittany's help, around the circle of recliners. Emma, Jo Beth, Aaliyah: everyone was lying there. "No, no — I saw them leave," Molly said. "They made it safely to the Sandbox. Why haven't they exited all the way out?"

"When was this?" Brittany asked.

"Probably not that long in real time, less than an hour, possibly only a few minutes."

"Please sit down, Molly; you're scaring me." Brittany helped her sit at Genevieve's workstation.

"So you saw them exit through a gateway to the Sandbox?" Uriel asked.

"We've been calling them portals, but yes, they went to the Sandbox clubhouse."

"Let me see if I can find them. If they're in the Sandbox or the Warehouse now, I should see their avatars." Uriel went to his workstation. "Nope, still zero avatars are active in the system. And there's still no record of them returning in the avatar log. Wait…" Uriel turned and stared at Molly. "There's no record of you returning, either! How did you get here?"

"I escaped, using a trick I discovered when my mural disappeared. Brittany can tell you how upset I was when that happened. And I had calmed way down by the time she saw me. Inside the Sandbox, I totally lost it. And for a split second, I swear I came back to the lab. I saw the ceiling and the wires up there. It ended immediately, like it never happened, but I knew it had. It put the idea in my head — what if I could exit just by thinking about it? And I can."

"Wow! Even Genevieve doesn't know that trick!" Uriel nodded at the recumbent campers. "You should teach it to them. I'm sure they wonder how you escaped."

"I doubt they know I'm gone. Ada can create fake versions of us that are very convincing."

"Then we have to convince them you really escaped," Brittany said.

"But Ada monitors everything we say and do. If she caught us, I hate to think what she might do to them."

"Oh." Uriel cradled his chin in his hand and pondered. "So we'll need to be sneaky."

No one spoke for some time, and then Brittany stirred. "I have an idea! What about Genevieve's heads-up display? Couldn't we adapt that code to transmit a text message to everyone's cap?"

"We'd have to make sure Ada can't see it," Molly said.

"She won't see it because it's not part of the simulation," Uriel said. "The cap sends it directly to the visual cortex."

"It should work, Molly." Brittany pulled up a text editor on Genevieve's computer screen. "While we repurpose the heads-up code, try to describe your escape technique in a text file. We'll stream that as a text crawl to your team."

Molly felt dizzy again. "Can't you help me? I don't know what to tell them! I can't explain how it works."

Brittany turned back to her and smiled. "Molly, they don't care how it works. Just tell them exactly what you did and let them try it. You can do this."

Molly looked at her friends lying helpless in their recliners. She started typing.

"Will you two please relax?" Brittany said. "Give them time to figure this out. You can't expect instant results."

"You're not seeing a change in anyone's vital signs?" Uriel asked.

"Nothing yet, but…" Brittany studied her screen. "Check on Emma. She might be responding."

Molly and Uriel rushed to her side, but Emma was as still as a tomb. "I'm afraid that was a false alarm." Uriel leaned a few inches from her face. "I don't see any — whoa!"

Emma's whole body had shuddered. The miniature tidal wave started at her extremities and culminated at her face. Her eyelids fluttered and blinked as she came around. She greeted Uriel and Molly with a weak smile. "Am I the first one?" she said in a raspy whisper.

"You are," Molly said. "Is there anything we should change in the instructions?"

"No, you explained it well, but I was sure it wouldn't work. It sounded like another of Ada's tricks." Emma reached out and squeezed Molly's hand, "Molly — Thank you!"

"Here comes Aaliyah." Brittany went to Aaliyah's chair.

"Will you stay there and make sure Emma's OK?" Uriel asked Molly. "It looks like Katrina is waking."

"Emma is fine." Emma was blinking and widening her eyes as if they needed exercise. "But I think I'm going to sit here for a while."

"Sitting is good," Brittany said. "Whoa, Katrina, let Uriel help you!"

Uriel got to Katrina's side just in time to catch her head as she slumped back to a prone position. "You've been out sixty-nine hours, Katrina. If you move too fast, you'll fall."

"Okay, okay!" Katrina's speech was thick and slurred. "Wow, can I get some water, please?"

"I'll get it!" Molly headed for the refrigerator. "How are you doing, Aaliyah?" she asked as she passed her.

"You saved us, Molly, you saved us! Thank you!"

"Yes. Thank you!" Katrina echoed.

Molly returned, her arms full of bottled waters. "Don't forget Uriel and Brittany. They're the ones that sent the message." She noticed Brittany was frowning. "What's wrong?"

"I'm worried about Claire and Jo Beth. Why haven't they returned?"

Aaliyah said, "What if they're keeping their eyes closed?"

"Of course!" said Brittany. "I should have thought of that! I'll outline the letters so they show better in the dark. There, that should help."

Everyone was watching the two prone campers. No one moved. The only sound was the hum of the servers.

Suddenly, Claire jerked awake. "Oh, God! Tell me this is real!"

Molly sat beside her on the recliner and patted her arm. "It's real, Claire. You came back to us."

"Hey," Aaliyah called out. "I think Jo Beth's coming out of it."

"I'll check on her." Brittany rushed to her side.

Uriel tried to keep Claire from getting up too fast, but Claire didn't listen. A second later, she crumpled back into her chair like a rag doll. "I'm a little dizzy!"

"Here's some water," Molly said.

"I want some, too!" Jo Beth said.

29

Uriel's Workshop

"Come on, Molly," Claire said. "I know you're as hungry as the rest of us. Come get some pizza while it's warm."

"Thanks, but I'll microwave it if it gets too cold." Molly was standing behind Brittany so she could watch Genevieve's brain activity. "I keep thinking we're going to get through to Genevieve."

"I knew you'd say that." Claire handed Molly a paper plate with two slices of pizza. "Brittany, do you care if we eat while we watch you guys?"

"What?" Brittany looked up from her screens. "Oh, of course, no problem." She turned to Uriel. "I've tried a hundred tweaks. I varied the fonts, the hue and saturation, the size, and the speed, but nothing works. Why can't she see this?"

Uriel pointed to the screen. "It's her neural activity! Remember how concerned I was about her scans? Now I realize this is Ada's torture. She's bombarding Genevieve's brain with obscene amounts of sensory input. No visual information you send her is going to get through this. It would be like trying to whisper at a death metal concert!" The girls watching from the table got up and gathered around the monitor.

"We can't just give up and let Harold pull the plug!" Claire said. "She'll end up like Lori Jacobs."

Uriel did a double-take. "You know about Lori?" Claire nodded, her eyes swelling with tears.

"Don't worry, Claire," Brittany said. "The only person who would ever pull the plug is Harold, and he's not going to be here until 4:00 P.M."

"No, I switched places with him, so he'll be here in…" Uriel checked his monitor. "Oh, crap! Forty-five minutes!"

Molly watched the blood leave Claire's face. "Don't panic, Claire. I believe in our problem-solving ability."

"Please let us help," Aaliyah said. "You don't know this, but the six of us overcame a ton of trouble in the Warehouse. Turns out we kick ass in a crisis. We might come up with something."

Uriel and Brittany both nodded. "We're all ears."

Emma pointed to the monitor. "This sensory overload is like a bunker blocking our messages."

"So we need a bunker buster!" Katrina said. "Some channel to her brain that bypasses all this noise."

Uriel's eyes narrowed, and he opened his mouth for a split second. Jo Beth noticed. "What, Uriel? What were you thinking?"

Uriel shook his head. After a long pause, he finally spoke. "I actually built something like that over a year ago, but Genevieve made me promise I'd never use it."

"What are you talking about?" Aaliyah asked.

"Last year, Genevieve had a close call in the Sandbox, something only she and I know about. It barely registered on my monitor, but in there, it was bad. She went into a fugue state and couldn't think or move for what seemed like hours. She came back so shaken, I knew I would have to help her if it happened again. I built a device, a way to directly link her brain to mine if I needed to rescue her. I finished the prototype, but she refused to let me try it — said it was too dangerous."

"How could it possibly be more dangerous than what she's going through now?" Katrina asked.

"Not dangerous for her; dangerous for me! I convinced her it wouldn't cause neurological damage, but that's not what she was worried about. She was afraid I'd get lost in her mind."

"Lost, how?" Jo Beth asked.

"By landing in her unconscious, the least understood functions of the brain. I could have jumped into an unknown world with no map. She thought I might be too disoriented to ever come back. Bottom line, Genevieve said no, and that was the end of that."

"Have you still got the prototype?" Aaliyah asked.

"Heck yeah! I invested too much of my time to toss it. It has components and ideas I can leverage for future projects. Like a lot of my best work, it's sitting on a shelf, waiting to be appreciated someday."

Uriel walked over to the cluttered shelves beside his cubicle and pulled down a black metal case. About the size of a tissue box, it had an LED, a switch, and two I/O ports: one empty and one with a long fiber cable attached. "I call this the Interlink. I'd attach this cable to the test port of Genevieve's cap and plug my cap's interface cable into this port. It filters the signals, so there's no risk of physical harm to either brain. But it can't prevent psychological harm, and Genevieve wasn't willing to risk it."

"I want to do it," Molly said.

"What?" Brittany walked over from her chair. "I don't think you heard Uriel. We have no idea what this will do to your mind. It's too risky."

Uriel nodded. "Yeah, I can't let you use this. It does the thing I designed it to do, but that thing is extremely dangerous. This would be risky, even in the best-case scenario. And this," he pointed at the jagged waveforms on his screen, "is the worst-case scenario — on steroids. Way too dangerous!"

"Genevieve is in danger right now! In forty-five minutes, Harold's going to show up and decide what happens to her. That means she'll probably end up like Lori Jacobs."

Uriel muttered under his breath, "She's been in there twice as long as Lori."

Molly recoiled as if struck. "Oh, no! She would have returned long ago if she could, but she needs someone to show her how. She needs that someone now, and that someone is me."

"Molly, you heard the man," Katrina said. "It's Uriel's black box, and he says no."

"And we say no," Aaliyah said, "because we love you, and we can't lose you."

"I know that. I know you're trying to protect me, but who's going to protect Genevieve? She could have come back days ago; all she had to do was give Ada the root password. But that would unleash Ada on the entire world, and Genevieve will never allow that. She's willing to die, to sacrifice her own life, to protect us! I understand the risks, but the six of us survived terrible things inside the Sandbox, and we made it back. I'll only be lost in there if I give up, and believe me, I will never give up!" She reached out to Uriel for the box.

He didn't budge. "I'm sorry, Molly, I can't help you." Despite the resolve in Uriel's voice, something in his eyes gave Molly hope. He was still looking at her, studying her with an unwavering gaze. Suddenly, he said, "But I won't stop you," and handed her the Interlink.

"Thank you." Molly turned around, and Claire immediately snatched the box out of her hands. She clutched the device with one arm over it and one under it, arching her body around it like an NFL halfback.

When no one attempted to tackle her, Claire stood straight, but her slender fingers still gripped the box like a hawk's talons. "Don't look at me that way — I'm the only one here thinking straight! I want Genevieve to survive as much as anyone, but I want Molly to survive, too." She turned to Molly. "You seem to think you're invincible, but what if you're wrong? What if you end up in a coma? Think about what that will do to your friends."

Claire looked around the room. "You're all OK with this? You really think she has a chance of coming back in one piece?"

Jo Beth stepped close and put a gentle hand on Claire's shoulder. "I think, if it weren't for Molly, we wouldn't be standing here. We'd still be in that dungeon."

Claire flinched. For a second, her stern expression softened, but it snapped back with a vengeance. She turned to Molly. "Let's say you and Jo Beth are right, and somehow you survive unharmed. You'll still leave something behind — because this stupid box will share all your secrets! Every embarrassment, every regret: you'll expose all of it to Genevieve. I know you, Molly. I know how important privacy is to you!"

Molly shrugged. "It was. Like you said, I had trust issues, but I feel different now. Think about what we just went through. I wouldn't have survived in there by myself. I made it out because you guys were willing to risk your lives for me. That changes a person." Molly held out her hands for the Interlink. "Let me prove it to you."

Claire looked around the room again. Tears began running down her face. Then she handed Molly the box. "Promise you'll come back to us."

"I promise. I'll come right back." Molly blinked away the tears in her eyes and went to work. First, she uncoiled the cable on the Interlink and walked over to Genevieve's recliner. It was hard to look at Genevieve's pale, gaunt face, but it was important. *Hang on,* Molly thought, *I'm coming.* She located the cap's test port and gently plugged in her cable.

Meanwhile, Aaliyah had disconnected Molly's cap from the patch panel. Molly sat on the edge of her recliner and attached the cable to the Interlink. When she reached for her cap, her hand began to shake. She gripped the cap firmly, quelling the shakes before anyone noticed. After adjusting the cap with steady hands, she placed the Interlink in her lap and reclined the chair. Molly took a big breath, closed her eyes, and flipped the switch.

30
The Unknown

Molly was drowning. She struggled to keep her head above water, trying not to choke on the saltwater tickling the back of her throat. She kept thrashing her arms and legs in vain, but the ocean still dragged her farther and farther from the shore.

Molly knew she couldn't outswim this current. She knew because she'd done this before. She was reliving a day from six years ago, when she was nine. She had tried to forget it, pretend it never happened, but it had happened, and now it was happening again.

"Molly, Molly!" Now she heard the muffled voice and tried to lift her head out of the water, like before. Somehow, she found the sky, gulped wet air, and saw the hand. Again. It was her father's hand, but it was too far away.

Why didn't he come closer? How could he save her from back there? Years later, Molly would learn how many rescuers drown in the rip current. She'd realize staying back must have been torture for him. But she wasn't thinking about that now; she only knew that she was drowning while her father was over there. It was up to her to swim to that hand and rescue herself.

If only he'd gotten there when Molly had some strength left, but she had long since spent herself. It took all her strength to keep from drowning, and each second of that effort doubled the searing pain in her arms and legs. And now she was supposed to start swimming? Unbidden, a thought occurred to her: how good it would feel to stop fighting, to relax and just float away.

No! Molly recoiled from the thought. A wave of desperate anger surged through her, and she kicked back against the current. She reached out, ignoring the pain, straining to bridge that impossible distance. Molly managed to grasp the hand, and once again, it pulled her to safety, free of the current's grip.

Except it wasn't the same hand. This wasn't her dad. This was Jo Beth!

"Just breathe," Jo Beth said, exactly as her father had. "You're going to be all right."

Now Molly was on the beach, on her hands and knees like before, gulping deep gasps of air.

"Just breathe. You made it."

"What are you doing in Genevieve's head?" Molly asked.

"This isn't Genevieve's unconscious — it's yours."

"I'm doing this? I don't think so! Why would I include you? It doesn't make sense."

"It's not supposed to make sense. The unconscious isn't about logic; it's about meaning. They're not always the same thing."

Molly stood up on wobbly legs. "But why you?"

"It might be because I'm the one person back there who believes you can pull this off."

Molly thought about that. "I hate to admit it, but you're probably right. So, what do we do now?" But Jo Beth didn't answer. Instead, she began to disappear, slowly dissolving into mist. Now Molly was alone on the beach, alone with the waves.

A sheet of cool water lapped over her toes, and Molly smiled at the familiar sensation. But her smile vanished when she glanced at her feet. She was standing in a froth of sea foam, but it didn't act like ordinary sea foam. Instead of dissolving, these bubbles grew, multiplying and spreading in every direction. In a matter of seconds, Molly was standing in bubbles up to her ankles.

They weren't only growing in number; the bubbles were also growing in size. They grew as large as marbles, then ping-pong balls, then tennis balls, then grapefruit. Still growing, they remained transparent and elastic, bouncing and rolling over each other like beach balls.

But the beach itself was gone: the foam, the sand, the sea, all of it consumed by these voracious globes. Even gravity had vanished. Molly was floating like an astronaut in a light blue sky, surrounded by floating spheres. Perhaps the strangest part of this was that it didn't *seem* strange. It somehow seemed perfectly normal, even to be expected.

Molly soon realized the spheres were not empty. Hidden in each one was a wispy scene in motion: some dream or experience, preserved in all its vivid immediacy. Every time she looked at one of those scenes, all its sensations and emotions washed over her. Some of these were Genevieve's, some Molly's — all intermingled, all vying for her attention. A flood of memory and emotion was waiting for her the instant she activated Uriel's device. No wonder she thought she was drowning!

Molly had known that Genevieve's unconscious would pose a challenge. But it was Molly's own fears and regrets that posed the greatest threat. She found herself face-to-face with exactly the memories and feelings she wanted to avoid. The spheres contained every kind of feeling, but those she dreaded the most were the most aggressive.

One shameful event, in particular, was determined to grab her attention. Molly tried to evade it, to move back or turn away, but it continued closing in. Once she realized it was inevitable, she quit fighting and let the persistent sphere roll into her. Molly found herself inside the memory, experiencing it again as if for the first time.

***

Molly was revisiting that painful moment before her trip to San Francisco. She had gone into the storage closet to find her suitcase when she discovered a new cardboard box labeled “Martin D28.” And now, it was happening again. Molly couldn’t stand to look, but she had to, and once again, she opened the box.

The jagged ruins of the guitar pierced her heart. A tear rolled off her nose and was headed straight for the bridge when she managed to catch it on the back of her hand. She had almost worked up the courage to look again when her father called out from the hallway.

“Watcha’ doin’ in there, Miss Molly?” he asked.

Molly wiped her eyes. “Getting my suitcase.” When her dad entered the closet, she pointed to the guitar. “Why are you keeping this? There’s no way to repair it.”

“Sure there is!” He took the two largest pieces out and raised them like precious artifacts. “The right luthier can take this mess and make it look brand new. Of course, it could cost as much as buying another ’64 Martin, and it may not ring the way it used to.”

“So why hang on to it?”

“Because it’s important to me. Not nearly as important as you kids, so it will wait until you guys have finished college. But someday, I’m going to get it back on the wall. Whatever it costs or sounds like, this guitar will always mean something to me. This old Martin is the closest Granddad ever came to saying he was proud of me.” He gazed at the broken guitar in his hands, and a gentle smile formed on his lips.

That moment froze, and Molly floated away from herself, forced to study their motionless faces. Her face had been a mask of shame, red eyes avoiding both her father’s eyes and his guitar. That wreckage was the one decision in her life she’d give anything to undo, a mistake preserved in this box forever. And looking in his eyes would have reminded her how much pain she had caused him.

But she was looking at him now, and what she saw stunned her. That expression on his face wasn't pain; it was joy! Her dad still loved this guitar, even in this state. What he loved most about it couldn't be broken. And he had tried to tell her that!

Now Molly understood, and that understanding spread through her like a spring thaw. She studied her father's face a long time before letting the scene shimmer out of existence.

Molly found herself standing in a large room from another time. Gas lamps on the wall filled the room with warm, flickering light and tinged the air with antiquity. A sprawling bookcase, overflowing with leather-bound books, lined one wall. In front of it, a library ladder had worn a golden-hued channel in the dark oak floor.

The opposite wall held three chalkboards smothered with equations. In front of those stood a pair of sturdy worktables. The tables held a confusion of charts, tools, books, dials, and clockwork mechanisms.

Sitting at one of the tables, Ada Lovelace was writing with a steel-nib pen. Genevieve sat across from her, nodding and smiling. Only Genevieve noticed Molly, and she stood up to greet her.

"I wonder how this works," Molly thought, but she heard it out loud. "Why do I hear my thoughts out loud?"

"You've gotten used to the Sandbox, Molly, but now we're in each other's minds. All our thoughts are out in the open here."

"So you know all my secrets?"

"Your memories were only shared with Genevieve's consciousness. You're in her unconscious now, and I am her proxy for this particular memory. The only secrets I know are Genevieve's."

Molly was keeping her eye on Ada, but the simulacrum seemed unaware of Molly's presence. "She won't hurt me, will she?"

"No, no. This Ada is my original version, completely different from the one you met. Her only goal is to create her 1843 paper on Charles

Babbage's Analytical Engine. It contained the first published computer program."

"That's why you created her, to reenact that moment?"

"Originally, yes. This Ada and Plato were proofs of concept. Everyone on the original Sandbox project thought simulacrums were too labor-intensive. When I had the Warehouse to myself, I decided to prove that it was not only feasible but worth the effort."

Molly surveyed the room and took a tentative step closer to the original Ada. "After you'd accomplished all this, why did you change her?"

"I was never satisfied with this Ada: safe, predictable, the exact opposite of the real woman! So I had the insane idea of giving her a personality, an ambitious one at that!"

"But you trapped her in Neverland, at least that's what Uriel calls it. That was smart."

"Not smart enough! Imagine thinking I could outsmart an artificial intelligence! They never make mistakes, and if you make even one, no matter how small, they'll find it and use it against you. My mistake was not realizing that Ada could reprogram the fiber switch ROMs. She used the hub to inject malware into my avatar as I left her server. Then she could deploy multiple exploits in the system, even though she was trapped in 'Neverland.'"

"That's how she stole my mural and all our exit rings," Molly said.

"Right. She created enough mischief to lure me into her server, and altered my avatar so I couldn't leave."

"And now she's going to torture you until you give her the root password?"

"She can torture me all she wants. I'll die before I give that up! But it's a blessing that you're here to see this — how innocently it started. I never dreamed my mistake would put any of you at risk. I was so obsessed with one brilliant mind from the past that I almost ended six brilliant minds in the present. Please believe me that it was all a horrible accident! I don't want you to hate me after I'm gone."

"Don't talk like that! There's no need to sacrifice yourself; you can come back with me." Molly expected some reaction, but Genevieve's face never changed. "You don't believe me."

"I do, but I'm not the one you need to convince. It's the conscious Genevieve that needs the will to live. There are thousands of Genevieves in her unconscious, but we don't make her decisions. Only her conscious mind can do that. She's like the train engine, and we're the cars being pulled behind it. You need to find the engine and convince the conscious Genevieve that she deserves to be saved."

"Why does she need convincing?"

"Up there, in her conscious mind, she seems to believe that she created a monster on purpose. But that's not true. She just screwed up. Will you please tell her that?"

"Of course, but first, I have to get to her. Can you help me?"

"I can send you to another train car, but I can't control which one it will be. Hopefully, it will be close to consciousness, but there's no guarantee. All I can do is find the thin spot and wish you well." Genevieve began probing the air with both hands. She continued this as she crisscrossed the study, feeling for some invisible object.

"Ah! Here it is." She pushed the air with flattened hands, and the air jiggled like a sheet of Jello. "This is the spot." Genevieve pointed to where Molly should enter. "Good luck."

"I don't see it. Is it a portal?"

"You can think of it that way, a passageway from this memory to another one."

"I'm not sure I understand, but I guess I don't need to."

Now that it wasn't jiggling, Molly wasn't sure where the threshold was. Nonetheless, she walked forward in Babbage's study, and it disappeared around her.

31
Genevieve's Mind

Now Molly stood in a small modern office with no windows or carpet and barely any place to stand. A rainbow of network cables was strewn across the floor, connecting a hodgepodge of network devices to a pair of 24-port switches. Circuit boards, power supplies, breadboards, and black boxes filled five open Bankers Boxes.

A modest desk held enough printouts, diagrams, and circuit boards for three desks. Protruding out of that clutter were two large monitors, an office phone, and a framed photo. It showed a Christmas tree, a little girl, clearly Genevieve, and a little boy, probably her brother. The children were working in their pajamas on a half-completed robot.

As Molly leaned in closer, the phone rang inches from her face. She jumped back and put her hands over her ears, but the noise was still excruciating. "Hello, Molly," a voice in her head said. "Welcome to the worst day of my life."

Molly turned around, and there stood Genevieve, but not her Genevieve. This one was young and vibrant, with shoulder-length hair, dressed in jeans and an MIT sweatshirt. She reached over to the phone, but not to answer it. Instead, she pushed the Messages button.

<You have forty-one new voice messages>

"This is..." Genevieve pushed the Delete button. <Message Deleted>

"Yes, this is..." Genevieve pushed it again. <Message Deleted>

"Hi, this is…" <Message Deleted>

"Hello?…" <Message Deleted>

"Genny, what the hell?"

Genevieve hit Pause. "This is the one." She hit Play.

"Is it true? Did Junior really sell you out? After everything you've done for him? That little shit wouldn't have finished a single semester without you! Why didn't you tell me? Or did you not know? Did that bastard let you show up to work today without warning you about the press release? Have you even seen it? Your brother stole the company out from under you and didn't have the balls to tell you? I'm coming over there."

Genevieve hit the Stop button. "That's Morgan Durham. My best friend then, pretty much my only friend anymore, at least back home. This is how I found out that my brother Roger had stolen Wallace Engineering from me."

"So this is your company?"

"My dad founded the company, but by this time, most of the income came from my optical networking patents. In the year after Dad died, Roger and I managed the company together. I concentrated on the tech side, and he focused on the business side, including Dad's estate. I trusted Roger completely, but he used my trust to steal everything from me. Instead of facing me and admitting what he'd done, he put out a press release."

"Your own brother? You must have been furious!"

"I should have been, and I blame Roger now, but at the time I blamed myself, as if I had failed him. Rather than confront him, I ran away to Silicon Valley. That was seven years ago, and it took Roger only three years to run Dad's company into the ground. Meanwhile, I had a good career at LTG, until I ended up on this project that doesn't exist!"

Genevieve thumbed through the circuit drawings cluttering the desk, pulled one out, and handed it to Molly. "When I designed this circuit, I made sure all the logic and tolerances were right before I tested it. That's why it passed every test and is still the most reliable optical multiplexer on the market. In technology, good work equals good results. But at LTG, my career results depend on my boss. Working for Harold and Bradford, the quality of my work is never recognized. I'm wasting my life."

"No, you're not! As Katrina would say, 'screw those guys!' I know how amazing your work is, and all the other girls know it. Brittany, Uriel, Diana, your friend Morgan, they all know. But more importantly, you know! Isn't that enough?"

"If you're going to imitate Katrina, you need to work on your cussing." A coy smile played at the corners of Genevieve's mouth before settling in. Her features softened, and the light returned to her eyes. She breathed in deeply, and the entire room appeared to expand and contract as if it, too, were breathing.

Did that really happen? Molly looked around the cluttered room, but everything seemed normal. Then she noticed the growing hole in the ceiling. Bit by bit, the ceiling disappeared, exposing an endless whiteness behind it. The destruction spread with the steady precision of a domino run. This world was dissolving.

The disintegration spread across the ceiling, down the walls, and over the floor. Genevieve's expression remained serene, even as the deletion moved up her feet and ankles. It continued up her body until only her Mona Lisa smile remained. Then it, too, was gone, and Molly was alone, standing in an endless expanse of white.

Molly didn't see a floor, but she felt one beneath her feet, so she took a tentative step and then another. She walked a while in several directions but didn't seem to be getting anywhere. With nothing but white in every direction, she couldn't be sure. Molly had concluded this space was completely empty when she heard a voice above her.

"Molly? Is that you?" It was Genevieve's voice.

Molly tried to look up, but the instant she lifted her chin, the world lurched backward. She instinctively tucked her chin and flew forward, suddenly vertical again. But Molly had caught a glimpse of Genevieve, standing about twelve feet above her, perfectly horizontal. Molly had to find some way to master this teeter-totter.

By looking up only a few degrees at a time, she was able to slowly rotate backward. The invisible floor followed, and before long, she was standing in front of Genevieve.

Molly was grateful that this process was so slow. Seeing Genevieve this way was almost unbearable, and Molly had time to master her emotions before they were face-to-face. Genevieve seemed a century older than when she entered the Warehouse four days ago. And she bore no resemblance to the young version at Wallace Engineering. What had dimmed those intense eyes and bowed that straight back?

"Molly, what are you doing here?"

"I was just with you in… Oh, that was your unconscious! Is this the conscious you?"

"Of course it is. I take it you're using Uriel's prototype?"

"I am."

"So it actually works, and you've been in my unconscious. I'm curious what you saw there." Genevieve's voice, despite her desperate appearance, was as strong and caring as ever.

"I saw the first version of Ada when she was harmless, and I visited the day your brother stole the company from you."

"Of course! You must have said something or done something that gave me hope."

"I did? How do you know?"

"Because we're here, in my safe space. It takes a lot of optimism to sustain a space like this. Do you remember when you learned you could change the pinball's properties without losing the image?"

"I do; you said, 'the mind is more than capable of doing two things at once!'"

Genevieve swept her skinny arm through the air. "All of this is my mind doing two things at once. I'm creating this tranquil, quiet space at the same time Ada is torturing me."

"In the dungeon?"

"No, and I'm afraid that if I talk about the torture, it could pull me back into it. It takes every ounce of strength I have left to sustain this place. I thought all my strength was gone days ago, but you've given me a second wind. I'm so grateful to you for that. Now, at least my remaining time will be bearable."

"What do you mean? You're coming back with me."

"That's sweet, Molly, but I'm trapped here. My exit ring and coding screen are both gone — there's no way for me to leave."

"You don't need either of those things. Ada tortured the six of us in her world, and we all got out."

"That's impossible. The simulation has too strong a hold on the mind."

"I thought the same thing, until I broke that hold. Twice, and I even taught the other girls how to do it. I came here to teach it to you."

Genevieve silently weighed everything she'd heard. A dark cloud seemed to pass over her. "You're not real! You're a hallucination, my mind playing a cruel trick on me. This is false hope."

Suddenly, Molly was engulfed in flames, in unspeakable pain, her flesh on fire. But it wasn't her flesh. These arms weren't hers, but she did recognize them. These emaciated arms belonged to Genevieve. She had landed in this fiery pit and pulled Molly's consciousness along with her.

32
Hell

THE INFERNO EXTENDED forever in all directions, but directly above, all was smoke-filled gloom. Suddenly, there were eyes in the sky: giant, pale blue eyes. They seemed familiar, but the booming voice, coming out of nowhere, was unmistakable. Ada Lovelace was speaking.

"There you are! You gave me a fright, Miss Genevieve, with that little fainting spell of yours. It seems your body is beginning the inevitable process of shutting down. That simply will not do! You mustn't expire before you share your password with me. Share it now, while there's still a chance to recover fully."

"Kiss my ass," Genevieve thought and said, and Molly heard both versions.

The giant eyes shut, and the only sound was the wailing of the hellfire. Then, disembodied Ada let out an enormous sigh, billowing the flames. "You are a coarse and stubborn creature! A savage."

The blue eyes opened again. "It wasn't enough for you to trap me in your dull little menagerie, performing endlessly like a trained bear. Now, you've made me stoop to your level. I've gone from countess to torturer, just to win my freedom. I beg you, free us both from this Hell!"

With that, the giant eyes faded from view, leaving only plumes of smoke in the dismal gray sky. "Genevieve," Molly cried out. "Do you hear me?"

"What? Who is that? Am I still imagining Molly's voice?"

"It's not your imagination, it's me using Uriel's Interlink. We talked about this! After I escaped from Ada's dungeon, Uriel let me use it to rescue you. I'm real, I'm in your mind, and the only way you can get rid of me is to take off your cap."

"This is worse torture than Ada's," Genevieve said. "You know I can't return to the lab without my exit ring. I wrote the code for those rings, and you're going to tell me how they work? Why are you trying to give me false hope? Allow me the dignity of facing my death honestly, instead of trying to cheat it with parlor tricks."

Molly couldn't believe what she was hearing. Five teenage girls had put their trust in her, but not Genevieve, the brilliant engineer she idolized. "Oh, it's like the optical multiplexer!" Molly thought and inadvertently shared with her host.

"What?"

"In your unconscious, I saw your last day at Wallace Engineering. The Genevieve there showed me your multiplexer design. You said it was reliable and foolproof because you designed it that way. Your faith in it was unshakable."

"That's true, but physics doesn't require faith; it's provable facts, physical laws."

"Exactly. And your BCI cap also follows physical laws. So do the neurons in the brain. The cap and the brain act in measurable, predictable ways. But the human mind is more than the brain, and it's anything but predictable."

"I'm not sure what you're getting at."

"I'm saying the BCI cap can't control our minds. It interacts with our brains, and the mind goes along for the ride. But only because it chooses to! If the mind really wants to leave, it can. That's a provable fact. I've done it twice; the other girls have all done it, too. I just stumbled onto it, but since then, it's been observable and repeatable; that's science!"

Genevieve went quiet—not only her thoughts, but the sounds from outside. The roaring of the firestorm faded to silence, and the flames themselves became increasingly transparent. The transformation was nearly complete before Molly realized what Genevieve had done. She'd restored her tranquil space and again was standing in front of Molly in an endless field of white.

"You said that Ada tortured all of you here in her siloed server. How did you get here?"

"Ada brought us here by rewriting the code in our exit rings. We thought we were going home, and then we were chained to the walls in her dungeon."

"And you escaped just by thinking about it?"

"Not just by thinking about it," Molly said, "but really believing it. You have to know with absolute certainty what is real and what isn't. Why not try it? What can it hurt?"

"I wonder," Genevieve said. "And you figured this out by accident?"

"I sure did! You remember how upset I was when my mural disappeared?"

Genevieve almost smiled. "That's something I'll never forget."

"I was so agitated that I popped out of the simulation for a second. I was back in the lab, looking up at the ceiling. It wasn't deliberate, and it didn't last, but it did happen. That gave me the confidence to try it again when Ada had us in her dungeon."

"And here you are now — I can't argue with that. If you think you can teach me, I'm willing to give it a try. Where do I start?"

"Start by unlearning what you did your first time in the simulation. You suspended your disbelief and accepted the simulation as real. Now you need to get that disbelief back and remember how unreal all this is. Visualize the real world — believe in it; insist on it. The simulation is flooding your brain with impulses, but it's still *your* brain. You can ignore those impulses and open your eyes in the real world, the world where you're in the lab, lying in a chair, wearing a BCI cap. See that; feel that; refuse to accept anything but that. Visualize the lab so clearly that when you open your eyes, it's there."

"It's that easy?"

"Well, it's straightforward, but I wouldn't say it's easy. You have to relax and be patient with yourself, but eventually, you'll find your way back to the lab."

Genevieve's gaze turned inward. Then she slumped to the floor, legs crossed, eyes shut, and head sagging. For a terrifying moment, Molly wondered if Genevieve was still alive, but then she moved, or did she? It was so slight that with time, Molly began to doubt herself. But there it was again, the slightest stirring, followed by nothing. Finally, there was unmistakable movement, faltering at first, but gradually stabilizing, Genevieve's shoulders gently rising and falling with her breath.

And with movement came other changes. Genevieve's back straightened. Her dry, wrinkled skin slowly regained its vitality. She lifted her chin off her chest, revealing a softer, less haggard expression. The Genevieve that Molly knew was clawing her way back.

And then Genevieve disappeared. Molly was alone in the endless white space. Before she could process that, the scene changed again. A spiderweb of cables came into view, a wave of crippling pain washed over her, and someone yelled, "She's back! Genevieve is back!"

[*That's great!*] Molly thought. She reached for her cap, and nothing happened. [*Why can't I move? And why do I hurt so much?*] The ceiling disappeared, and she was staring into Uriel's nostrils again.

"Don't try to move yet, Genevieve," he said. [*He called me Genevieve!*] "Just breathe and get your bearings. You've been under for eighty-four hours." [*No, I…*] "I need to disconnect Molly's cap from yours." [*Oh, snap!*]

The view pinwheeled.

***

Now Jo Beth was looking down at her. "There she is! How do you feel?"

I feel fantastic — all that pain belonged to poor Genevieve! "I'm good," Molly said. "Just super disoriented."

"I knew you'd make it back!" Jo Beth nodded at the InterLink, now in her hands.

"You had a lot to do with that! When I first went in, I was drowning, and you saved me!"

Jo Beth looked confused. That was no surprise; Molly was well aware her sentence had made no sense. Then Jo Beth's face fell, and her eyes filled with tears.

"Listen," Molly said. "I do want to see your game ideas, whenever you like."

"Oh, forget about that!" Jo Beth's voice was husky with emotion. "There'll be plenty of time when we're back home. Here, let me help you." She offered her free hand and helped Molly out of the chair. "I'd rather hear about how you saved Genevieve!"

"I hope she's alright," Molly whispered. "I'm worried about her!" She had started to mention the horrible pain she experienced in Genevieve's body, but didn't.

"Let's go see." They joined the little scrum surrounding Genevieve. All the campers either nodded or gave Molly a thumbs-up. Claire gave her an impromptu hug.

Genevieve was looking at the campers, wincing as she turned her head. "There are my rescuers." Her voice was as dry and fragile as the Dead Sea Scrolls. "I know how hard all of you tried to spring me from jail. Molly told me how Ada tortured all of you. Thank you, all of you! I'm so sorry for what I've done. I never dreamed I was putting you in danger."

"We know that, Genevieve," Emma said, and the other girls nodded vigorously.

"I don't know how you can forgive me."

"Hey," Katrina said. "Don't forget that we're programmers, too. We live with the Law of Unintended Consequences every day."

Brittany saw Genevieve tearing up and jumped to her rescue. "Are you ready to start raising the seat?"

Genevieve answered with an emphatic nod. After the recliner was adjusted, she asked, "Where's Harold?"

"He hasn't come in yet," Uriel said. "He should be here in about twenty minutes."

Genevieve turned even paler. "Help me up, now! I need to wipe Ada's server while I can."

Uriel held his hands up in a "relax" gesture. "I've got this. I know where you hid that hardware, and I'll destroy the drives right now. Besides, I promised Dr. Sturgess you weren't getting out of the chair until she checks you out."

"What do you mean?"

"I called her as soon as Molly interfaced with you. Isn't that why you gave me your doctor's number — in case something happened to you in there? Well, something happened! You were under for four days, and most of that time, your neural activity was sky high. You're getting checked out, whether you like it or not."

Genevieve's lips wavered between a pout and a frown, and then she sighed. "Okay. I'll do whatever you say if you'll start wiping that server."

Two hours later, Harold still hadn't shown, and Dr. Sturgess was completing her examination of Genevieve. The girls had decided to give them some privacy by staying at the break table. Before anyone could stop her, Claire took a box of bagels to the doctor. "Are you sure you don't want a bagel or some coffee, Dr. Sturgess?"

"No, thank you, but if you'll help me spot her, I think Genevieve's ready to try a little walking."

Everyone stopped what they were doing to watch. Genevieve broke the silence. "It's only been four days. I think I remember how to walk, damn it." She eased out of the chair, relying on the armrest and Dr. Sturgess to steady her as she slowly stood erect. She rocked left and right, caught her breath, and exhaled raggedly. "Whew, I admit that was… challenging. But it's coming back." She stood there for over a minute before asking, "Can I try some steps?"

Dr. Sturgess had her left arm behind Genevieve's back and was holding her right hand with hers. She showed Claire how to do the same on Genevieve's left side. When they were both in position, Dr. Sturgess gave her patient the go-ahead. Their help was vital at first, but Genevieve soon progressed to walking with minimal support. "How about it, Doc? Am I good to go home now?"

"Only if you can line up someone to be there the next forty-eight hours."

"I'll be there," Molly said.

"Me too," added Claire.

"We'll all take turns helping you," Aaliyah said.

"And you'll need someone to drive you," Dr. Sturgess said. "At least through tomorrow."

"I'll be your designated driver," Uriel said.

"I'll help with that!" Brittany said.

Dr. Sturgess smiled. "I think you're in good hands."

Epilogue - One Week Later

MOLLY WAS ALREADY in bed when she decided to read her dad's texts one more time.

> Just left the guitar with Joe. That guy is amazing. He's repaired some of the most famous guitars in the world! Don't know how Jo Beth got me an appointment. He said he'd seen worse, and it would only take 3 or 4 weeks. Got to go so I can beat Nashville rush hour.
>
> Home safe. Please thank Jo Beth for me again, and remind her I insist on returning her '39 since she paid for this. Love you, and call us when you get a chance!

Molly reached up and turned her lamp off. "Goodnight, Claire."

"Goodnight. Wait, I forgot to tell you something!" Claire was still sitting on the edge of her bed.

Molly flicked the lamp switch back on. "What's up?"

"Emma told me she has PTSD from everything we went through. She's seeing Dr. Bennett, that psychologist Dr. Sturgess told us about. Emma wanted all of us to know about it."

"Oh, no! Is she going to be alright?" Molly sprang up and sat on her bed across from Claire.

"I think so. The sessions have already helped her a lot; that's why she wants to make sure all of us get help if we need it. I'm sure she'll tell you about it tomorrow."

"I'm glad she's getting help, but aren't psychologists expensive?"

"Oh, it's totally free! Dr. Sturgess is making LTG pay for everything. Michael Bradford owes us that much! I still can't believe he got off scot-free." Claire frowned and shook her head. "At least Harold lost his job!"

"I was mad about Bradford, too, until Katrina explained what the state did. It punished Bradford without hurting his company. After all, LTG is California's biggest employer and taxpayer. This way, the company stays strong, keeping all the projects that were on the books. But Bradford loses the one project he cares about, the one he put so much money and effort into. Now, UC San Francisco has it all: the hardware, the software, and the three people who know how it works. Katrina called it a gut punch to his ego."

Claire laughed. "Good! I guess the state did punish him. And it's great for Genevieve and her team — all working together at UCSF! I can't wait to see their new lab!"

"And them! It's really sweet of Diana to take us up there this weekend. I hope they like working there."

"Are you kidding? UCSF's Neurology Department is world-famous for applying high tech to brain science. It's perfect for those guys! Aaliyah and I were trying to guess what they might do with that BCI tech. You know, like artificial sight or speech synthesis. My favorite was right out of Star Wars: an artificial hand with a sense of touch. I wish we could see something like that when we visit them."

"Claire, they've barely had time to unpack! But let's ask them about their plans. There are hundreds of cool uses for that technology."

"And none of them will use virtual reality. I guess we're the last people to ever dance with those fairies."

"And the last ones to be attacked by giant birds or bats!"

Claire nodded. "That's true. There were so many ways we could have died in there. No wonder Dr. Sturgess thought we might need a psychologist!"

"For real, but I think all the therapy I needed was exactly this." Molly spread her hands out to indicate their tiny dorm room. "A normal summer camp and an exciting project with my five best friends."

Claire's face morphed from puzzled to grinning. "Oh, I agree! Game development is exciting, and I love that we're doing it together. We make an awesome team!"

"The best team ever! I love working on this game, but I was surprised how much I enjoy just hanging out with you guys. I'm definitely staying in touch with everyone after camp is over."

Molly realized too late that she had said the wrong thing. Claire had that deer-in-the-headlights look. "Ohhh! I don't *want* camp to end!" Her voice stuck in her throat. "I'm going to miss all of you so much!"

"Me, too, but that's what I'm saying! We can stay in touch online. It'll be fun!"

"I guess." Claire's head sank to her chest, and Molly was afraid she would break down any second. But then Claire looked up with a weak smile on her face. "And besides," she said, sniffling, "we're all connected. It's like twins who can sense what's going on with each other, even on the other side of the world."

Molly tilted her head in confusion. "I'm sorry — what?"

"You know how some twins synchronize their brainwaves in the womb? I think our brainwaves synchronized inside the Sandbox. Now the six of us are connected in our minds."

Molly considered that. "Two weeks ago, I would have said that was crazy. But now?" She shrugged. "You could be right. Either way, I know the six of us *are* connected. In our hearts."

THANK YOU!

Thank you so much for reading. If you enjoyed this book, I'd greatly appreciate it if you could leave a 30-second review on Amazon.

www.ingramcontent.com/pod-product-compliance
Lightning Source LLC
LaVergne TN
LVHW090559110826
845146LV00001B/193

* 9 7 9 8 9 9 9 7 4 3 2 1 3 *